Galactic HELL CATS

BY MARIE VIBBERT

GALACTIC HELLCATS

Cover art © 2020 by I. L. Vinkur

Design and interior by ElfElm Publishing

Available as a trade paperback, hardcover, and eBook from Vernacular Books.

ISBN (TPB) 978-1-952283-07-9
ISBN (eBook) 978-1-952283-08-6

Visit us online at VernacularBooks.com

*For my original galactic girl gang:
my evil twin Grace Vibbert and our best friend
Shannon Heffner.*

01:

KI GETS HER RIDE

A STARSCAPE TURNED BEFORE KI—BREATHTAKING, BANDED WITH blue and green nebulae. She reached toward the velvet black and the stars abruptly became a glistening slab of marbled meat. Ki covered her face. She was starving, and the food ads on the projection wall were pure torture.

Ki crouched inside a dumpster frame, thighs aching, waiting for the trash bot to trundle by. It didn't smell great. The Mars Tourism ad was her only distraction in the rotating video line-up. Few people were in the shopping center this late, scurrying on their way to someplace else under the fuzzy grey sky. A chubby girl pressed her thumb to a doorplate and walked through a hologram urging her to wave her hand at it to try different styles of pants. The hologram thought the departing store worker was interested in bright colors and shorter lengths and spoke eagerly to her departing form like a horny hustler. Ki made a mental note to tell Ethan about that. He'd think it was hilarious.

"Hey!"

Ki froze, veins turning to ice. She couldn't afford another mark on her record. Two strikes already as an adult, and the third would send her to hard time. Running footsteps, pelting up behind her. Could she make a break for it? Her joints ached, she braced to jump.

The figure ran past her, chasing after the chubby girl, who turned and waved in recognition. They linked arms and continued to the train stop.

Relaxing without giving up her crouch hurt. Her foot slipped on something that felt like chicken skin. The display urged her to travel the galaxy at Café Andromeda.

The trash bot wobbled around the corner at last, a barge with a flat face and two arms at one end, taking its own sweet time picking up each trash container and inspecting it. It reached Ki's dumpster, the one with a Ki-sized hole in the bottom. (That had taken four separate trips to cut at the bin and check that no one noticed or cared.) Ki squeezed her arms tight to her sides and hoped the bin would lift clean around her. The bot lifted the bin, as it did with all of them, and the back of the hole only brushed Ki's hair. This bin would register empty, but the bot still shook empty bins over the compactor on its butt. Perhaps it was programmed like that to make it look busier.

While the bot shook the bin, Ki jimmied the lock and climbed into the bot's center compartment. The greasy interior had the particular acrid stink of sour beer and fermented soda pop.

The bot continued on its way with Ki in its belly. Her shoes slid in unidentifiable goo. She tried to hold herself in place with one fingertip pressed hard against the compartment roof and kept her eyes on her wrist-screen. A green dot (representing her) approached a little blue flag. The bot dropped a bin in its storage space and Ki wriggled to keep her spot by the door. The bot swayed and paused. Ki held perfectly still. The bots had a function to detect unwanted passengers—usually rats—by shifts in content weight, but Ki thought she'd killed that when she'd uploaded her malware that morning.

The bot continued, whatever had momentarily confused it forgotten. It inspected another empty bin. The leading edge of her dot touched the flag on her screen. Ki kicked the door open and rolled out into the fresher air, her heart in her teeth until she could look up and see if she had been discovered.

A security bot whizzed by overhead, having just scanned the space Ki now occupied. Right on time for its schedule. The little red dot on her screen. Perfect. Now she was in the "employees only" alleyway and had two minutes to get out of sight.

Ki peeled a sticker off the back of her hand. It was a conductive plastic circuit with sticky goo on one side. Printed illegally at the local library after hours. It fit the lock perfectly and it gave with a soft click.

She pushed the handle, however, and another bolt caught. Oh balls. Did no one trust their door locks anymore? Ki felt offended on behalf of the MedeCo lock company. She fished her longest lock pick between the door and frame, feeling for the offending bolt. A shadow fell over her.

She froze and shrank against the wall, staring up helplessly like a mouse caught in a trap. The shadow glided gracefully over the next building. Not a cop, not a drone, but a late shopper heading home in a gorgeous solo-flyer. A ShadowKat 88. Ki knew the shape as intimately as the interior of a four-tumbler lock. The 88 was smooth as a river pebble, elegantly elongated around its driver with this delicate hint of vestigial fins, like a curve cut on the underside. Ki found herself staring at the patch of sky it had left, at the void where someone had gotten away from gravity.

Now she was going to get caught for dreaming. Ki didn't bother to check the time. If she didn't get in, she was as good as arrested. The pick found the bolt. It wasn't a drop, it was a pull. She wriggled her magnet wand out of her sleeve and passed it over, feeling the slight tension as the bar was picked up.

One more glance to make sure no one was in the alley watching, and she was in. The back of the store had what she needed: duffle bags, jackets, and security tie-downs that hadn't been upgraded in years. She always stole a duffle bag these days; one of her favorite fences collected them.

She stuffed her wig in the first bag she found. Then she freed items from their packaging and dropped them in until the bag was full.

She stopped and considered a cap emblazoned with Ethan's favorite team. Ethan used to get presents for her. One time a rich john left him an extra night in a deluxe hotel room. Ki had drowned in towels that were unreal in their softness and they'd split tiny bottles of liquor playing "Never Have I Ever" on the big bed. They both lied so much the game was meaningless, but that had definitely been the best gift. Four years they'd been best friends. It should have been longer. They should've met as little kids.

She left the hat. She couldn't give a petty theft as a gift—it felt like passing along the guilt. Stealing a lot of things, selling them, and using the money, however, didn't ping her conscience in the slightest.

The duffle could barely zip closed. Time for the dangerous part.

There was a release on the front door for staff or customers caught by the automated closing. She hit it with her prize possession: a signal scammer that had a recording of some poor Joe's palmprint. He was probably long dead, but still getting caught in shops all across North America. "Gate will open for five seconds," the cheery voice of some also long-dead woman announced, and a floating five appeared, flooding the shop with blue light as it mutated to a four. Oh! Her sticker! She dashed to the back of the store. She didn't want to have to print another.

Holding the sticker aloft in two fingers she slid through a fading number two like a baseball player stealing home.

"Did you see that?" she announced. To no one. She got to her feet with a sigh, wishing there had been someone to see, to share the moment with, even if it was a cop.

Ethan was going to laugh so hard when she told him about that.

Ki walked out the front entrance of the shopping arcade in a blue cap and black tracksuit, carrying a duffel bag full of merchandise. This was the real risk, this moment here, walking casually past the human security, blending with the shop drudges.

Ki didn't know if normal people looked at security guards, or how long, or if they smiled. It was a question that occupied much of her time. She let her eyes glide over Officer Splendig and scan ahead like she was looking for someone. "Nick!" she called, raising a hand. She hurried her pace.

She felt, as she always did, a delicious jolt of pure excitement as she crossed the threshold of capture: past the guard and his area of responsibility, out into the public street. She knew she had a dorky grin on her face, but hopefully that would be interpreted as her relief at having found "Nick." She didn't know anyone named Nick, which is why she chose the name. She hurried, picking out a particularly oblivious man at the train stop, hunched over a hologram. She ran up to him. "Nick! Nick it's . . ." She reached him and stopped. "Oh, sorry. You're not Nick."

Ki bit her tongue not to laugh at the man's confused expression. She turned to the ticket bot and flashed her pass.

The RTA had upgraded security again and her fake ride pass didn't work. Balls. She couldn't stand there attracting attention. She started walking along the tracks. It was a gamble. The cops never liked people walking with bags, and doubly so on the tracks. But if she made it, if no one tried to rob her on the way, if the fence was generous, her month of preparation would pay off with a month of food and shelter. If she haggled right, maybe even something extra. Something sweet. Something for Ethan.

Ki first met Ethan on a street corner. She was running for her life, having gotten identified by a store's security bot, and a human security guard was chasing her. She turned a corner and there he was, just gorgeous, bare chest, leaning up against a building like it was a personal friend of his. He'd blinked heavily made-up eyes at her and she'd grabbed onto him and said, "Hide me."

He turned her to the wall and gave her the best, slowest, longest kiss of her life. If the security guard saw it, he must have decided not to interrupt honest commerce.

She'll never forget the languid way he ended the kiss, lifting his soft lips from hers and looking down at her bliss to ask, "Where are your parents, kid?"

She punched him in the dick for that. She made to run off but he grabbed her ankle and then she was down and she thought he was going to take her to the cops, but he held up his hands. "Hey, sorry. Sorry. I'll make it up to you. Do you have a place to spend the night?"

It wasn't exactly a coincidence that she was between homes.

Ethan's roommates were out. He had a 3D projector and a subscription to *Knights of Saint George.* Warmth, indoors, and her favorite show. She was miserable with wanting it. "But . . . you were working."

"I can take a night off."

She didn't like how he looked at her, like she was helpless. A kitten he'd found. "My mom's on Mars," she said, because her mom had always wanted to go to Mars. It was a lie she'd been telling long enough to half believe it herself.

"Emigrated all by her lonesome?" Ethan wasn't buying it.

Ki quickly changed the subject. "You like *Knights of Saint George?*"

"There are only two types of people in the world: those who like *Knights of Saint George*, and assholes." Ethan lay on a sofa and made the gesture that started the show. He was laconic and gorgeous, a cat in a sunbeam.

Ki told herself she wasn't going to make a pass, that her ego had suffered enough already at Ethan's hands, but did it have to be *Knights of Saint George?* It always got her going. Since freaking grade school. The sleek little phallic solo-flyers penetrating ecstatic nebulas. The idea of freedom they represented, flying off into the galaxy, nothing but her and her ship. She never made it through the opening credits without wanting to grope someone, and Ethan was there. He grabbed her hands. "Seriously, how old are you?"

"Eighteen. And a half."

He stretched out his full length, which was quite a lot of length, and threw back his long neck. "Bullshit. I'm nineteen and I'm Methuselah next to you."

"I really am older than I look." She tried to get close to him again. "You didn't mind kissing me on the street."

He let her kiss him, then, but pulled her off as she started rounding third base. "I'm sorry." He kissed her chastely on the forehead. "It's not that I don't want to. I use it all up with the clients. I have to save my energy."

Ki suspected most of the women Ethan dated didn't take that for an answer, but she respected him. Damn it.

They started meeting once a week to watch the serial. When Ki found two tickets for the space elevator in a data cube she'd palmed, she immediately asked Ethan. "A present. You showed me the stars on a projector. I'll show you them for real!"

How lovely the elevator car was, how clean and new and shiny. How beautiful the people were in their clean, unwrinkled clothes. How accidentally she let slip, "If we can't find tickets back, do you want to live up here forever?"

Ethan stiffened. "You don't have return tickets?"

"We'll figure something out?"

He jumped up, pacing, ruffling his hair, scaring the other passengers. Ki worried he'd throw her out an airlock.

At Top Station, she shrank into her seat as the other passengers filed out. Maybe, if they stayed in their seats, they'd be taken down?

Ethan scooped her up and dragged her to the ticketing counter. In a posh voice she'd never heard him use, he said, "I demand to see a manager. My round-trip ticket claims to be one-way! No, I will not sit down. I will not be quiet. This is my birthday!"

Ki had never intentionally drawn attention to herself in her life. She cringed and hung as far back as Ethan would let her. Somehow, the crazy scheme worked. Or at least got them dumped on a shuttle to Laguna Station, where the transport company main offices were. She drank in every second of the stars and a sliver of blue Earth in a tiny porthole.

On Laguna Station they had enough money for one meal, no

berth, and the station guards stared hard at Ki the second she was in sight and never looked away.

Ethan lifted her against his hip, reveling in his strength in the lower gravity. "My little space pirate! I could kill you!" He was laughing. It was heaven.

They were really in space, even if all they could see were corridors that could have been in a subway station, the same feel of many people passing, the diminutive stores crammed into corners. Ki felt tall for the first time in her life, and not just because of reduced gravity. She didn't want to come back down to Earth. Ethan did. He had a job, an apartment, friends. He charmed the pants, literally, off a delivery ship pilot to get them back. Her weight returned with a feeling of finality, like losing wings.

For two days, they had been part of a larger world.

All Souls Hospice was a swank place. As such, they didn't care for Ki. The employees never said as much, and the robot attendants were programmed to be polite, but the retina scan at the front door continually forgot she was the invited guest of a resident. She knew she hadn't been banned for breaking rules, because she regularly hacked into the security system and confirmed she hadn't been caught. There were no notes or warnings from the staff on her record. Still, every time she came, the door refused to let her in and she had to call the desk and wait while the robot attendant contacted a real live human with the authority to override the guest settings. Real live humans always gave Ki the stink-eye.

Ki found it easier to climb the building and slip in through the window. Fortunately, Ethan had a private room one floor above a decorative band of stonework.

Ki lifted the sash and held it up with her knee while she ducked under, nearly over-balancing because of the duffel on her back. She fell to the floor with a crash.

She jumped up and raised her hands over her head. "Ta Da!"

The pile of musty blankets shivered, then rustled, and a tousled head peeked out. Ethan was getting much too thin; he looked like fuzz on a stick. Ki dropped onto the end of the bed and opened her new duffle. "Look what I got!" She triumphantly produced his favorite chocolates.

Ethan turned a slightly greyer shade and she knew she'd misjudged how welcome candy would be. He covered his head again.

"Come on, it's not like you need to worry about your figure." Ki curled up in the space beside Ethan on the bed.

There'd been a nasty trap in Ethan's DNA, a genetic malfunction that coated his lungs and stomach in a protein. It made him not want to eat and it made his breathing hard. There was some stupid name for it. The doctors had been all "oh yes, it often strikes in the early twenties," like they knew the very depth and breadth of the muck destroying Ethan. Probably they did.

All Ki saw was her friend getting weaker and thinner. All she could think about was how there was free healthcare on Mars. "Don't you want to eat anything? What can I get you? Anything at all. You say it, I'll bring it. It'll be a challenge."

He gave her the stink-eye. "You could steal . . ." Ethan's tongue dragged on his lip, dry on dry. "You could steal the squeak out of a rat. I'm past eating, you little kleptomaniac."

"Don't say that. I went to the good grocery on Vine. I got saltines and soda and even some things that are green, or, well, look like things that are green in their natural state."

He shook his head, but she opened her bag and set crackers

and soda in front of him. "You took care of me when I needed it," she said. "So, it's my turn. You're going to love this."

She smeared some pink meat-paste on a saltine and held it out to him. He pushed her hand with the back of his. "I want to give you something, while I'm still conscious."

"Now you're pissing me off."

Ethan turned in bed. Each movement was slow and protracted—a gasp, a lurch, a pause. Ki had no choice but to step over him and reach in the direction he was yearning. "Just point. Ethan, just point at it. Don't try to get up."

"Now . . . you . . . are pissing *me* off."

It was obvious he was going for the knapsack on the floor so she picked it up and spilled its contents in front of him.

Ethan's crooked fingers pushed silk fabric and a gaudy belt aside. He almost fell out of bed. Ki supported him. He was hot. That wasn't good. He nudged a little silver box, a ring box. Ki opened it. It was empty.

"Under the . . . the stuff. Flocking."

She peeled the fake velvet lining back and found a slim chip with a number. She hurriedly closed the box and held it tight. "This is a storage locker key."

Ethan lay back. "It's all I have left. I want you to have it."

The box felt too fragile. Like Ethan. All fuzz on cardboard. She felt like she would crush it with her anger. "If there's something in there we could have sold for treatment, I will kick your skinny, dying ass!"

That was the worst thing about seeing Ethan like this; enough money could buy treatment, real treatment that repaired the damage his unlucky genetics was doing to him and let him live, instead of what his savings could afford: a comfy bed and pain-killers that made him waste away, stop eating, and die a little more slowly.

He put his hand over hers. "Let me have a legacy, Ki."

What could she say to that? She tasted tears and snot at the back of her throat. Her face was completely wet. She hoped Ethan couldn't see well in the dark. She smeared her nose on her sleeve. "Okay. Damn it. I mean . . . thanks."

He smiled. She'd thought he'd never do that again, but the muscles were still there, lifting that corner of his lip. His face recovered some of its ravished beauty. "That's my mercenary," he said.

"You owe me. Eat a cracker. Just one."

He groaned. He did look better. More like himself, rolling his eyes. "Beast. This is why I never married you."

Ki kissed his sweaty forehead and thought that yes, he really was going to get better. This time for sure.

Ki slipped out the window when Ethan was asleep again. She kept off the streets, taking fire escapes and balconies and railings where she could until she got to a favorite spot of hers, an old, graceful bridge. Too beautiful for the neighborhood, but then, they didn't exactly tear things down for that reason. The water below was an opaque oil slick reflecting the city, but it moved like a living thing. How was it people were so fragile and things like that just kept going? She wiped her runny nose with the back of her hand. She could toss the storage locker key in. It would be a grand gesture. It would feel good.

She knew she wouldn't. Ethan was right—she was a mercenary. She would do the awful, dreary thing and sort through his stuff and fence what she could and count it all up and check black market prices for retroviruses and gene therapies. It wouldn't be enough. Nothing ever was.

She had to think bigger.

Ki walked across the bridge on a balustrade that was outside a chain-link fence meant to keep people from walking on it. Big boats chugged by, the size of buildings, always looking like they weren't in a hurry. A boat heist? Could she steal enough to let Ethan keep his things? How would she haul it?

Ethan wasn't going to die. Not now, not ever, so he didn't need a legacy. It wouldn't hurt to check out the resources he had on hand, though, if they would prevent the whole dying thing. There'd be something in there to buy time. To plan a real heist. To finally have enough.

The street was indifferently paved in a variety of asphalts like giant toddlers had had a mud and concrete fight and their parents moved away rather than clean it up. Ki left it for a dirt track along the riverbank. Sometimes, in a city, you could forget there was dirt under everything. She liked the funk of it, of the river, and the tough, prickly things that managed to grow between the smooth path and the corrugated metal of the river channel.

The storage building was squat and old with exterior framing that marked it as a former parking garage from the dangerous old days when just about everyone had a powered vehicle. The ground floor held a fish and produce market where live chickens squawked between fat cement columns and you could practically hear the money changing hands. Haphazard lights in every color and ad-hoc awnings of printed scarves made the area feel like a festival.

The entrance to the storage facility was at the top of a wide ramp at the back. The door was quality, steel and ceramic set into a poured concrete wall a shade lighter than the ramp. Ki almost didn't try it. Better to find a loose window than battle that. But it was a long walk back down the ramp so she pressed her hand to the lock. It blinked green and the door slid back. Ethan must have already keyed her access. When had he last been up and about? Ki felt a warm flush. She'd never planned anything in her life that far ahead.

Ki entered the airlock and pressed her hand to a second scan pad. The door behind her closed, a light turned on overhead, and after a hum and a shudder, the inner door opened. A series of green arrows glowed on the concrete floor, leading her past door after door set into walls of poured concrete. The corridor turned hard right at regular intervals, ever inward and ramping slightly upward. It would feel good, looking through Ethan's prized possessions. His secrets. It would be like seeing him healthy again. Knowing him.

The green arrows slid under a door. A tiny slot the size of her key chip glowed green. Ki slid the key home. It asked for a thumbprint, and a rattling old chain drew the door upward. This place would be hard to rob, but she was already imagining how she'd do it.

Ki suspected she'd find lots of clothes, stuffed animals, the things Ethan liked to collect. Maybe a piece of furniture from his never-mentioned family's home. Something she'd have to sell at a loss to the antique store.

Not even close. (Well, there was a chaise lounge and a set of bar stools at the back, but she didn't notice them at first.)

The gleaming hull of a red solo-flyer dominated the front of the locker, looking like a freshly painted fingernail and costing more than all the things Ki had ever stolen in her life. Her knees gave out. Her vision blurred, red and wet and wavering.

She sniffled, wiped her eyes, and reminded herself she was a hardened criminal. "Oh boy," she said, out loud. It echoed back at her, tinny and fake. "Look at that." She almost couldn't touch it. Her hand hovered, but then she stroked the nose, felt the smooth ceramic, not cold to the touch as she'd expected, but warm. "Someone loved you," she said, and she reckoned that could be interpreted three ways.

02:
MARGOT GETS HER RIDE

WHEN GENERAL QUARTERS WAS CALLED, MARGOT SANTIAGO-
Nguyen didn't think anything of it. It was a drill; it had to be, because they drilled so much.

Margot ran to her post and processed orders. She brought fourteen rounds of N24 to the third port gunner. She refilled all munitions to starboard. She didn't think about anything but making sure she got each order right and under the required time limits. She didn't wonder that she kept shipping ammunition out and it didn't come back. She didn't suspect anything was out of the ordinary until she was hurrying down the corridor pushing a cart loaded with bombs and saw an officer looking scared.

She brought another parcel of rounds to the fore gunner, and the woman pushed her away, leaning back from her harness, eyes still reflective-white from the targeting display. "It's over," she said.

And that was when Margot knew for certain she'd been in a battle.

She returned to the depot to take stock and report, like they were taught. One of her fellow munitions crew, Cho, sweating profusely, slapped her on the back and said, "You are *stone cold*, Nguyen!"

But I didn't know, she thought. Can I panic now? Her knees knocked. She held onto her station for support and gave Cho a tight smile.

She'd often sat up at night, anxiously wondering how she would face real battle—if she would cry or freak out or visibly show her fear to the derision of her teammates. She hadn't. Despite herself, she'd done just fine and could do so again.

She pushed herself back onto her feet. Being in battle was the scariest part of being in the Navy, and it was over. Fearing her own cowardice had been the worst part of the anticipation. That was over, too.

At dinner she let Cho tell the tale of her calm under pressure, while the truth sat silent inside her. Everyone else seemed to have a more communal experience, and they finished each other's sentences and embroidered stories of heroism she hadn't seen. Everyone else had narrowly missed a falling bulkhead or been rocked by an explosion with a live warhead in their hands.

Cho said, "Dude, why was it live? You have to insert the M-385 into the housing to prime the explosive."

Rayes answered, "I didn't say it was an M-385."

"Well that's what you were shipping, you bullshitter."

Margot felt left out, but she was glad to have missed all that. She left dinner as silently as she'd come into it. She had her first real solid night of sleep that night, despite the smell and discomfort of sleeping in the previous shift's warm body depression and the belches and snores of her rack-mates.

"I'm going to get through this," Margot thought, with relief.

Like a self-guiding torpedo on a delayed course, though, the fear was still there. It took three more General Quarters to hit her. The sled she pushed, the handle biting blisters in her palm, was as insubstantial as cream, waiting to effervesce into the vacuum of space. The clang and din in the cargo hold made the walls seem so solid, but they weren't, and the weight she had just hefted and turned to deposit on its rack was designed to destroy that thin wall and send a woman just like her into the tearing emptiness.

It was like hitting water at the bottom of a high dive. She stopped mid-step. Crewmates rushed around her like fish around a rock. Someone shouted, "Get a move on, sailor!"

It felt like each joint in her body had to break through ice to bend, and each part of the ship felt more dangerous than the one she had just left. The depot was full of explosives. The gunnery bay was close to the hall. The corridor had lots of area to be breached.

Somehow, she did her job, sweating cold the whole time and shaking.

An idea, once thought, was hard to let go of. Margot was in five more battles, but toward the end, every day on ship felt like a battle.

Margot was startled by how tiny her hometown was. Approaching Luna, it was just this texture, straight lines against the organic craters. Then they landed and the door opened and she was looking at the dock she had left four years ago and it was enormously open, all this space you never got on a military base, but it didn't feel big, it felt like everything inside it was tiny. She caught herself afraid to brush the ceiling as she bounded out of the troop transport, grabbing the "earthling rails" instead of pushing off the floor and ceiling alternately like a born Lunatic.

Her parents overshot her and had to check, her mother's hand brushing the top of the dome briefly, and then they were hugging her, dragging her back down to Luna's good old surface. Her father was crying. Her mother was crying. For a moment she felt so solid, so heavy with their tears, that it was like she'd been a cloud for the past four years.

"I'm okay, I'm okay. I'm here," she said, over and over. Things were going to be different between her and her parents now, she realized. Warmer. More affectionate.

That was four months ago.

Margot's alarm woke her in time for nothing, the same as it had the day before and the day before that. She turned the alarm off and laid back in the bed she'd slept in since childhood. It smelled greasy. She would have to wash the sheets soon. She piled all the covers on every night because the weight made her feel a little safer.

Her father poked his head into her room. Margot flinched. She feared doors opening.

"Do you have any interviews today?"

Margot covered her head with her pillow.

"Breakfast in five," he said, voice tight with irritation, and slid the door shut.

Well, so much for sleeping. Margot had been having an annoying dream, anyway. She'd been stuck in a maze. It was the same one she dreamed about as a kid, a combination of the school corridors and the colony corridors and it didn't take a genius to figure out why a kid would be scared of getting lost, but she wasn't afraid of that anymore. The monsters chasing her were gone, too. What did that say? That her imagination wanted to bore itself to death?

She waved her information display on. There was a message in her inbox from the Sol System Navy Veterans' Administration. Advice on conducting a job search, part five million. She trashed it. She used to read all their tips, but they were getting repetitive, and the constant reminder of her failure was not helpful.

Going through the motions, she checked each of the places she'd applied to. There were only two warehouses in Isle Imbrium, Margot's hometown. One was inside the habitation area with artificial gravity, but it was laid out the same as the one outside the gravity field, which was laid out the same as the storerooms on navy ships. Narrow racks with narrow walkways and every spare piece of space used. She knew the daughter of one of the owners. Still, they hadn't been hiring.

The VA guy said that showing up in person was the only way to stand out from other applicants, so she'd taken day trips to each of the other Luna colonies and their warehouses. Same story. They had already hired all the former military stock clerks they needed. Tranquility City had eight warehouses, so that visit had been grueling as well as useless.

Two weeks ago, she'd gone to the warehouse asteroid Aten. That was a zero-gravity warehouse. Completely different skill set. She'd barely been able to look around their spirals of racking without puking. The hiring manager hadn't even let her speak. It had been a long, cramped journey both ways. She still felt tired from it.

Everything was tiring. She thought after the navy, Luna would feel full of bright color, but her friends were gone and every light and sign was in the same place it had ever been, so that looking at anything was the same as looking at nothing at all.

Margot's parents kept gravity low in the main area of the habitat. They liked it that way. Something about making the food fluffier. Also, it was cheaper, keeping the unit turned off. Her dad stood at the table, one foot hooked over a chair-rung like he hadn't decided whether to sit or not, eating an egg pocket.

Margot's mother bounded in with her environment suit half-on. "Do you have an interview today, sweetie?"

Margot knew her mom was trying to sound friendly and not pushing. She wasn't succeeding. Margot tried to think how to break the lack of news.

She didn't have to. She saw her parents read her silence, disappointment settling on their features. "Apollo's sake." Her father wiped a corner of his mouth. "It's been half a year."

"Four months," Margot said.

"Go to the promenade," her mother said. "Store to store to store. You'll find something. You just have to be persistent."

Margot had been to the promenade. But she nodded.

Her parents kissed each other and her mother bounded out.

Margot picked an egg pocket from the bowl on the table. Her father gave her a look like he was about to remind her of the price of an egg. "I'll go to the promenade," Margot said.

"You were watching *Knights of Saint George* last night."

"For an hour."

"Seems to me if you have time to relax, you have time to find a job." He wiped his fingers on the soft fiber cabbage they kept for cleaning crumbs and went through the door to her parent's private room. His feet landed heavily in the higher gravity. It wasn't an angry stomp. It was just the way the rooms were. But Margot felt anger in it, and in the dismissive door closing.

Margot had already been limiting her recreation time to an hour or two a day. It wasn't like she had anything to do. Or anyone to hang out with. Her high school girlfriend sent a few messages, but they had nothing in common anymore. The girl she'd dated in the Navy was dead. They'd racked together one week, saw each other maybe fourteen days in total. It was odd grieving someone you had just started to get to know. The VA said to talk to other vets.

Margot didn't want to talk to other vets. She'd tried, but all she could think during group sessions was "How did I end up lumped in with these people?" They were all so depressed and not like her at all.

So . . . nothing to do but read or watch entertainment and that was considered lazy so she worked out a lot—but not at the gym because that cost money, and at home she looked like she was wasting time so she did sit-ups or jogged in the colony maintenance corridors.

Margot was spending more time trying to look like she was looking for a job than actually looking for a job. Hours of "research" and community classes and strolling into stores that had already told her they weren't hiring. It was exhausting.

"Widen your search," her VA counselor had said.

Where could she go? Luna and near-orbit were all shut down. She either had to drop down to Earth or start looking at Mars and other asteroids.

Mars had voted against sending the navy to fight the rebels on Planet Ratana. From what she'd seen on the news, Martians were still pissed off there'd been a war at all. So . . . Earth, then.

Margot sat, in her best clothes, in a tiny partition-office in the corner of a warehouse that intimidated her with its open plan. Earth was decadent in its use of space, filling up a single layer like the planet's surface was infinite. Enclosing all that space in rectangular sheeting like they were storing air. Margot could not stop looking up.

The sound of load-lifters and humming hover-sleds made it hard to hear the grey-haired man behind the desk. A picture of soaring eagles dominated the wall behind him with the caption "Achieve." Margot had hoped to see birds on Earth.

The man behind the desk asked, "What excites you about stock clerking?"

Margot forced herself to re-focus on his face. Had anyone, in the history of humankind, ever been excited about stock clerking? "Uh . . . I know how to do it? I really need the job," she said.

The man frowned.

Margot put her hands on the desk. "I really, really need this job, and it's a lot like what I did in the navy."

The man set down his flimsy screen. "Ms. Nguyen, I just don't think you're what we're looking for at Sports Warehouse."

"I thought . . . they said you would consider veterans first for this position."

"And I've had five other veterans apply."

"But I'll work hard and I won't complain and I'll pay for my own relocation."

His smile was already dismissing her. "My other applicants said the same, and they had good management skills and experience. Good luck applying elsewhere." He stood, hand extended.

Margot took his hand limply.

"I'm sure you'll find your niche," he said.

Margot walked out into the bright, sunny day and, as she always did when on Earth, blinked in confusion at the sky. It was baffling how it didn't show any stars. How it was flat and solid like a roof but you couldn't tell how far away it was. She always felt like she might fall into it.

She'd hoped Earth would make her happy again. The first time she'd come to Earth had been for a family funeral, but her parents had arranged it so that they could spend a weekend at an amusement park as well. A tiny part of Margot still expected Earth to always be about roller coasters and death.

Margot sat down on a low curb and checked the time. It was only two in the afternoon. She had planned on her three interviews taking until four or five. Her return ticket on the elevator wasn't until 5:40.

Luna hung in the blue sky, a washed-out crescent, mocking her uselessness.

Four years of army pay in her bank account, plus combat bonuses, and her parents would still lecture her about the expense of traveling to Earth. She knew that. She also knew they wouldn't lecture if she'd gotten one of the jobs.

She stuck her hands in her pockets and went for a walk. The gravity was hard, but that was good. Margot liked working out. She liked the ache in her joints making her feel solid. This would be like a free bonus trip to a heavy gym. She'd try that on her parents, maybe, to help justify the expense.

Margot walked between chain-link fences back toward the center of town, back to the bus station that would take her to the elevator. Short, heavy steps like chopping through mud. Like dragging a sled in ship-gravity. Plants grew everywhere, between cracks in the pavement, between posts and walls and under the benches of the bus station. They just left the plants there. Leaves moved with the wind. Maybe that was why, they showed you there was wind. Still, if Margot were in charge, she'd have Earth employ people to dig out the plants and cover the exposed dirt with grating. It was so sloppy and ugly the way it was!

And she hadn't seen a single bird. There were sounds. Chirping. It scared her because it was similar to an alert. She stopped under a tree and tilted her head back and forth, trying to locate the origin of the chirp. Something moved, but it might have been a leaf. The chirping stopped.

Margot walked past the bus station because it was only 2:15.

After several random turns she found herself in front of a spaceship dealer. A solo-flyer held pride of place behind the plate glass window. It was a narrow oval, caution-sign yellow but glossy like melting sorbet. The hatch was raised to reveal the chocolate-colored leather interior.

Margot walked into the building, up to the flyer. She touched it. No one stopped her. A sales rep was talking to a couple on the other side of the showroom. Margot ducked under the open hatch. There was something sexual about straddling the seat. It was soft and organic between her thighs. Everything was new and clean and expensive.

"She's a beauty," a voice said. Margot flinched, nearly hitting her head on the hatch. The sales rep smiled down at her. "Go on, lie down." He rested his hand on the canopy. "Feel what it's like."

Margot felt vulnerable lowering her body to the seat, but it seemed rude to say no after she'd been caught feeling up the upholstery.

The hatch sealed with a gentle pressure on her ears. Instantly the noise of the street, of birds in the trees, of the hum of electric wires, was shut off. She was snug and comfortable. Safe. She was something new: a cocooned butterfly. She felt her back unclench, her body melt into the pillowed leather.

She'd be polite to the sales rep when she said no; she wasn't getting it.

There was nothing practical about a solo-flyer. It didn't have enough cargo space for a trip to the grocery store, much less between worlds, and yet that is what it was designed to do—carry a single passenger through interstellar space. There was no reason for Margot, jobless, hopeless, directionless, to even dream of such an extravagant purchase. She didn't need a spaceship; she needed a job! She could take public transportation wherever she needed to go. Luna Colony was designed for pedestrians. She had nowhere else *to* go if she could.

After an all-too short time, the sales rep opened the canopy again. He smiled at her like she'd already turned over the credits. She supposed it was on her face—she was in love.

"I don't . . . I don't really . . . I shouldn't."

"This is the lowest price you will ever see on this model," he said. "Demand is down in anticipation of the new designs coming out at the industry conference next month." He petted the smooth yellow ceramic as though consoling it.

Her sergeant had warned her about this exact situation. "When I finished my first tour," her sergeant said, "four of my buddies blew all their saved up pay on solo-flyers and within a year, three of them were dead from crashes and the fourth was paralyzed the rest of his life at twenty-two years old. Stupid kids with money for the first time! Don't be like that. Save your pay like it was somebody else's money and get a job fast or you'll be back in the service within a year. Like me."

Margot wasn't a stupid kid. She was a good girl. She'd always been a good girl. Top third of her class. No disciplinary hearings in the military. Honorable discharge. She'd done everything right.

The sales rep tilted his head. "You're from the moon, aren't you?" He snapped his fingers and pointed at her. "I knew it, moment I set eyes on you. That's a Lunatic face. Is it all right to say that? Tell me, kid, how are you getting home? This baby could have you at your airlock with no waiting, no timetable, no fellow-passengers, no elevator sickness."

No two more hours to wait. Margot licked her lips. "I'm not . . . not that I'm considering this, but if I did, do I have to pay it all at once?"

Like a priest inducting a neophyte, he led her to a comfortable chair, set a glass of water within easy reach, and instructed her in the arcane ways of "affordable payment plans."

Like the fear of battle, it didn't hit her until way too late to be useful.

03:
HOW KI MET MARGOT

Ki only knew one guy who might be able to buy a solo-flyer: Mookie of Mookie's Robot Repair on East 160th. Mookie let her fly his cousin's solo-flyer whenever he was fixing it. Solo-flyers were tricky, prickly beasts and needed constant mainte-nance. Mookie's cousin, obviously, couldn't afford a real ship mechanic and went to him instead. Mookie was a pushover, so he let her be his "assistant." Ki got to loop it around the block for multiple "test flights." He even let her watch while he bled the hydraulics or replaced a small part. Swell guy, all around. Married, though. Damnit.

Mookie let out a low whistle. "Wow. That's a ShadowKat 80. Cherry condition. I wish I could give you half of what she's worth." He scratched his stubble. "I . . . how hot is it?"

"It's not hot. It's Ethan's. He didn't say where he got it."

Mookie gave her a pitying look. "Always assume it's hot until it's not." He pushed up a sleeve and tapped on his forearm key-board. "Checking the registration . . ."

Ki had never seen anyone go from 'drooling' to 'dejected' that fast. "What?"

"It's not hot." Mookie flicked a display into the air above his arm. "It's worse. There's a lien on it."

"A what?"

"It was put up as collateral on a loan that's past due. You can't sell this. Well, you can, legally, but the lienholder . . . aw shit. There's . . . there's more than one. Ki, your friend owes this ship to two different people for the full price. So, okay, I know a gal who removes registration numbers . . . shit."

Mookie flicked his display off, grabbed Ki's arm, and threw her toward the flyer. "Dinger's coming. Get out of here."

"Who?"

"Repo man. I'm sorry. One of my searches must have gotten sniffed. Ki, they're coming to take this hog and I don't want it to happen here."

Ki wasted precious time staring blankly at Mookie before climbing back into the flyer.

On the way to Mookie's, Ki had flown as carefully as if she were wearing borrowed glass slippers. Now she opened the throttle all the way and didn't look where she was headed. None too soon as a hoverbike with a mounted machine gun was coming in hot, straight for her like a guided missile. In case she had any doubts, the damn thing said "Dinger" in rhinestones across the windscreen. She pushed the flyer straight up. Dinger wouldn't be able to fly above breathable atmosphere on his bike.

She hit the clouds and a siren went off, letting her know that law enforcement and air traffic control were unhappy. She held down the throttle and ignored the screaming alerts and prayed no one was flying directly over her.

The atmosphere parted like a curtain and exposed the deep, bold space beyond. She could almost reach out and touch the velvet black. Ki squealed in delighted panic. She was Chantoya from *Knights of Saint George*. She was Chantoya's mysterious girlfriend from the planet without a name. She was . . .

She was under fire. The ship shook and warning bells and lights competed for attention. Okay. She had to get this under control. It was hard not to bounce with glee because it was so much like she had imagined!

A shot zinged the hull. She flinched and let go of the controls. The ship dropped, dizzyingly, and she threw up. Her vomit hit the canopy and then little droplets were floating around her.

Not so fun. She rolled the ship, cooling with the seriousness of the danger she was in. A police drone was honed in on her, and she was in space. There was nothing to dodge behind in space.

So she turned her nose down. More warnings. Heat sheeted off her canopy as visible light. The ship bucked like a stone skipping on water. Something was going to break if she kept this up. She turned up again, shot out at random, and nearly collided with a satellite.

Her vomit slapped her in the face, and she knew she deserved that. The drone was gone, however. She opened the throttle and flew blind.

Ki parked in orbit somewhere just beyond Luna-controlled space. The alerts and threats petered off and stopped. Maybe she was out of jurisdiction. Maybe they had to circle back and get a warrant or contact Luna control or something. She had no idea how long she had.

What did she have? The clothes on her back. A genuine spacesuit she'd bought used and kept in pretty good repair. It had felt like playing dress-up putting it on to take the solo-flyer to Mookie's, but now she was glad for her childishness; she'd have fewer options if she were wearing her usual shirt and shorts. She had her tool pack with her signal jammer and lock picks, which were about as useful as a lace doily in the present situation.

The solo-flyer was on five percent of battery, but it soaked up solar power now that she'd parked. The solar battery ran the sub-light system. She also had the stardrive, but she was saving that. Stardrive was only good for one shot before you had to realign the wave harmonics. (Chantoya and the Knights sometimes squeezed a dangerous second jump in when the situation was really dire. Fan boards were mixed on whether that would really work.)

How often did Ethan check his messages these days? No, he couldn't help. She should write him anyway, in case she didn't get out of this. But she didn't want him to worry. She opened a text editor. "I can't believe you held out on me like this! I'm orbiting Jupiter right now, literally! I'll bring you back a space rock. See you soon!"

She'd used way too many exclamation points. He'd see through it.

Her stomach clenched, churning on emptiness. She ought to have shoplifted a candy bar on her way to Mookie's. What an idiot. How was she going to get back to Ethan?

First things first, she needed food, water, and a way to erase the flyer's registration. Unload the ship, sell it hot, and run home with the cash.

Feeling calmer with the beginnings of a plan, Ki headed toward Luna. No atmosphere meant less energy expended landing, and there were service stations and restaurants in the sprawling colonies.

Ki skimmed along the moon's surface, planning a sneaky approach to what was probably the most unused entrance to the colony, when she saw another solo-flyer out on a joyride.

Almost instinctively, she scanned the registration. Legit. Even better—purchased that day and the insurance information said "Warning: operator under-twenty-five!"

A well-to-do kid with a shiny toy. A mark. Ki felt a small tension release in her belly. At the very least, this kid would get her dinner. She changed course to follow and radioed the other flyer.

"Hey, fellow soloist! How are you?"

The other pilot sent an acknowledge receipt, which was better than nothing. Ki shadowed him. "I'm Ki. Is that the ShadowKat 88? That's less than a year old! I never thought I'd see one this close. It's gorgeous. Love the color. Fierce Mango, right?"

Ki was just about to give up when a rough voice replied, "Yeah, I just got it."

Hook set. No one could resist a compliment. "Sweeeeeet. Let's see what she does. Try to catch me!" Ki fed the throttle and led the other pilot, just a little—she didn't want to escape, and she didn't want to run out of energy, but she had to look like she was getting away. The instinct to chase would draw the mark in. Ki glided, let inertia carry her, used the moon's gravity to fishtail and spin. Not only was it fun, it would *look* fun.

Ki kept one eye on the mark. After a long second, the mark sped up and matched trajectory. "Now you're loosening up!" Ki said.

After a pause, there came a reply. "I don't . . . I don't do this much."

Hooked! "Could have fooled me. So where are you from? What do you do?"

"I don't do anything. I mean . . . I was in the navy."

Ki almost pulled away right then. Ex-military? That didn't sound like an easy mark, but she was almost out of battery again and didn't have a clean exit strategy. She slowed and straightened her course. "Fresh out of the navy, eh? What were you? Fighter pilot? Astrogator?"

There was a long pause. Please, please, Ki thought, don't say special forces.

"It wasn't interesting or anything."

"Come on, you gotta have stories," Ki said. "You were in the Ratana War, right? Did you get to see sky wolves?"

"I was an ordinance technician."

Ki blinked. It took her a moment to decode. Something about bullets? Technician? That sounded geeky. The con was back on. "No way! Does that mean you know all about blowing stuff up?"

There was a frustrated puff of breath. "I delivered ordinance to people who asked for it. I know all about how we label the boxes."

Perfect. A stock clerk. "Listen to you! You carried high explosives and you're so badass you're blasé about it."

"It's not like that," came the pleased reply.

"Whoa. Hey, bomb-tech-expert-badass, my machine's about starving. This has been fun, but I need to pack it in. We're just about to . . . Isle Imbrium. Wanna hit that?"

"Not . . . really. What about Tranquility? We could get food. Or Laguna station's not far."

Ki relaxed, the plan pieces were falling into place like tumblers in a lock. "That's even better. Follow me, I know a good place to park."

Interesting that the mark didn't want to stay on Luna, but the station really wasn't far away, sitting opulently on the Lagrange point between Earth and the moon. It was probably a cooler place to hang out. A local would know.

There was an out-of-date auto-park on the far side of the station. Or there had been, when Ki had been there. The delivery pilot who had taken them back to Earth had parked there, rather than at a commercial dock, because the security was busted and it was easy to get berthed for free.

Ki set the coordinates and fumbled through her pack for her signal jammer. The battery indicator flashed EMERGENCY, but she could coast the last little bit.

Her first sight of the garage door was encouraging—it was the same banged-up steel it had been last time. She started the jammer and dialed up the program to open the gate.

Ki's hand rested on the retro rocket ignition, approaching the gate that was still closed. Keeping it casual, for the mark. She watched the data read out on her jammer. Same old . . . wait, there'd been a software upgrade. Shit shit shit. She didn't have power to start again if she braked.

Heart pounding, she flipped through files and commands, hand still on the power button, the mark still following confidently behind her at a regular pace.

Just as she was about to bail, the gate began to rise. Ki signaled her mark. "Slow thing, this gate. Follow me in and stay close unless you want to pay extra."

The mark's ship practically kissed Ki's as she swung into a free space that looked inconvenient to the cameras. (Assuming her detector was correct on where the cameras were.) Ki double-checked that the pay-bot was fooled by her script and added the charge for the mark's ship, too, just to be generous.

The giant flashing red lights slowed, then turned green after the outer door sealed. The atmosphere detector binged. Ki opened her canopy and jumped out, anxious eyes on the shiny new solo-flyer next to hers. The canopy opened.

Brown skin, narrow eyes, and brown hair in a smooth bob.

Round face. The mark looked muscular and taller than Ki. Padded with health and wealth so she almost glowed. She also looked anxious.

Ki smiled and held out a hand. "Nice to meet you. Call me Ki."

Margot had pictured someone like her high school gym teacher, robust and peasant-healthy. Her voice had sounded big, brusque and confident. Instead the other flyer disgorged a tiny, bird-like woman with jaundiced skin and ragged patches of multi-colored hair standing out like a child's art project from her head. Her spacesuit was shabby, scuffed grey-black with bits of other colors patched into it—shiny red sealant glue and denim-blue swatches mostly. One arm of the suit was colored in with black permanent marker. It almost matched.

Margot looked doubtfully at the thinness of the woman's arm and the off-size padding of her glove, and felt the moment dragging and her pause creeping toward rude. She reached her hand toward the shiny leather palm.

Ki's grip was hard and sudden. She hauled Margot out of the flyer like she weighed nothing more than a box of handgun rounds. Margot was startled, wobbling on her feet.

Ki grinned fiercely. "And you are?"

Confused? Not in the right space dock? Margot cleared her throat, straightened, and forced herself to say, "Margot."

Ki slapped her on the shoulder. "Let's get some grub, Margot. I'm starving and the flyers are more patient."

Margot looked from Ki's patchwork suit to the exquisite red solo-flyer parked beside hers. It was an older model, but there was no way that person paid for it. Margot had recent and intimate knowledge of the price of solo-flyers. She shook herself, locked her canopy, and followed. For someone so short, Ki walked at a brisk pace. Margot had to jog to catch up.

"Where . . . uh, Ki? Where did you get your solo-flyer?"

"Oh, that's for me to know." Ki swayed between a parked vehicle and the exit gate to the lot.

"Wait, we didn't . . ." Margot ducked close and lowered her voice as they waited in the docking bay's inner airlock. "We didn't pay."

Ki waved her hand leisurely. "I got it covered. You can make it up for me with lunch. You ever been to Lola's?"

The airlock opened onto the main station corridor. Instantly, suspicious glances fell on Ki. A merchant hurried to stand between them and her storefront.

Ki didn't seem to notice. She sauntered down the middle of the corridor like she belonged there. Margot would never have been so brave on her own. The force of other people's disapproval pressed down on her as she hurried after Ki.

⚡

Ki had only visited one restaurant on Laguna Station, and that was Lola's. It was a crescent-shaped cafeteria with a long window on the outer wall so customers could sit at the counter along it and marvel at Earth, which always filled one quarter of the view. There was a better window one level up and a little over, in a fancier restaurant, or so Ki had gleaned from advertisements plastered all over the station restrooms. Ki had tried to peek into that place, but the security guards stopped her before she was even close to the entrance. You could smell the expense coming off the printed wood grain.

Lola's smelled of steam and spoiled milk and Ki hurried Margot through the food line before she could have any doubts.

"Oh yeah, get the shwarma. It's the best thing they serve. Make it two."

"I don't know," Margot frowned at the self-service bar. "None of this looks very healthy."

A man in a Laguna Security uniform—and boy had Ki learned what those looked like—paused in his path across the room and turned. Ki quickly looked down and brushed a hand over her head. She should have worn a cap. "Get it to go," Ki said.

"What? I thought we'd . . ." Margot gestured vaguely toward the window.

Oh yes, the security guard was looking directly at Ki. "This place can be pretty lawless," Ki said. "We should keep an eye on the ships. It'll be like a picnic."

Margot looked to be considering it.

"Great," Ki said, and leaned forward to grab the 'to go' wrappers. They were flat spongy rice-bread. Ki dumped the spiced meat and rice Margot had picked into them, folded them up, and hurried Margot to the pay counter.

With one hand on Margot's back she watched the security guard take a seat, less concerned now that money was changing hands.

Soon they were ensconced on the noses of their flyers, unwrapping the steaming, spicy meat. The flyers themselves hooked into power, generously provided by the station's bad security.

Margot's drab green military-surplus (or, Ki supposed, not so surplus?) flight suit made her look like a stem, or maybe a leaf, lying across her mango of a ship. She had one leg dangling, tapping gently against the side with her calf. Margot was turning out to be quite the easy-going chick.

Though she kept looking at the doors. "What if someone comes in to dock?"

"There'll be an alarm and it'll give us plenty of time to get into the flyers. Relax."

"I just don't want to spill my shwarma," Margot said.

That sounded like a lie. "Heh. Yeah." Despite her long list of worries, Ki felt great. It really was like a picnic, and the food was good. Maybe she could give it a go, being homeless in space. Though up here, if a place wasn't inhabited, it wasn't habitable. At least not all the time. Maybe she could rig herself a series of airlock berths, hop around the local cops, palm a few tourist baubles for food . . . be a real space pirate.

Margot said, "This sauce tastes like real earth yogurt." She licked her thumb, and looked, again, at the dock doors.

Margot was so nervous it was making Ki nervous. Best to get her mind off depressurization. "This is the life, isn't it?" Ki asked. "Freedom. Just going where you please and eating when you're hungry."

"No, you need more than that. You need security for the next day and the next. I should never have bought this thing." Margot scowled at the shiny ceramic between her legs.

That was a pretty good opening. "Why not sell it? There's gotta be someone who'd take it. You might even make a profit, if they don't know what you paid."

Margot didn't say anything.

Ki pressed, "Don't know any spaceship dealers? How about parts and repair guys? Anyone who deals with registrations?" She was losing her. "Well, maybe if we head back to Luna . . ."

A service door screeched open. "Hey!" A man pointed at them. His environment suit had the security company logo on it. "No eating in here! Where are your helmets? Let's see your ship registrations."

Margot, like a dumb rich kid, set down her food and raised her hands and faced the cop.

Ki folded her food up and tucked it in a suit pocket. She smiled tightly, waving at the cop. Trying not to move her lips, she said, "He can't see my registration."

Margot's eyes got big. "Just send it to him."

Had she not gotten her super-subtle hint that the ship was hot? "Get your helmet. Fast."

Ki jumped into her ship and started it up. The cop was shouting. Margot didn't have her suit helmet on. The system refused Ki's request to open the outer doors because it detected there was a person without a helmet in the dock. Ki's ship hovered. Margot was still staring dumbly at the cop, shwarma on her lap.

Ki flipped through the options on her scrambler, bypassing the security lockdown and safety lockdown until the red lights flashed all around them.

"I'm going to kill you!" Margot's voice shouted from the ship-to-ship radio.

Well, good, that meant the stupid mark had gotten into her cockpit at last.

The cops were sending all sorts of angry chatter that mostly came down to "stop now or we shoot." They generally shot even if you did stop. Ki flew forward the second the doors opened wide enough, heading full speed to the edge of jurisdiction, wherever that was.

What she could not understand for the life of her was why Margot followed.

Margot wanted a gun. Any gun. A flare gun. A ten-millimeter slug-thrower. A front-mounted recoilless X-47 Cannon. Her vision was red and her anger was pure and she didn't feel afraid for the first time in four years, listing off to herself all the weapons and ammunition that she would definitely use to kill Ki.

She'd trusted this girl. Thought she'd found a friend, a sympathetic ear. She hadn't felt completely useless for about four minutes, and then she'd had her worst fear thrust on her.

An opening airlock.

She tried not to think too hard about her panic. It felt better to be angry.

Ki slowed down. Margot caught up to her and started running through all the buttons and controls on her dashboard. There was nothing on this ship she could use as a weapon. The best she could throw was foul language. She briefly considered ramming the red flyer.

No, that might chip her paint. She was going to bring this ship back to the dealer and apologize and ask for her money back. Maybe. Eventually.

What was Ki doing? They were . . . nowhere. Margot looked at her in-system map. They were just past Luna. It was a small crescent of hard light behind her.

Margot had to stop and think. She didn't like stopping and thinking. Should she call the police? Would they come out here? What then?

Ki radioed. "This ship needs to charge. Solar sub-light runs dry fast."

Just like that. Like they were on a trip together. "You are coming with me back to Luna and the proper authorities."

"What, is this a citizen's arrest?" Ki gave a short laugh. "You're going to want to reconsider that plan. Which authorities? What will you tell them? Did you stop to think what they'll ask you? What they'll want to know about you? You think it's going to be easy, like in a serial? You think you'll just say 'book her'? No, my friend, it does not work like that . . ."

There was something odd about Ki's words. It sank in slowly. She was just . . . talking. Fast and random. "What are you doing?" Margot demanded.

"Looking for a fence, and I found one. Later!"

Ki's ship arched over Margot's and sped down, toward Luna. Of all the impossible things!

By the time Margot got to the lunar surface, Ki's signal had merged with that of Isle Ibrium and vanished. Ki was inside Margot's hometown. Margot slowed her craft and hovered, looking down at the too-familiar domes and corridor spokes. She knew every inch of that tiny, awful colony. There weren't any fences. Fences were an Earth thing, for separating space without walls. Was that some outlaw lingo? There were no outlaws in her town! They barely had graffiti.

If she landed, she would have to face her parents. She felt safe only so long as she was in her flyer. A dim, irrational part of her was sure Ki's betrayal had been Margot's fault for leaving the cockpit.

This was exactly what the VA warned about. Irrational thinking. She had to calm down and take control. She flew into the public dock and logged herself as a visitor.

Fred Lakwana looked up from the duty desk. "Margot! What are you doing coming in on a visitor registration? I could have moved you to a closer berth."

"Sorry. Uh . . . in a hurry. Sorry."

There was a button to call station security right there next to Fred. She could stride up and hit it. But what would she say?

Fred looked at her oddly. So did Levi Sault, who was pushing a cargo sled. People were starting to stare and whisper. Margot had to find Ki fast. She bounded out of the dock lunatic style, grazing her fingers on the ceiling as she went, little push-offs to keep going. Ki would be going slow, earthling-style.

But being faster didn't help if Margot didn't know where she was going. She found herself in the promenade. She'd gone there out of habit. Shoppers milled. Food smells came from the automat. This was terrible. Any second now her father would walk by, or one of the kids from high school.

A fence? Margot stopped and asked her uplink for any alternate definitions of "fence."

One who buys and sells stolen goods? Where would you find that on Luna?

She should just go home, tell them everything, get yelled at, take the ship back.

The idea of losing her flyer felt like giving up her own skin.

Capturing Ki and taking her to justice wouldn't stop her from having to give the ship back, but at least it was something to do *before* giving it back.

She went back to the dock. Ki's ship wasn't there. "Mr. Lakwana, sir? Where else could a guest solo-flyer land?"

"Is this a club of yours? Someone lending those out?"

"Please, sir, I need to find . . . my friend."

He rubbed his bald spot and mumbled about kids and freedom and wasn't that nice. Margot felt Ki's lead stretch with every second.

"Oh, yes . . . a solo-flyer came in on a guest dock over by the research center. Say, is your mother working on the solar farm today?"

Margot left without answering, which felt rude and awful, and she stumbled trying to turn and explain herself, but Mr. Lakwana was already back to watching his screen.

Margot got in her flyer. It would be faster to fly around the colony than run through it. She made it to the guest airlock outside the research center just as a red solo-flyer flew out of it.

Ki was a better pilot. Margot had to stop and check the

manual every time she made a course correction, and then all these error messages were screaming at her as she approached Earth-controlled space. She lost Ki completely before she hit the cloud layer. Her vision went red; her head ached like it would explode. A traffic control bot talked her through landing.

The bot kindly told her that yes, there had been a red, unregistered solo-flyer with no logged flight path, and told her where to find it.

She was flying through the streets of an unfamiliar, run-down Earth city, panic like a cold fire in her chest, when she saw Ki's flyer, just sitting there next to a building.

And Ki, herself: climbing the building!

Margot couldn't believe it. Was she in an action serial? She forgot, for a moment, to be afraid. She ran into the building. A hologram in a nurses' uniform held up one hand. "I'm sorry, please scan your ID to visit All Souls Hospice, or state the name of the patient you are visiting."

Margot's heart pounded with the exertion of running in Earth-G. "I'm not here to visit anyone. I'm chasing this woman climbing up your building!"

"I'm sorry, please scan your ID to visit—"

Margot ran through the hologram. All the doors off the lobby were locked. She shouted, hoping a human attendant was nearby or at least had an audio feed. "Someone is climbing your building!"

A door opened. A disgruntled, wiry guy with pink dreadlocks waved Margot forward. "Come on, I know where she's headed."

He led her to an elevator. Margot sank gratefully against a scratched chrome bar. She hadn't wanted to think about running up stairs in this heaviness. The elevator was cramped and smelled of engine oil and opened onto to a corridor that was weirdly tall and narrow, cut with random angles like it had been assembled piecemeal and without care.

He unlocked a door and pushed it open. "This is the last time," he said. "Tell her that."

It was an empty hospital room. The bed was stripped down. Ki, looking very small, her face completely wet, sat in the middle of the floor. She hugged a sack almost as big as she was, labeled "Deceased's Belongings."

04:
GETTING OUT

LIGHT YEARS AWAY ON HIS HOME PLANET, PRINCE THANE OF Ratana held as still as he could. As still as a statue. The makeup went on cool and wet, but dried thick and itchy. If he blinked, the glitter would end up in his eyes, and royalty did not squint, cry, or wipe.

A door opened and despite himself he flinched. "Hold still!" The makeup artist hissed. She had ways of punishing him that left no marks. It was why, he suspected, she'd lasted longer than other groomers. Thane strained to see the door without moving his head. A shadow on the floor was all he could make out.

"That's my son, unable to do something as simple as sit still."

Of course it was his mother. "Sorry," Thane said, trying not to move his mouth. He tried to make it sound sincere, but it came out a petulant mumble.

The queen came closer. This time he didn't flinch. It was just nerves. Her shadow wasn't actually colder than the room. Her hand was on his shoulder. He was a statue. Perfectly still. No matter who touched him. A royal's body wasn't his own.

"What are you getting dolled up for?"

The groomer, thankfully, answered for him. "There's a library dedication."

His mother's fingers dug deep into the flesh of his neck. "Cancel it. Your aunt is here for the summit. As soon as you're done, come to the viewing gallery. I need you to look pretty and be distracting. And pay attention."

Distract everyone but pay attention. Her instructions set him up to fail. "Yes, mother."

"This summit is important. If I catch you chatting with your friends on your implant . . ."

"I won't. I haven't. Ow!" The long thin brush that was applying paint poked him in the eye as his mother smacked him.

"All the work I put into you." His mother grabbed his jaw and inspected his eyes. "I should have saved the money spent on your eyes, nose and teeth and gotten you a brain." She let go and marched out of the room.

He tried to stay still but tears welled, despite all his training, because of the sting of the paint.

The makeup artist grabbed his chin hard and poked his eye with a cotton swab. "That went well." A hard, rough swipe, and the tears were gone. It was magic. The artist looked him steadily in the eye, her face almost touching his. "Any mistakes in your makeup are *your* fault."

"Of course." Thane lowered his lashes and hoped he looked submissive and contrite. After a moment, the artist climbed off his lap. He heard her picking up new tools.

"Let's hope your jaw doesn't bruise. She grabbed you hard. I'm going to put a coat on it, just to be safe."

Thane caught a glimpse of himself in the mirror. He looked exactly like his father had in all the royal portraits. Like his father's father's father. Had they been born closer to the perfection demanded by their rank? Was there really any way to tell?

Behind him, the monster stirred. The camera-spider that followed him everywhere. Perhaps it detected emotion and wanted to get a shot of tears. Or it was ordered to provide a candid shot of the preparations for the day. Its many tiny eyes had watched every bad thing that had ever happened to Thane, and reported them to people who consistently did nothing.

With the barest smirk, as the makeup artist gave way to the hairdresser, Thane activated his implant and let messages swim into his hand.

The hospice orderly said, "You have two minutes. Then get out." Margot barely heard him. He left.

Ki looked about four years old. Margot didn't know how to be angry with someone who looked like that.

Also, now that Margot's rage was dissipating, she felt so very heavy and tired. Almost too tired to care the door was open. Almost. She closed it. Ki didn't move. Margot let the high gravity press her into the floor. Lying on her side, she watched Ki continue to cry and hug the bag. "Um . . . are you . . . ?"

"He was getting better," Ki said. "He was going to get better. We were going to explore the galaxy. Together. We were. I . . . I . . . look at me!" She threw her hands out like she'd spilled something on herself. "I'm in a stupid space suit. The money and time I spent . . . I'm useless and I'm too late and I didn't . . . I was going to . . ." She punched the floor. She pulled her hair. She punched herself in the chest, the arm.

Margot stopped Ki's fist as it flew wild. She gathered the tiny body to hers and held it. "It's okay," she said.

"No. It's not." Ki made an alarming sound, like she was chok-ing, but then she hiccupped and laid her head against Margot. "You came for me. That's . . . sweet."

Margot decided against telling her she'd come to kill her. "I have to get back."

Ki's arms tightened. "Don't leave . . . I mean . . . can I come with?"

Margot cleared her throat. "I live with my parents. They're going to be mad I've been gone all day without checking in." She was pretty sure they'd be mad if she did check in. Hi Ma, Hi Ba. I'm hugging a fugitive from justice, so I'll be home late.

Ki sniffled, leaving the conversation one-sided. Margot tried to explain. "They don't know I bought a flyer. They're going to make me sell it back."

Ki pulled back and gave her the weirdest look.

"What?"

"Don't do *that*." Ki straightened, no longer the helpless waif. "Sell it back? No. That's giving up. That's saying it was all for nothing!"

That resonated. Some planet kept its government and some trade agreement was destroyed and re-made and Margot Santiago-Nguyen went right back to where she'd been the day after graduating high school. Yeah, she knew what it felt like when your efforts were all for nothing.

Margot scooted back. It wasn't easy. She felt pressed into the floor and her joints ached. "I'd better get this over with." She pulled herself up against the wall.

Ki hopped to her feet. "Don't give up. Come with me. Please. I couldn't save him and I have to save *someone*." She winced. "Don't look at me like that. I mean . . . what do you have to lose?"

"Uh . . . everything? My home? My parents' respect?"

Ki shrugged like that didn't sound like much. "You know

what parents love? Money. Come home rich, and they won't care how late you are."

"That's stupid."

Ki swung her leg out the window and straddled the sill—heavy gravity, heavy emotions, and all. "Maybe. I want to do something stupid. Something brave and crazy. Worthy of . . ." She trailed off, then smiled sharply. "You're welcome to be stupid with me." And she jumped out the window.

Margot ran to the window, a scream caught in her throat. Ki was making her unhurried way down the building. Margot felt dizzy and exposed, hanging over the long way down. She was abandoned in a rickety structure made mostly of decayed plant material on a planet with no dome over her.

In a weird mix of compassion and anger, she returned to her flyer.

A strange man on a hover bike was next to it, looking at it. His face was obscured by a reflective visor. Margot felt awkward approaching the stranger, but he was the one practically drooling on her ship. "Excuse me?"

A reflection of the building slid across his visor as he looked up. If she looked hard enough, would she see Ki climbing in miniature on his face? "This yours?" the man asked.

There were oily black machine-gun muzzles on his hover bike. A ship thief? Margot trembled. The man looked down again. "Dinger" was written in chrome speed-slanted letters on his bike. It sounded like a euphemism she didn't want to know the meaning of. "Yes, it's my ship. Excuse me, I'm meeting someone."

"You expect me to believe a Luna registration? In this neighborhood?"

He dismounted, the leather of his bodysuit and saddle creaking. "I'm taking your ship." He reached to pull something from a holster on his side.

Margot dove into her open cockpit and hit the police panic button. Nothing happened. The man stood over her, gun out. He cocked his head. "That's adorable. Maybe you are from Luna. You think car alarms work."

A shadow swooped over them. Ki in her red flyer. Dinger craned his neck to follow the shape and holstered his gun. "Hello, old friend."

"Hello, asshole," Ki returned in the same quiet, admiring tone. "Let her go. She's legit."

"Of course. Soon as you hand over that flyer."

"This? This isn't the flyer you're looking for. I left that with a chop shop on Luna. This one just looks exactly like it. Check the registration."

"Bullshit."

Ki leaned over the side of her ship, looking somehow older and taller. "You want to waste time decoding my fake? It's flawless. I'll mail it to the judge myself."

The asshole looked back at Margot and shrugged. "I don't get paid by the hour," he said.

A text buzzed on Margot's dash. "That means move it now while he's feeling lazy. Go go go."

Ki lowered her canopy and rose into the air with all appearances of no haste. Margot cleared her throat, said, "So . . ." and slammed her canopy shut and took off.

She caught up to Ki two blocks away. "You know that man?"

"Wish I didn't."

Margot couldn't believe how close she'd come to being robbed and left abandoned on Earth. All her back pay from the military turned into some ship thief's bounty. On her dash the "call police" light was still blinking. She turned it off. "Why didn't the police come and help?"

Ki cackled like this was a rare joke. "Because they're the

police. Come on, let's circle back. It'll be dangerous, but I need to get some things."

Thane's aunt was the head of Ratana's military, as stiff as her uniform, which was more than half couched silver thread. Thane watched her greet the queen with all the flexibility of a yardstick. Thane's sister Jolica, the heir apparent, dropped into a liquid curtsey at their mother's side. Jolica was a fantastic faker. You could almost believe she was delighted. Slowly, the most important women on the planet arranged themselves into a tiny parade and made their way up and down the gathered dignitaries, themselves standing in rank precedence along the banquet tables. Behind them, the camera bots swayed, craning for the best angles.

Thane was up in a balcony overhead with his uncle and two unmarried male cousins. Uncle Reg sat against the wall, arms crossed, looking disdainfully at nothing at all.

"Politics," Thane's cousin Amir said, sliding up to him. "Boring as fuck, isn't it? I'm glad we're up here and not down there." Amir was beautiful. Darkest skin in the family, and ropey muscles that shifted luxuriantly under his robe. They'd been friends, once, when they were too young to know better.

"You're standing too close," Thane said, expression cool, voice pitched low. Even if the camera-beast picked this up, it wouldn't matter too much. Thane didn't have to be polite to his male cousins.

"You should be nicer, cuz," Amir said, draping an arm around his shoulders. "You're down to one sister."

Amir was so careless. They weren't kids anymore to be seen touching. Thane pushed his arm off. "Is that a threat to the royal heir? Please, please tell me that was a threat."

"I'm expressing sympathy, you frozen prick." Amir settled his arms on the railing, robe sleeves trailing, and looked down at the female party below. The nape of his neck was breathtaking. The bastard. "I've still got two sisters, more's the pity, and either one of them would love to be queen. They aren't going to care much if they feed you to the sky wolves to get it. Me, I care. We have to stick together or they'll walk all over us."

Thane hated when other men talked about 'us' and 'we' like he owed them something. And all Amir would do was talk, anyway. Talk and bite his succulent lower lip and then run off to kiss some female cousin's ass. Thane checked his implant, cupping the hand inside his sleeve so it wouldn't show.

Amir sighed, holding up his hands. "Fine. Let's not relieve the boredom. It might be above our manly station."

More stupid talk. Thane had an account on the underground freenet—the ultimate rule-breaking. The top posts were about the summit, protests and demonstrations against it. Thane hated when the freenet got political. He could care less about that stuff.

He switched to the fan discussion for *Knights of Saint George* to see if anyone had commented on his post about his favorite character, Galahad. Thane was of the opinion that Galahad was the real main character, not his sister Chantoya. And here was another knob arguing that Galahad was boring. BORING. Thane brought up his keypad to retort.

Amir leaned into his line of vision. "Hey, cuz? Whatever you're doing? Your mom saw it."

Thane closed the link, closed his fist, and looked with icy horror down at his mother, who spared him a brief glance.

Behind him, the camera-beast stirred. A palace guard approached. She tapped her spear on the ground. "Prince Thane? Your presence is requested."

Thane wished he had an eye-display so he could type without being seen. He wished he could wipe his device's history.

He wished Amir hadn't seen that. The other man shook his head, smirking, and went back to watching the women below.

When Ki and Ethan last celebrated their birthdays—was it really only a year ago? Her birthday was two weeks before Ethan's so they always picked a date between to celebrate. Not a weekend, those were Ethan's busiest working days. A Tuesday, usually.

Last year as her birthday approached, Ki had robbed and fenced and saved to take Ethan out on the town—a real restaurant dinner and drinks on a rooftop club. They were so shabbily dressed everyone thought they must be celebrities. They laughed at the whispers and toasted their dying youth. Ethan wasn't that sick yet, but somehow they both knew they wouldn't live much longer.

Dinger could be setting a trap. Taking his time because he knew he had her. Ki checked all her feeds and sent out sniffers. This meant she saw the date. Her birthday was in two weeks. She hadn't been thinking about it, this year. She hadn't made any plans to celebrate with Ethan.

Not having plans to cancel felt like the worst betrayal.

Ki led Margot on a circuitous path through the city, to give herself time to stop crying.

Margot knew she was letting life pull her along again. She followed Ki to a storage locker, and then to a disreputable junk dealer. In the shop, Margot kept her distance and exchanged nothing more than disapproving glances. That Dinger person could show up again at any time. Or another like him. "Is this really necessary?"

"You want to leave Sol system, don't you? Can't do that on one order of shwarma."

Ki had saved her from Dinger and all, but . . . "No one said anything about leaving the system."

Ki tilted her head down at a tiny opening in the bullet-proof glass separating the junk dealer from his customers. "Come on, Tomsik. It's worth twice that. They're collector's items." She looked calm, amused. Somehow, that made the pain she was covering up more obvious.

Maybe Margot knew a bit about that.

Ki turned away from the counter and shook three fat triangular pieces in her palm. "Trines. These are good in most of the colonies."

"Do you even have a plan?" Margot asked.

Tomsik, behind the glass, barked a sarcastic laugh and walked away.

Ki didn't seem to hear him. "We'll go to Ratana. Richest planet in the galaxy, and not that far away. We fly in, steal something, fly out. Real space pirating."

Margot had a patch on her uniform from Ratana. She had not seen the planet, of course, just the ordinance room. Every battle looked the same from inside the belly of a ship. Still, the name "Ratana" made her think of explosive decompression.

There was something comfortingly familiar in that. "Sure," she said, "Let's do that." If the suggestion had been any place less meaningful, would she have said no?

Ki tucked the coins in a pocket. "I have some supplies hidden near here, but we'll need other stuff. Do you have any cash? You can't be too careful going interstellar."

Margot checked her bank balance on her bracelet. Forty credits left. Not a fortune by any means. Her bank informed her that the exchange rate on the Triad Trade Association Winged Trine was one trine to 13.2 credits, currently. So she and Ki were about even on funds. "How many supplies are we talking about?"

Ki frowned and looked away. "Well, I wouldn't ask you to spend more than you're comfortable . . ."

"Give me a list," Margot said. "I'm good with lists."

"You are amazing at this," Ki gushed.

The lack of organization in the Army-Navy store set Margot's teeth on edge. "Compared to finding one box of ammunition in a storehouse of boxes of ammunition, it's... somehow worse."

Margot found the whole list without touching the trine coins. She felt powerful. This was what it was like, then, to take care of someone else.

Packages in hand, they paused to look up and down the street for Dinger or his ilk. Ki ran off—west. They'd hidden the ships in an abandoned garage to the east. Where was she going? Feeling exposed and under fire, Margot followed her.

Ki led her under a bridge. It was filthy—cold, leathery mud underfoot. A makeshift shelter of garbage and twine clung to the highest, driest spot. Ki scrambled into it.

Margot lifted the plastic sheeting with one finger and thumb, not wanting to touch more than that. Inside, Ki squatted on matted paper. She lifted a rock, took a small, silver thing from under it and tucked it in a pocket. She pulled a cap from under a folded blanket and put it on her head.

Margot let the flap drop. Ki lived here. This was where she

lived. Margot almost couldn't breathe. Did Earth people live like this?

Ki duck-walked out. "One more thing to get," she said, and half-crawled along the slippery rock edge to the side of the bridge, where she removed a brick to pick something out of a hidey-hole.

"Okay," Ki said. She slapped Margot's back. Margot tried not to recoil. "Off to adventure!"

Adventure, indeed, Margot thought sarcastically as she wiped her fingers on her thigh and stomped the mud from her boots on the sidewalk. Everything was grubby and dirty and their ships were in a grubby burned-out garage with more plastic sheeting.

She forgot to be afraid until they were pushing their ships out of said garage and saw something very like Dinger's hoverbike flicker by on a cross street.

Margot felt a tickling of excitement. Like when she'd left for the Navy. Adventure, indeed, she thought, without sarcasm this time.

She got into her ship feeling like she'd died in the war, and her corpse had been floating along in her trajectory. In the flyer, however, she could steer, and steering made her alive again. Going home, facing the consequences of all she'd done, would be to go back to being a corpse.

Ki couldn't believe her luck, punching out of Earth's atmosphere with a full hold of emergency supplies and no official warning to halt in the name of the law! Yet. The registration scrubbing from Luna must have worked. Ki looked over at Margot's orange flyer. The shiny egg could be anyone. It should have been Ethan.

"Excited, rookie?"

"I . . . no. But I feel . . . I feel free." The last word came out a sigh. "Like I had this leash on me and I didn't know it until I took it off." Then, more her rough self, Margot said, "And I'm not a rookie."

It was almost something Ethan would say. Ki felt a hole punched through her careful preoccupation. She was making plans just to make plans. Was it fair to this random Lunie she'd just met?

An official alert from air traffic control snapped her out of it. Someone had filed a complaint, a reasonable doubt about one red solo-flyer.

They needed to move fast. Ki aimed for the out-system gate and dropped all her qualms. "I'm telling you, rookie, get down to the surface of Ratana, scoop up a handful of dirt, and there'll be a diamond in it. Last time I was there, I got an emerald as big as my fist."

"What happened to it?"

Ki was not in the mood to construct a backstory for her lie. She made a noncommittal noise and hoped Margot would drop it. "Wait until you see the crystal canyons and the wastelands!"

"If you're not making this all up, you had an emerald the size of your fist but now you live under a bridge."

Damn she was persistent. Was that accusation or pity in Margot's voice? Ki didn't like either. "Oh, is that an embarrassing story! I can't keep hold of money to save me. But trust me, if we get to Ratana, we can get a big enough score to get us both to the next thing."

Margot said, "What do you mean, 'if'?"

Right on cue, another challenge from the authorities, and this one with a note that a ship was coming to intercept them. Ki felt like she was coming apart at the seams. "You're one of those people who likes to plan everything, aren't you?" She checked the cops' trajectory. It was close, but they could beat him to the gate. She started a search for information on Ratana so she could answer Margot's questions. "Have some sense of adventure. Look, that's the safety limit buoy. I'm going FTL. Oh no! Is that Dinger behind us?"

Please follow, she thought, and yanked the ship into stardrive. Don't leave me alone.

Margot saw Ki's ship abruptly slip out of sight.

Margot dangled over nothingness, her responsibilities and parents behind her, the unknown ahead.

"I already regret this," she said, and told her ship to follow Ki. Everything shrank to a point in front of Margot's view-screen—the long, illogical tunnel of FTL. She'd only seen it before in training. There were no windows in a navy ship, not outside of the rec deck. Margot stared at the point and tried to wrap her head around the math. She couldn't. She darkened the canopy.

"That's a girl," Ki sent via ansible, the text somehow conveying her smug tone. "I knew you'd take the leap."

Margot grinned despite herself. She'd never gotten an ansible transmission before. Her parents had preferred to send messages to her inbox in Sol system for the military to relay. It was cheaper than waiting in line and paying for the military ansible. But with two private transmitter-receivers in the same jump space, it didn't cost a thing. Margot typed back. "What do you do to entertain yourself during the tunnel?"

"I'm already reading a book. Take a nap if you gotta. We'll have a warning before we come out."

Ki was so cool and confident. Margot felt a thin edge of her anxiety coming back. Ki's words reminded her of the fragility of her flyer, the distance she was traveling, her past falling behind her.

She closed her eyes and breathed slowly, in, hold, out, like the VA counselor had said. This time, it actually worked.

$$\text{\Lightning}$$

Ki was reading the search results from the onboard wiki. The history was long and dry. Ratana means "Crystal" and the planet is known for its mineral wealth. This geologist became the first queen. These people tried to overthrow the queen. Then these people did. These people actually overthrew her for, like, a day. Then they were wiped out. Seemed like control of Ratana wasn't worth what people were willing to pay for it. None of this was distracting her from her loneliness. Also, there were no mentions of getting rich quick. Ki switched to a tourist article. "What you need to know before visiting Ratana."

"Respect Ratana's strict cultural norms. Male visitors should always have a female escort. (See our companion article for men traveling alone on Ratana.) Avoid physical affection in public, especially same-sex couples. But the food is fantastic!" The rest was all about how to eat politely and how far away to stand when talking to people and some weird thing about eye makeup, like you shouldn't wear any unless you read this whole other article on eyeliner etiquette.

You'll get a diamond just from digging up the dirt? What was her mouth thinking? Ki went back to the official wiki, skimmed for mentions of border control. She switched to her copy of Crimeopedia: All the information lawbreakers needed, provided by lawbreakers.

"Do not try to evade border control on Ratana. Decades of war and generations of resource-robbing travelers have left the planet paranoid and shrewd. You may be killed. If you can, obtain a false citizen identity before entering the system. On Earth, a good supplier is . . ."

Well, that was nice and distracting. Ki skipped ahead to the "less recommended strategies" section.

$$\lightning$$

Margot was awakened by the rapid expansion of light as they dropped out of FTL.

"Tack off with me over the pole," Ki said over the radio. "That's how I got in last time."

Ratana opened below them, smooth as a billiard ball and dusty-tan. Its sun shone redder than Sol, and a blood-orange gas giant lurked nearby to increase the ruddy effect. Margot got telemetry from Ki and followed her precise course for Ratana's north pole where a thin cap of ice gleamed an odd, intense teal.

As they approached, Ratana's seeming sameness broke into jagged traceries—glints of rivers and lakes—a branching network of dark canyons.

"It's beautiful," Margot said.

Ki's response was an awed, "Yeah."

Margot was going to see Ratana as a place, not a war. It was real. It did matter. The fear and death were not for nothing. It was for this. The canyons beyond the daylight terminus gleamed brilliantly with electric lights, like the world was a cracked egg, illuminated from the inside. This was the peace she'd felt zooming along Luna's surface, alone (more or less) with stark, natural majesty.

"Unidentified solo-flyers, you will level off at this altitude and transmit your entrance visas."

The voice cut right through Margot's thoughts. She started to change course, but saw Ki hadn't.

"Ki. Slow down. We're being hailed."

"Unidentified solo-flyers. You have ten seconds to change course or we will fire on you."

"Ki! Slow down. We have to stop for the border patrol."

"Don't chicken out now." Ki veered sharply, a dart of red light.

Margot realized a second later that they were, in fact, running from the cops. Something bright flashed in the corner of her vision. And again. Tracer rounds? Lasers? They were firing on her? Someone was attacking her, personally, not the ship she was on. It was insulting.

Margot slowed down and hailed the police.

"Shit. Margot. Margot, what are you doing? Speed up, Margot. Follow my course and SPEED UP."

"I'm sorry, I can't do that. I'm going to apologize and hope for leniency."

"Margot! This is a fascist planet! You can't—"

Ki's voice cut off mid-breath. Either they were too far apart now, or the police were jamming as they closed around Margot.

Margot would explain her situation and the authorities would see how there was no harm done and no harm meant and send her on her way. "Hello? My name is Margot Santiago-Ngyuen. I'm from Luna."

The signal was not received. Margot frowned. She didn't understand radios that well, but it was clear nothing was getting out or in. Her ship jolted sharply and veered left. The controls did nothing. Her ship obediently hovered close to a police ship, moving with it. The police had control. Well, that was good. They'd know what to do. Margot watched the landscape. Each valley they passed seemed deeper than the last, and each rock spire higher. It was a wonder the planet had looked so smooth from orbit.

She hit the ground with a jolt. She hoped that didn't scratch the paint. The canopy opened. She started to straighten and felt herself grabbed. She was thrown onto hard dirty ground, the air pressed out of her lungs. She couldn't scream. Rough hands twisted her arms. Metal closed on her wrists. "You are charged with illegal entry and suspected smuggling," an angry woman said. "Be silent or you will be shot."

They wrenched her to her feet. She blinked away dust and tears. Her hair was sticking to her cheeks. "I—"

"This is your last warning." Someone punched her in the kidneys. She stumbled forward, and continued stumbling as she was pushed and pulled until she fell into a dirty little room. They closed the door and she was alone.

She never got a chance to start the explanation.

05:
HOW KI MET ZULEIKAH

ZULEIKAH MANGAN EXISTED IN A STATE OF WELL CRAFTED, CARE-
fully maintained boredom. When she did work up some interest in something—metal repair or zither music—her mother
would crush that interest in mountains of equipment and tuto-
rials and advice. It was best not to.

Lately, Zuleikah was not showing interest in solo-flyers.
She'd picked up a vintage solo-flyer from an art dealer and
her mother had obediently flown in, buying the best of all the
best parts and tools to fix it up and sending Zuleikah to slouch
unwillingly through spaceship repair classes and flying lessons.
Zuleikah enjoyed the spaceship repair and flying lessons, but it
was exhausting, pretending all the time that she didn't.

Stretched out on the sofa in her home, Zuleikah trolled the
solo-flyer fan boards, trying to decide if she really was interested
in the latest model release rumors, or just less uninterested.

Her father's voice interposed itself. "Are you home, darling?"

Zuleikah waved an acknowledgement and her father received

a pre-recorded video simulation of his daughter paying dutiful attention. Zuleikah moved back and forth between the flyer board and celebrity news, pictures of the crown prince's moue as he stood in the back of the queen's council. She was relieving her boredom by watching someone else being bored. It was tragi-comic.

Her father sighed. "Your mother asked me to nag again. I hate doing this, but she has a point. Your brother isn't getting any younger, and it wouldn't hurt you to get out more. I don't understand why you don't have more friends. You're so tall!"

Zuleikah wondered what the average variation was on her father's conversation openers. She checked the stats as her simulation dutifully answered that she was doing all she could to throw eligible young ladies in her brother's path. Or him in their path. According to the stats, her conversation simulator had 7% more variance in phrasing than her father.

Zuleikah regarded her father's hologram. Was her father also using a simulation for their conversations?

He was mixing himself a drink and it was still mid-day. So, no. "Your aunt and cousins are coming for Founder's Day, and I was hoping we could turn it into a big to-do. It would be a good time for you to talk with your cousin about the export business."

Zuleikah made another gesture, and her simulation told her father, sincerely, how very little she wanted a job working for or with or even over her cousin. Yes, even if her cousin had lots of friends with unmarried brothers. The argument escalated and moved so politely Zuleikah suspected her father wasn't really paying attention, either. "Your mother expects me to keep you on track. You think I enjoy playing the nag?"

Prince Thane was gorgeous, though. There was an interest her mother couldn't buy. It would be amusing to see her try. Almost. Zuleikah's family was wealthy, but as far below the crown as dirt was beneath the stars. What if she said she only had eyes for the prince? Her father wouldn't dare try to secure an invitation to a royal function, but her mother? She was immune to humiliation.

Zuleikah saved the best pictures of Thane to her secure server.

An alert pulled her eye from the handsome prince's pout. Someone had posted an urgent, anonymous message to the solo-flyer community board. That wasn't boring. She read it and it wasn't boring at all. Zuleikah cancelled the simulation. It would appear to step out of frame to check on something and then she stepped into frame. "I have to go, Dad."

"Did someone call you? JJ Arbourgh's sister? Another boy's chaperone? Another girl?"

"A friend is in trouble. I'll call you when I get back." Zuleikah laughed. Her father looked so proud and excited, and Zuleikah was going to go break someone out of jail.

Ki never looked back after Margot hailed the cops; there was no glory in getting yourself caught trying to save an idiot from themselves. The magnetic storm at the pole did its trick, as the wiki had promised, confusing the cops' instruments so she could get away. In the short window before the planetary defenses could lock in on her again, she cleverly set off three controlled bursts and cut all power. Hard to track, she fell toward the surface. Sweat broke out all over her body, her blood thumping in her ears as she forced herself to count to five slowly before starting the power again.

Roll, orient, fly . . . she was too busy to feel anything until she found a remote, rocky overhang to hide under. She turned off everything but her passive data sniffer. Ki breathed out slowly. She was safe, for now.

Safe and more alone than she had ever been.

Poor, stupid, naïve Margot. They should have gone over the plan. Okay, if Ki had made the plan before hitting light speed. They could have gone over *possible* plans.

And she could have explained that no matter what, you don't go to the cops.

Ki had a long, long file on her personal drive titled "Next Time." Ethan had suggested it. She really should go back and sort its entries by situation. Add a keyword system.

Next time.

The passive data scanner flashed and fluttered. Ki thought she'd lose her mind watching until it darkened and died. If the cops were still sweeping for her, they'd given up on this area. She counted to sixty for superstition's sake, and then started up her active scanner. Please, someone, be out there.

The local public network was . . . intensely secured. It wanted a citizenship ID number to start a connection, before a triple-factor password. She narrowed the focus of her scanner to find other data streams. There was one—bouncing around, redundant secure packets with no apparent origin. Paranoid, but not secure. Anyone could log in, but no one could see who was logged in or from where. Underground network. Nice. It didn't take long to find the local solo-flyers' club. Ki used all the security protocols the message board required and bounced her post off a soft drink manufacturer just to be safe. It never hurt to be more paranoid than the paranoids.

"To anyone reading this board: This is Klepto, fresh from out-system and short one buddy. Border cops got her. Anyone up for a rescue mission?"

She waited.

"You really have to start planning more than one move ahead, Ki." She fidgeted, hardly able to take her eyes off the screen. How was she supposed to predict Margot would do such a crazy thing? She'd seemed so steady!

Ki was about to give up and try a different message group when a reply came in, vocal: a bored female voice with the typical Ratanese lilt. "Are you talking about breaking someone out of jail?"

Ki felt awash in relief. "My friend's a rookie and I got her into this, so I gotta get her out. I'll go alone if I have to, fair warning." Please don't call my bluff, she thought. She couldn't do this alone.

"What did she do?"

"Not a damn thing, other than fly into Ratana space without asking. Cops always have it in for us solo-flyers."

Ki held her breath, hoping it was the right tactic. Hell, it was nearly the truth.

"Sounds interesting. Let's talk more. Offline. Somewhere secure. Hm . . . how about . . ."

A series of coordinates flashed on Ki's console. She couldn't start her engine fast enough.

The coordinates were on the shores of one of Ratana's many poisonous lakes, this one turquoise with bands of what looked like gold flakes floating in it. Thanks to the guidebook, Ki knew better than to touch. The shore was encrusted with crystals and mud flats. Ki parked on a dumpling-shaped rock that was a nice, safe-looking shade of brown.

A stylish black solo-flyer, a vintage Hawk Angel, skimmed the surface of the lake and landed next to her.

Ki whistled low. Brand-new the Hawk Angel had been worth a fortune. Now? It was priceless. Ki had no idea how many were even *left*. It was the best of the pre-war flyers, and the most stylish, with its swept-back wing-shapes on the sides. Back then, only the insanely rich travelled between stars. Well, the insanely rich, corporations and governments. That amounted to the same thing, though.

The smoky glass canopy opened and a Ratanese girl rose from the seat. She pulled a black, old-fashioned helmet off and shook her head. She had the very dark complexion Ratanese people tended to have in dramas, with her head mostly shaved, a lone braid laying on her scalp, dyed light green. Her eyes were outlined in glittering lime paint.

Well-fitting, new clothes. Now this was a mark. A Happy Birthday to Ki, mark. Ki kept her eyes, mostly, on the flyer. "That is a classic! What is it, fifty years old? How do you get replacement parts?"

The girl frowned, severe as a prison guard. "Do you have a plan? For your rescue?"

"What's your name?"

"Zuleikah."

"Nice to meet you, Zuleikah." Ki set one hand reverently on the gilt hawk-beak on the nose of Zuleikah's flyer. "Call me Ki." She smiled at her own audacity in giving her real name. "I *always* have a plan."

Zuleikah didn't look impressed. "A foreign woman was arrested an hour ago in a brand-new solo-flyer. I presume that is your friend? Margot Santiago-Nguyen?"

Ki nodded, slowly. She bit hard inside her lip to keep from smiling. She had a feeling this gal would react best to serious and somber. "If you can get me where she is, I can get her out."

Hopefully. Ki had a habit of burning her bridges when she got to them.

The longer Margot was left alone the more worried she got. The room was narrow and bare, with nothing in it but a hard bench and a phosphere for light. Her tears dried and itched and she had to go to the bathroom.

"Hello? Anyone? Is there a camera on me? Hello? I need to use the bathroom!" She waved and paced and repeated her pleas until her mouth was dry.

She was squirming when the door finally opened. She jumped to her feet, only to be pushed back. Two officers entered the room. They had broad-shouldered, embroidered jackets. Silver wings flew out on their lapels and pointed up on the sides of their caps. Dark blue wings of makeup fanned out from the eyelids of the foremost officer, outlined in black, making her appear bird-like and predatory. All the officers she'd seen had these eye-wings in varied shades of blue and green. Margot wasn't sure if it was the fashion on Ratana or part of their uniforms. It was hard not to stare when they blinked. The officer said, "You may write a message to be transmitted via ansible. If someone is willing to cover the expense, you will be released to return to Luna."

She handed Margot a tablet and stood, waiting.

"Could I go to the restroom?"

The officer didn't respond. Margot felt stupid, writing out the message, erasing it, revising it, while these large, unimpressed people watched. After a few minutes, the officer abruptly snatched the tablet away.

She'd written, "To Javiar Santiago-Nguyen and Thi Nguyen,

Isle Imbrium, Luna: This is Margot. Went to Ratana. Just a joy ride. Don't be mad. Cops need to know that you'll vouch for me and pay for return trip. Sorry. Don't know what I was thinking. Please don't—"

She hadn't figured out what she was hoping they wouldn't do. Punish her? Hate her? Kick her out? She regretted using the word "cops" which seemed almost an admission of guilt, like she wasn't on the law's side.

The officers turned to leave. Margot had to grab a sleeve. "Please. I need to use a bathroom."

The officer backhanded her and the door closed. Margot curled on her side on the floor. Her bladder hurt. She tried not to move.

Finally, the door opened again. An officer pulled her up by her arm. Margot felt like she was going to wet her pants just from moving, but she hurried to comply. She was pushed into a room. The door behind her closed and locked. In front of her was a second door like an airlock, but it obviously wasn't an air-lock because the second door didn't reach the floor nor ceiling. She opened it and found herself in a washroom. Three sinks and three partitions with doors. Like an old-fashioned movie version of a . . .

Margot pushed open a door and was so relieved to see a toilet she almost fell over.

The officers were waiting outside the bathroom. They put her in a different small, featureless room to wait. This one didn't even have a bench, just a floor and walls and a light. She had a headache and a strange, hollowed-out feeling. The worst that could happen had happened, hadn't it? And she was still there.

Or maybe it wasn't the worst. That was the problem. She should have been blown into space during the war. Then she wouldn't have to keep waiting for the worst to happen.

An official whose uniform lacked silver wings opened the door and tossed her a data cube. "Congratulations," she said, "No sign of contraband in your flyer. Either you did a good job scrubbing it, or you're just as stupid as you look." Her eye-wings were dark, almost purple, and her eyes were hard to see inside the heavy makeup, making her look blind. "Press your thumb where indicated. By doing so you verify that we were in our rights to search you and accept our findings. This is not a legally-binding statement of your innocence, but it may be admitted as evidence in a court of law on other worlds."

She spoke in a rapid and bored monotone, the voice of many repetitions. It took Margot a few minutes to catch up. "Oh. Okay." She turned the cube over until she found the big red "Thumb here" sign and pressed it.

The officer snatched the cube back and dropped it efficiently into a pocket. "This doesn't mean you're off the hook. It means we're going to actually wait for a response from your ansible before sentencing you. Who was the other flyer with you, and where did they go?"

"I don't know."

"You do realize that if we find out you have lied to us, that's a crime. You are being recorded."

Margot didn't have a lot of experience with lying. Her parents always knew when she did it. She'd never lied to a teacher or a superior officer. Ki had saved her from that Dinger person . . . so what? It wasn't like she owed her anything. In fact, Ki owed her! For food and provisions.

An eye-wing lifted expectantly. Margot ducked her head. "I swear. She . . . or he . . . just tagged along. I didn't say anything because solo-flyers like to group up. For safety. You know?"

It felt wrong to snitch on someone, even someone she'd just met.

The officer's painted wings seemed to tilt down for a dive. "And the party you contacted for the money? Who are they?"

"My parents." Margot felt small and young and pathetic. "It was a stupid idea. I wanted an adventure. I swear I'll never do something like this again. Never." She sniffled and hated herself for sounding so weak.

"We torture people on this world." The officer said it like she was proud of it. Her purple lips stretched. "If your home planet doesn't pay to have you back, it'll be easier to execute you than have a trial. Just think about that, and how little you owe your friend."

With that, Margot was left alone, again.

06:
THE JAILBREAK

THE POLICE STATION, LIKE MOST RATANESE ARCHITECTURE, WAS primarily underground, taking advantage of some natural crevasse or human-made mining pit. It looked like a peg in a hole. The squat structure was topped with solar panels like the head of a nail. A nail with a front door and a loading dock.

Atop a cliff half a mile distant, Ki and Zuleikah lay side-by-side on their stomachs. Ki squinted through her binoculars at the complex. She saw the door, the windows, the fence, the lights, but no matter how many filters she flipped through—ultraviolet, infrared, sonic—there was no sign of anything inside the nail head. "They have some serious shielding."

"I have internal communications. Looks like she's cooperating. They're going to fine her and escort her off the planet." Zuleikah removed an earpiece and sat back on her heels. "So much for that."

Ki peered at her. "What are you talking about? So much for what? We're still doing this thing. After all the trouble we went to getting on this planet . . . jeez, it's demoralizing if we let them kick her right off again."

The very slightest smile graced Zuleikah's lips. "I suppose it would be wrong to pass up a perfectly frivolous chance to endanger our lives."

It was the sort of thing Ethan would say. Ki set down the binoculars and turned fully to look at Zuleikah. "I . . . look, I don't know anything about you or your situation. I don't know what you're risking or what you have to go back to. You don't have to follow me into this if it'll cost you too much. And it could. Even your life."

Zuleikah shrugged.

Ki supposed that meant Zuleikah wasn't too concerned about losing anything. "Why are you here?"

"I was bored."

"And?"

Another shrug.

Ki laughed before she realized she was going to. She slapped her hands over her face, getting dust in her eyes, which just made her laugh more. It felt wonderful. She laughed up at the purple twilight. She laughed at the taste of dust and the smell of her sweat and Zuleikah's perfume.

Zuleikah poked her. "Hey. Stop. Stop that."

"No, no," Ki shook her head and got back on her elbows to pick up the binoculars again. "No." She had tears in her eyes and her hands were way too filthy to rub them. She took a slow breath, giggled, and got herself under control. "That's just the most perfect reason I've ever heard." Zuleikah nodded as if, well, duh, of course it was. This girl could be Ki's new best friend. "Okay. Okay. We're both in it whole hog. See if you can find out when they'll be moving Margot."

"What about her flyer?"

Ki clapped Zuleikah on the shoulder. "Of course! Find the impound lot."

⚡

"Your parents have forwarded your fine plus the price of retuning your star drive," an officer with gold wings on her hat pulled Margot out of her cell. Two more cops waited in the hall. They wrenched her hands behind her and cuffed them. Margot tried to console herself that at least the ordeal was almost over. She'd be back home, back at square one, but things couldn't actually get any worse.

No, no—she knew, academically, that getting killed would be worse, but right now she couldn't explain to herself why.

The police took her from the boring, beige cell to a boring, beige corridor, and out onto the boring, beige desert. Nothing to distract her from her impending doom. Walking on a far-flung planet should have felt amazing, like what she first envisioned when she joined the navy: seeing the galaxy up close.

There was a dark line in the sand. They marched her toward it. It widened into a chasm. Margot struggled, leaning back as they approached the sharp drop-off. Sand pooled in front of her and then fell over the edge to skitter down jagged rocks.

There was a stairway of stone cut into the side of the canyon—an extremely narrow stairway with no handrail and a sharp drop, and her hands cuffed behind her. "I'm going to fall!" They shoved her forward. She scrambled to keep her feet under her. The stairs were slippery with sand.

"Come on! Relax, would you?"

She tried to keep her eyes on the steps and leaned toward the canyon wall. She'd never been comfortable with open spaces. Cliffs? In high gravity? That wasn't even fair. Her head was spinning and if there weren't hard hands holding her, she might have pitched right over the edge despite herself.

Every step echoed. Crawling sounds of pebbles falling. The cry of some hidden animal. Tiny blue succulents filled the air with spice.

She missed the boring featureless room.

The stairs ended at a concrete platform jutting out of a cave. Chain link fencing blocked the mouth of the cave, and inside she could see her solo-flyer resting in front of a selection of other vehicles. Her knees wobbled.

One of the officers stepped forward to unlock the gate. The one standing closest to Margot said, "Your star drive is tuned to deliver you to Sol system. Once we bring the vehicle out of lockup, you'll get in and fly with us to the limits of Ratana space. At that time, you'll be on your own to get home."

"I understand," Margot said, hoping she sounded as serious and contrite as possible.

Two officers wheeled the flyer out onto the platform.

There was a scratch on the bottom of the nose. It wasn't deep, but she could see it when the officer's darker reflections slid over it. That was just great. She'd have to pay for that when she returned the ship. Her parents were definitely going to make her return it. And then . . . and then? Her life was over.

She settled into her flyer and had a moment of tearful self-pity that it would be her last time doing so. Two police flyers descended from above. They were rainbow-swirled neon-trimmed confections of pure bad taste.

"You may alight," said a voice on her radio.

She rose into the air. The police flyers tightened formation around her. It was easy to keep to their course. Margot wished it were harder. She had nothing to distract her from the heavy thoughts on her mind.

Funny how she wasn't scared of the canyon now that she was in a ship. She hadn't even noticed passing over it until they were climbing to clear the far wall. It was safer, more abstract, with the flyer comfortably around her. She was never going to feel that security again.

Something glinted in the corner of her eye. She looked that way and saw a solo-flyer, black and old-fashioned, diving toward her from a greater height. Was it another escort?

The new flyer zipped between Margot and the police ship on her right, then swung low and zagged between her and the police ship on the left, causing both escort vehicles to shade away from her to prevent crashing.

Ki's voice came from Margot's radio, on a private frequency. "Follow me, kid."

Margot said, "Oh no."

Ki's flyer swung directly into Margot's line of sight, wagging back and forth, and then darting upward.

Margot radioed the police. "I'm not with them!"

Ki wove in front of her again. "Margot! What are you doing? This is your get-away."

"You are crazy! They were letting me go!"

A sickening crunch sounded from the side of Margot's flyer.

A voice she didn't recognize said, "I have her. Disabling her control. Let's go."

Lightning flashed across Margot's instruments, leaving darkness and a scent of ozone in its wake. She rose from her seat as the ship fell. Margot screamed, sure she was plunging to her death, but then the flyer jerked, slamming her hard against her restraints. Margot was able to orient herself, but had no idea what was happening. Her canopy was solid, no view out of it without the polarization circuits running. The flyer was swinging, a dead weight with nose up and tail down. She tried to restart the control console. The button didn't light up when pressed.

She felt another jolt, a hard hit from the left, the sound of crumbling and cracking.

She was blind, in an enclosed space, with a battle around her. Again.

Margot felt the panic take over and screamed. She battered her hands against the canopy, desperate to get out, even if it meant falling to her death.

Thane laid across his bed on his stomach, his feet bare to the air, which was the only relief he was allowed for the burns. His mother and her preference for torturing his feet! Because the damage wouldn't show. He hoped whatever wife she picked out for him, the dream-wife, the best one she really wanted, was a foot-fetishist. That would show her.

This was Amir's fault. Thane had checked his messages a thousand times on that gallery. Amir must have noticed, and his mother noticed him noticing. You could never rely on other men.

A slight air current awoke a line of fire in his instep. He bit his lower lip and clenched his fists to keep from making a sound. The camera beast was watching and he suspected someone who reviewed the tapes liked to see him cry.

The door opened. More air currents. He hissed.

"That was really stupid, baby brother."

Thane gave up on his efforts to turn and let himself flop. "Go away, Jolica."

She didn't. She tugged the rope binding his implant hand to the bedpost, sending stinging sensations through his numb arm. "Kinky. Is your sex tutor visiting again?"

Jolica liked making him uncomfortable. She knew why his implant hand was tied. She started picking apart the top knot. It felt like she was plucking his nerves. "Stop that. You'll get me in trouble."

"Not if I have permission." She slid her knee onto the bed and really got down to untying. "Did Shahrukh do this? He's getting overzealous."

His chief steward and handler had not, in fact, stooped to bondage duty. Shahrukh had limited himself to haranguing Thane for the disruption he'd caused in his own schedule by requiring punishment. The queen liked to tie her own knots.

Buzzing insects of returning blood ran inside his skin. He wanted to squirm away from the too-soft touch of Jolica's robe, but that would be pointless. He held still and waited for her to cackle about her latest diabolical plan.

"Turns out one of the ambassadors coming to the summit is female, unmarried, and favorably connected," Jolica said. That was the diabolical plan? "I convinced Mother she needs you up and about and fluttering your eyelashes."

Shahrukh should have been sent to free him. Or some other functionary. "And you're helping, why?"

"Oh sweetie!" Jolica finally wrenched the last knot free and picked up his wrist. She massaged it with what looked like care but felt like lightning forking through tortured muscle. "Because I'm a good sister." She kissed his knuckles. "And you know, with all this disorder and dissent, something might happen to mother dear." Jolica's teeth gritted in a grim parody of a smile. "I might need you to do something *unmentionable* for me." Her hand stroked down, under his sleeve.

He stared at her, disgusted and trying not to show it. "I'm not going to help you just because you untied me once."

"Of course not." She pressed close, his hand still captured

in hers. He had to scoot back on the bed and winced as his feet jostled. "Which is why I'm using this opportunity to whisper in your ear." To his horror, she nipped the shell of his ear with her teeth. "You're going to help me because I know your little secret," she said, throatily, and laughed as he, despite his promise to himself that he wouldn't, cringed away from her. She followed him, crawling up onto the bed with her hand on his throat. "Mother's special little project, her perfect prince to marry off?" She squeezed very close. "Would rather kiss boys."

And then she let him go. Smirking proudly. Behind her the camera bot shifted like a child that needed to go to the bathroom, legs swaying, lenses flashing as they lifted and sank and re-adjusted. It wanted to have captured what Jolica said, but she had blocked it.

She waved to the camera and walked out of the room.

Ki hoped this local chick was really, really local. Zuleikah snaked crazily into ever-narrowing crevices. It was hard to keep a lock on her, even with Z's private beacon code—which was good, because presumably the cops were having an even tougher time of it. Zuleikah's beacon was a tricky, paranoid little thing, hardly there if you didn't know exactly where and when to look for it, but twice it had kept Ki from losing her completely.

Zuleikah swooped a sharp bank and Margot's dead-weight craft bounced on the wall of the narrow canyon behind Zuleikah's flyer. Ki winced, thinking of the shaking Margot had to be getting. She hoped the other girl had strapped down tight.

The cop sirens were still audible, faint in the distance, and Ki dutifully tracked them on her display, glowing dots through intervening columns and curtains of stone. When it looked like there was no clear line of sight in any direction, Ki dropped her scrambler through the manual waste chute. The dots on the display blurred and fuzzed, winking out of existence.

Expensive thing, and the only one she had, but the point of a scrambler was to use it.

Zuleikah's ship bounded up and over a thick wall of volcanic rock, jouncing Margot again, a spray of rock scattering as the solo-flyer glanced off.

Damn but Z could fly low and avoid detection. Maybe she wasn't the little rich girl she appeared to be. Maybe she was a mastermind pirate genius girl.

Ki tried not to get her hopes any higher than they already were. Still, Zuleikah was a good runner if nothing else, and Ki loved a good chase.

Zuleikah slowed down, barely skimming the bottom of a ravine, lazily wriggling along a dry streambed.

"We're clear," Zuleikah said, slowing to a hover near a cave entrance. She dropped Margot's flyer gently, right-side-up, too, and then popped the tow cable before landing herself. Fancy flying.

Ki hopped out of her flyer with a whoop and hurried to jimmy Margot's canopy open—only to see stars as Margot's fist hit her nose.

Ki staggered back, both hands on her nose, which throbbed with pain. Margot kicked and shoved her way out of her restraints. She had been strapped in. Good. She was okay.

"Ow, kid! That's no way to say thanks."

Margot threw her hands up. "What . . . what kind of idiot breaks someone out of jail as they are being released?" Margot stomped in a circle making grunting noises and half-screams like a cat that had been sprayed with water. She turned to look at her flyer, and froze. She said, in a quiet voice, "It's never going to fly again."

Ki approached carefully, hand out but not touching. "Kid . . . Margot, what would have happened? If you'd gone back? Back home in disgrace, minus all that money and nothing to show for it? You'd be at their mercy. You really want that?"

Margot smacked Ki's hand down. "Now I have a prison record! Now they'll cancel my military benefits. Now I'm not even going to get to keep. This. Flyer." She kicked the dented side of her flyer and then stopped, looking at it with the mortified expression of one who has just stepped on a wounded mouse.

Zuleikah, who had calmly dismounted and watched all of this with a stoic expression, said, "They're reporting that you were kidnapped, so there's that. They don't blame you."

Margot slumped to the ground at the side of her flyer. "Yet," she said. Tears wet her cheeks.

Ki crouched in front of her. "You're giving up awful easy. We've got everything we need."

Margot gaped at her. "Who ARE you?"

Boy was that a question Ki didn't want to answer. "We succeeded, Big M! We made it onto the planet of Ratana, free and clear. Dig up a handful of dirt and maybe there'll be a diamond in it."

Margot responded to this by picking up the nearest clod of dirt and throwing it at Ki. It was just dirt and crumbled apart as it hit her.

Ki shook clods from her hair. "Really? You're that mad I busted you out?"

Margot's nose scrunched up and she looked liable to deck Ki again, but Zuleikah wandered over, breaking the mood with her bored expression and cool tone. "This valley has a lot of metal deposits. Should hide us from a casual sweep, but we shouldn't stay long. I have a place where we can hide out. It's residential. If they don't track us on the way, they won't think to look for us there."

Saved by the new bestie! "That's perfect." Ki slapped dirt from her hands.

"Have fun." Margot sat down and wrapped her arms around herself. "I'm waiting for the police."

"No, you're not." Jeez, the kid would die.

"I am."

Zuleikah said, calmly, "You'd die."

Zuleikah had something of an honesty problem. Ki turned to sit next to Margot, shoulder to shoulder. Margot squirmed away, but not very far. Ki said, "We lost the cops when I dumped my scrambler. Sorry, but they aren't going to find you quick. If we leave you here, Margot, you'll freeze in the night or be devoured by the sky wolves." Zuleikah gave her such a look, like she hadn't thought Ki could read! *Sky Wolves of Ratana* was a classic. Although novels could play fast and loose with facts. "Sky wolves are real, right?"

Zuleikah's smirk gave no indication either way. She pulled open a panel in the nose of Margot's flyer and poked around in it.

Sky wolves were genetically-engineered bats the Ratana colonists had made to chase down an accidental rabbit infestation. The book wasn't really about them, but about this triad of love-sick geologists. Books didn't tend to lie so much about back-ground material, right? "Whatever. Margot, you have to stay with us. If the cops find you, you'll be back where you started."

Margot gave her a look of sheer incomprehension. "You're crazy and you're going to drag me along no matter what."

"No. If you really want to leave, leave. We'll see if there's a settlement in walking distance or, well, we'll try to fix your flyer. I'm just telling you how it is."

Margot set her face against her knees and was silent for a long time.

Ki nudged her with her elbow. "I couldn't leave you in the lurch. We just got here!"

Margot pushed a clod of dirt with her toe. "Sure. Wouldn't want to miss all this."

Zuleikah rested on the nose of her flyer, pulling displays out of her bracelet. "Before the sun goes down," she said, without looking up, "We'll want to take off fast."

Now, at least, Margot was glaring at someone other than Ki. "And who the hell are you?"

Zuleikah didn't answer so Ki said, "Local gal doing a good deed for us."

Margot marched up to Zuleikah's solo-flyer. "I'm not asking you. I'm asking her. Who are you?" Margot smacked the flyer hard enough to rock it.

Zuleikah looked down like a bird of prey deciding if she was hungry enough to attack. "I'm Zuleikah."

"You wrecked my solo-flyer!"

Another half-shrug. "I'll fix it."

"With what? Another mythical diamond?" Margot dug up a handful of dirt and threw it at the gold-plated nose of Zuleikah's Hawk Angel.

Ki sucked in a breath. "Sweetie, that's vintage."

"We'll go to my place," Zuleikah said.

Margot raised her hands over her head. "That's it. You both think there's always a way out."

Margot looked murderous, and Zuleikah was absorbed in her screens. Ki was alone again, even though there were two people there. Ki backed up, hands raised. "I'll . . . check our perimeter."

She made short work climbing a curving spire to a shelf that stood over the canyon like a viewing platform. The rock was hard under her hands, and knife-edged with little crescent cuts like a stone arrowhead, lots of little divots for her feet. Her companions would sort themselves out. She wouldn't let them take this from her. She'd done it. She was on another world, exploring. Maybe there weren't diamonds, but she'd find something better. An experience. She stretched her hand out beside her and imagined Ethan's on top of it. He'd sit just there, one leg out straight, his eyes wide, taking in the soaring view like it was wine and he was already drunk.

07:
THE FOUNDING OF THE GALACTIC HELLCATS

ZULEIKAH WASN'T BORED. THE ONLY ANNOYING THING WAS Margot anxiously hovering at her elbow as she transferred power to the disabled flyer. "Is it ever going to fly again?"

"Working on it."

"Are the cops coming?"

"No." Zuleikah had not been this trapped in conversation in a long time. If only she could turn on a conversation simulator for Margot. The flyer had survived the kill -9 without damage to its systems. They should be able to get out of there before trouble found them. Depending on how prompt trouble would be. Oh, there was an idea. "We'll need Ki to be down here so we can go as soon as this is done."

Margot dashed off and started climbing up to where Ki was. Perfect.

Prince Thane was online. Not his usual account, but the secret friends-only (supposedly) account her cousin had told her about. He didn't post from it often.

"Somebody save me from this circus," he wrote. "Rehearsing to be set dressing at a treaty signing. I may chew my own arm off to escape."

Zuleikah considered responding. Something funny, light, and not too interested.

Margot screamed. Zuleikah looked up to see her at the top of the cliff, throwing fistfuls of dirt at Ki.

Perhaps she would be more interesting to Thane if she wrote "I'm hanging out in the badlands with outlaws. Come join us."

Her eye hovered over the 'post' button.

She deleted it. Even on the underground net, Royal security had bots trolling. "Chew someone else's arm," she posted instead.

"That would definitely get me taken out of the room," he replied.

Zuleikah hated how excited she felt, getting a direct reply. She wanted to tell Ki and Margot, her brother, or one of her online friends. Re-post it. Anyone, everyone, see this? I got a reply from Prince Thane! But that would be childish. She held her breath. She'd play it cool. Like of course, she got messages from royals all the time. She wouldn't even mention it unless it came up. No, even if it did come up. She'd hold the knowledge quietly to her chest and look mysterious to everyone else.

Ugh. It was stupid, but Margot couldn't stay mad at Ki if she kept acting like a little kid. She danced backward from Margot's attempt to murder her with dirt clods, laughing so hard she was crying. "But *you* scared me!"

It was too much effort staying this mad. Margot barked, "Come on, we're leaving," and started the slow, careful climb down. At least the gravity here wasn't as high as Earth. She still felt all-over warm from it, like she'd been working out a long time.

Zuleikah was leaning against her evil-looking flyer, throwing smirks at Margot like she wouldn't jump if someone scared her at the top of a cliff. Her eyes were swaddled in green makeup with little round petals glued to the ends of her eyelashes. Margot didn't know how Ki had met this Zuleikah person. She didn't trust her. She did, a tiny bit, want to date her, but she didn't trust her. That danger was itself hot. Damn it. Was her skin naturally that toasted chocolate color? Were her eyes a lighter brown or was that the makeup playing tricks?

Margot dusted her pants off and tried to look casual wandering over to Zuleikah. "I hate both you of you."

Zuleikah half-shrugged. "The cops might have shot you once you were out of the atmosphere and called it an escape attempt."

Margot felt cold in her gut. "You think so?"

Another half-shrug. "They do that. Your battery will finish charging in time for dusk."

Wow. Had Ki actually saved her? Could she have mentioned that sooner? Margot tried to get a look at the screen over Zuleikah's hands.

Zuleikah glanced at her, a sweep of pink lashes, and then back down at her screen. "There."

"Excuse me?"

Zuleikah tilted her head toward Margot's hand.

"What does that mean?" Margot asked.

"Look." Zuleikah repeated the gesture.

Margot looked at her hand.

"Screen," Zuleikah said.

Oh! Margot turned on her screen bracelet. A file had appeared on her drive. Repairs needed on flyer, estimated time, materials needed. Most of those were marked "at home." Margot stared at her. Zuleikah continued to look at her own screen.

Why couldn't she speak more than one word at a time? Also, how had she even known the device's address? More sexy danger. Margot checked her security settings. She felt herself blushing, like the file transfer had been a more intimate pass.

She hid her face by bending to inspect her poor flyer. It had a dent, an actual dent, with bits of ceramic missing, and so many scrapes. Margot always kept the things she owned as pristine as she could. You never knew when you'd have to sell or return something. There was nothing she could do but scrub the dirt off with the pad of her thumb, so she did, working slowly over the nose.

The entire planet was after them, and her ship was destroyed. She had no money to repair it and no hope of returning it. "There's no way out of this."

Ki trotted up, covered in dirt and grinning like a cat. "I'm proof that there's always a way out."

Zuleikah flashed her lovely eyes at Ki. "How's that?"

Ki made a deprecating gesture. "It's nothing. This one here, she's ex-military. A bomb expert."

"Ordinance technician," Margot quickly corrected. "And I'm not anymore. It's not like you can find a job delivering bombs."

"You can," Ki and Zuleikah said, in unison. Then they smiled at each other. Ugh, how could they be shutting her out when they just met?

Margot took a deep breath. Just say it. "I think . . . I think I will stick around with you guys. For a bit. If I go home, my parents will kill me."

Ki stretched, her thin arms making alarming popping noises. "You don't look like the type who has parents who actually kill people. Maybe turn you away, disown you. You show up with a fat stack of cash, they'll fall over themselves begging you to stay and have a slice of fattened calf."

"Is that what your parents did?" Margot asked.

Ki found something interesting to stare at across the canyon. Margot was starting to notice the difference between Ki gleefully hinting at a dark, mysterious past and anxiously avoiding talking about her dark, mysterious past.

Zuleikah said, "My parents forgive me anything." She didn't sound happy about it.

Margot wished she could draw out more information. What makes you happy? Do you have a girlfriend? What came out of her mouth, though, was, "I thought I'd be done thinking about parents by now."

"I don't think you ever stop." Zuleikah rose gracefully. Wow she had legs. She walked to Margot's flyer. "Come here."

Margot rushed after her before she could think about how desperate that looked. No wonder Ki was talking her up. She wasn't hiding her attraction at all.

Zuleikah, not noticing this drama, pushed buttons and released doors Margot hadn't known were there. She pointed at a little green light and then twisted and pulled free two cables, which she rolled up and stowed on her ship.

Wait . . . that was it? She didn't want to talk? "Is it fixed?"

"It'll run." Zuleikah closed each of the doors in turn and motioned for Margot to test the starter. The controls lit up normally and the exterior lights flooded the overhanging stone, making her realize how dark it had gotten. Zuleikah shrugged, her answer for everything.

Stars were starting to appear in the reddening sky, dancing, dim and magical in a way they weren't outside of atmosphere. Margot felt like she'd cried herself out, fallen asleep, and woken again. "So now what?"

Zuleikah opened her canopy. "I'll take point."

Margot watched the other two get in their flyers. Was she being morally weak, following them? The right thing to do was to head back to the police—regardless of how bad that would be for her personally. Doing the right thing wasn't about protecting yourself.

Ki executed a fancy barrel roll against the side of the canyon, the gleaming red oblong nearly kissing rock, reflecting stars crazily as she looped. It was reckless beauty, an aria to adventure.

Margot dropped into her seat. Very well, she was being morally weak. Being morally strong hadn't done much good for her so far. Besides, Zuleikah had obviously gotten herself out of worse scrapes than this, to know so much about fixing ships and hiding in canyons.

"Radio silence," Ki sent over the radio. "Just to be safe."

Ki wished she hadn't said it the second she did. It was the safest option, but she hated silence. She needed words to fill the void. She needed Ethan. Someone to take care of who could also make her feel taken care of. Margot clearly did not want to be taken care of. Zuleikah didn't need taking care of. How could Ki keep these two wildly different people in her orbit if they didn't want anything from her?

The thought was embarrassingly needy. Was she so desperate to make herself a family that she latched on to the first two unattached people she found?

Well, fine. She was. Adventures were thrilling, and Ratana was beautiful, but what good was adventure, what good was beauty if you didn't have someone to share it with?

Margot was grateful for the silence, the meditative feeling as she leaned into lazy turns, following the ship in front of her. She could stop thinking for a while. Stop worrying. There was a plan and she was executing it. Follow Zuleikah.

She was setting all her worries in Zuleikah's hands. Stupidly. It wasn't like she had agreed to take them.

Zuleikah led them close to the ground, so close it was like she had invisible wheels. She bobbed easily over a tongue of black rock that lay like a fleshy limb across their path. Margot took the jump more gradually. The flyer was responding normally, but she was afraid to push it. The desert was painted in sunset reds striped with deep blue shadows. Margot kept her focus far ahead so she could make her adjustments slowly, swaying and turning . . . it was a waltz.

Oh how wonderful it was that she got to fly again.

They dropped into a larger canyon and Margot gasped when she realized the unusual, bright veins on the canyon walls were artificial—windows and balconies glowing with electric lights. As the canyon widened, the structures became larger, and the lights more varied in color, a crazy dream of a city, like the Ratanese places Margot had seen in movies, slicing the darkness with prisms of metal and glass. She'd assumed that wasn't real.

Zuleikah's flyer slipped neatly into a dark cave and parked on a concrete floor.

As Margot climbed out beside her, she held her breath, expecting a siren. The air smelled of oil and sawdust. Ki's flyer landed gently next to her.

Zuleikah waved a hand and said, "Secure garage."

Something groaned overhead and a segmented metal door descended, closing the three of them in. The air illuminated.

Irregular walls climbed up to a narrow V above them, half rough stone, half smooth concrete.

"Sweet place." Ki poked the flat wall at the back of the cave.

"This way," Zuleikah said. The wall Ki was poking rolled up exactly as the garage door had rolled down.

It revealed a plain room, windowless, with silver stairs spiraling upward. Despite the plainness something about it—the texture, the smell—felt expensive. Zuleikah led the way up the stairs to a room with a large curved window looking out on the canyon city. She dropped onto a grey flannel couch. All the furnishings were grey and black and as rectangular as possible. Zuleikah gazed out the window. Something large and dark briefly obscured the lights on the other side of the canyon. "We got in before the sky wolves."

"I knew they were real!" Ki exclaimed in delight.

Zuleikah waved them toward chairs. "Tomorrow night, if the border patrol haven't found us, we can slip through the defense network and get you off the planet."

"And go where?" Margot asked. "My parents received an ansible telegram that I'm in prison. They sent money to bail me out. I can't go home."

Zuleikah shrugged. "Where do you want to go?"

Margot didn't know how to begin to answer that, because "the past" wasn't an option. She looked at Ki, who looked to be scanning the room for something to steal. "Are you all right with that?"

Ki turned to face her, tucking something into her pocket at the same time. "What's that?"

"Are you all right with us leaving without getting that gem you wanted?"

"Gem? Gems shmems. We got something much more valuable than that." She jumped over the back of the couch, settling in next to Zuleikah. She raised both hands, waiting for one of them to take her bait. When Zuleikah and Margot kept staring silently, she gestured at both of them. "We got a gang!"

Margot sat down. "What on earth are you talking about?"

Ki pointed at each of them, ending with herself. "One, two, three criminals. You need at least three people to count as a gang. I always wanted one." Ki smiled proudly at them, like a parent. "It's just a suggestion, but how do you feel about the name The Galactic Hellcats? Closed membership to start, but we can each bring in one other member at a future time. Should we have the right to veto new members? I mean, if there's someone I love and you hate? Also, I have ideas about secret call signs and handshakes." Margot looked to see if Zuleikah was as surprised at this as she was, but Zuleikah was grinning as madly as Ki.

Ki laid her arms across the top of the sofa. "Now, what do you have to eat around here?"

08:
A TERRIBLE PLAN

ZULEIKAH HADN'T HAD PEOPLE OVER AT HER PLACE SINCE SHE'D gotten it. Had it always been so Spartan? She should have bought things for entertaining: trays, glasses. Some big, gaudy painting to cover the empty wall and give her fidgety guests something to focus on.

Zuleikah left them and their awkward silence and went to the kitchen. She opened her refrigerator: a jar with a single pickle floating in it and three takeout boxes.

She gestured for the attention of the house mind. "Recommendations for feeding my guests?"

"Younger female guest is severely malnourished."

"Younger?"

The AI kindly provided a live feed of Ki, who stood with her back to a cabinet in the living room, looking off in random directions as she opened the drawers and felt in them. Zuleikah said, "huh." She hadn't expected Ki to be the younger one. She looked . . . wizened. Of course, the AI was just guessing her age based on . . . biometric things. Whatever it was AIs cared about. "House, what do we have on hand that would provide the best meal for both guests?" The AI identified ingredients she could feed into the food-maker, including the take-out containers.

A message came in from her father. She told the system to tell him she was busy and it alerted her she'd never set a "busy" message.

That said something. Grimacing, she told the system to send the default message. She could already hear him saying how disappointed he was in her lack of manners.

When Zuleikah returned to the living room, Ki, to her credit, did not look like she was doing anything suspicious, or like she had just stopped doing anything suspicious as she loitered near the potted plants.

"This is a real nice place, Zuleikah," she said, smiling at the view of the canyon. "Real nice." Her hands were clasped at the small of her back, no doubt holding something Zuleikah neither cared about nor would miss.

"Food will be ready in a minute."

Margot looked pleadingly at her. "What do we do if the cops find us here? Can they find us here?"

Zuleikah had assumed the police wouldn't think to find them here if they didn't catch them on the way, and she'd been very careful about her path home. Was that wrong? She called up the police band on her heads up display and checked.

Yes, there was a general bulletin to look out for three solo-flyers, with all of Margot's information and very brief, vague descriptions of her flyer (black, old model) and Ki's (red, newer model.) Nothing else. Locally, there was a curfew and blockade on the ground-level neighborhood. Suspected dissidents. Zuleikah flicked through the news reports, frowning and unsure. Margot was watching her like she expected a solution but Zuleikah didn't even understand the problem. What if her neighbors saw them fly in and called the police based on the bulletin? What if a local police officer saw them?

Ki sprawled on the opposite couch. "There is nothing like a local friend to show you a place. If we were staying in a hotel? We wouldn't see Ratana itself, not as it really is when company isn't over."

Ki didn't look like she had the money for a toothbrush, much less a hotel, so Zuleikah suspected this was an attempt to sound sophisticated, though it was the sort of thing a low-class person would say. Zuleikah had never been this close to a poor person before. She wondered what Ki thought about her, if she knew what to do about the police. "You did a good job getting into the underground network."

Ki waved the compliment off. "Never paid for a data drop in my life. That's for chumps, right?"

"Not really." Zuleikah frowned. She didn't know how much she paid for data access. It was part of the utilities bill. Anyway, she didn't use what she paid for; the official network was useless and censored.

She wondered if stealing data was morally the same, whether you were fighting censorship or a paywall.

"What about our ships? Won't the police know what they look like?" Margot stopped pacing. "You're sure you can get us off-world tomorrow?"

Ki said, "Relax. Getting out is way easier than getting in."

"No, it isn't." Why did Ki keep lying about things?

Ki said, "I've evaded the police twice, today!"

Come to think of it, there was a big diplomatic . . . thing happening in the capital. Thane had been complaining about it. Officers had probably been moved to protect the royals, leaving this area under-staffed. "You were lucky."

"See?" Margot gestured at Zuleikah as though they were allies in this argument. "Lucky."

Ki said, "What I see is that we have an inside scoop."

"*We* don't have anything. *We* aren't a gang. You are a criminal and you've dragged me along in your wake and I'm leaving you as soon as I conceivably can."

Zuleikah raised a hand to get her attention. "You've decided where you want to go?"

Margot looked like she'd been beaned.

Zuleikah felt young and stupid. "I guess I should show you the spare bedrooms. After dinner."

Ki yawned. "Not that I'm looking to move in—that's not my style. I am not a mooch. But, if things get bad or we run into complications, how long can we stay here?" Ki ended her words with an anxious, almost wincing glance.

Stay? Zuleikah had never had anyone live with her . . . not since she moved into her own place when she was eighteen. Even back at home, her parents and brother never came into her suite. All that . . . having to talk and interact. It was terrifying.

Margot asked, "Do you think the police here have told the police on Luna about me? The police on Earth? On Jefferson? Everywhere?"

"I don't think so?" The idea of Ratana's government talking to anyone was absurd. When people disappeared on Ratana, relatives had to assume they'd been arrested by process of elimination.

Ki said, "Please. Cops don't even talk to other cities' cops in the same country on the same planet. If you don't break an international law, they have no reason to share your information. They don't even want to. Like, if you do become an intergalactic super-criminal, they want to be able to get something for your origin story."

Margot listened to this speech with an expression of horror, but Zuleikah felt it had a ring of truth. "Yeah, the less they say, the less to cover up if they kill you."

Ki and Margot stared at her. Zuleikah fled to the kitchen without a word of explanation.

⚡

After showing her guests to their rooms, Zuleikah sat alone on her sofa. She was usually alone in her home, but it had a special quality, being alone with other people nearby. It felt . . . warm. She watched them through the security feed. Ki dragged a pillow and blanket into the closet of her room and set herself up in the farthest back corner, facing the door.

That was odd.

Margot, on the other hand, got into bed like a normal person, but immediately curled into a ball, sobbing.

Zuleikah felt she had to do something for these two women. Something more than a meal and a place to stay. There had to be a way to fix them, while she had them, before releasing them to the universe.

A quiet alert informed her that Thane was online again.

He'd made a public post. "I am not joking; I would love to be kidnapped again just to get away from here."

Zuleikah looked at his post for a long time. Did he want to be reassured that he had it good or reassured his problems were important? Everyone knew the queen was mean and the court full of fakers. Or was that just the empty conjecture of gossips?

"I'd kidnap you," she wrote, and then deleted it.

She logged herself off and went to bed. If the police didn't come in the night, they were probably safe.

Margot woke in a luxurious bed, sunk deep in satiny pillows, unaware of how she'd gotten there.

Then it came back. She wished it hadn't.

She was sore. Her back ached, and her head, neck, wrist—everything ached once she moved it. She covered her head with the comforter and tried to reclaim that sense of peace she'd had a moment ago. It wasn't coming.

The heavier gravity made it feel like she was at the bottom of an ocean, struggling to get upright and slog the long walk to the little private bathroom connected to her guest room.

She'd washed her underthings with soap in the shower. She found them still wet and ran them under the room's drying light. They felt dry, a little crisp, but there was a damp patch on her undershirt where it touched her neck.

She put her dirty, stiff flying suit back on over the damp undershirt and followed an increase in light down carpeted stairs. The house was empty and quiet, but Zuleikah had left a display running on the coffee table. It looked like celebrity gossip. The place smelled like the inside of a new environment suit. Zuleikah couldn't have lived here long. There was nothing personal, nothing to give a sense of who she was.

Kind of like Zuleikah herself.

Margot heard a sharp clang from the direction of the garage. She walked down the stairs to the entryway, listening carefully. She thought she heard a sound like grinding. How had Zuleikah opened the door last night? Margot waved her hand along the featureless wall, feeling for the control spot.

The door to the garage flew up with a blast of high-pitched noise: a squealing buzz, and a sulfurous smell. A plume of pinkish smoke rose from the far side of Margot's solo-flyer.

Zuleikah crouched next to Margot's flyer, passing a round tool over the scarred metal. The sulfur smell was joined with sharp spikes of acid now and then, as different colored sparks arched from Zuleikah's gloved hands. Some whitish material had been filled into the dent and Zuleikah was buffing it smooth, marring the yellow paint with a mix of metal and compounds that came out cotton candy pink. Margot came as close as she dared, holding the neck of her shirt over her mouth to block out the smoke.

Zuleikah switched off the grinder and turned around. She had a white dust mask over her mouth and nose and goggles over her eyes, rendering her menacing and inhuman. She pulled the dust mask down revealing her sudden, youthful mouth. "What?" Zuleikah asked.

"You're fixing my ship."

Zuleikah set the grinder down and stood. She stretched and rubbed her shoulder. "Yeah. Said I would."

"Um . . . thanks? Are you . . . ? I mean, this won't invalidate the warrantee, will it?"

Zuleikah dropped her safety glasses around her neck and gave her a long, slow look. Margot felt foolish.

Today her eyes were painted pink, complete with new petals on the lash-ends. She'd done all that just to put safety goggles on? She walked across the room. "I removed your identifiers. Ki's were already gone."

"Um . . ." Margot was sure that was illegal. She turned to follow. "Can you undo that?"

Zuleikah opened a cabinet. "What color do you want?"

A row of square containers sat on the top shelf of the cabinet, each a different brilliant color on its face. "Do you have the same yellow?"

"They're looking for a yellow ShadowKat." Zuleikah plucked a bottle. "How about green?"

Margot bit her lower lip. "I like yellow." Also disguising the bike made her feel . . . complicit.

Zuleikah shrugged. "Could go orange-yellow or green-yellow. Could do flames. Something different."

Margot paced as Zuleikah set out bottles and tools. "I don't want you to feel I'm not grateful. You're very kind, taking us in, feeding us. But . . . well, I can't return the flyer with the identifiers wiped, can I? Anyone I tried to sell it to would think it was stolen."

"Government doesn't need to keep a tab on every vehicle. I remove my identifiers on principle." Zuleikah wiped over every surface of Margot's ShadowKat with a soft chamois. Margot felt jealous—she hadn't owned the flyer long enough to have devotedly cleaned it herself. Zuleikah ducked low and crawled around, doing a thorough job. Margot didn't know what to say. Zuleikah didn't appear to have any desire to break the silence. Margot wondered what that was like, to be able to just . . . not talk.

"So," Margot said. "Thanks, you know, for the shower and bed and everything."

Without looking away from her work, Zuleikah half-shruged.

"I'll pay you back, if I can, after I get out of all of this and find a job."

Zuleikah waved one hand dismissively. She set aside the chamois and tested the smoothness of the flyer with her bare hand. She nodded to herself, turned to Margot. "Color?"

Margot should remind Zuleikah that she was not interested in breaking any laws, ever again. She should demand the same paint job and hope the dealer wouldn't notice it had been re-done when she tried to return the flyer for its purchase price and get back to where she was two days ago.

What came out of her mouth instead was, "You can paint flames?"

Zuleikah's impassive face cracked into a warm grin. She nodded and went back to the paint cabinet.

Margot hated how much she liked being the object of that smile. A lassitude spread over her, like her muscles said, *Okay, we're going along with this. No more need to worry about making a decision.* She sat down on a stool by the wall.

Zuleikah sprayed small spots of three different reds on the flyer and waved at them with her other hand, frowning. Margot watched the blotches change color slightly as they dried. Zuleikah returned two of the reds to the cabinet.

Zuleikah painted the ship with broad sweeps of her arm, holding a flexible sheet of plastic against the edge of the canopy when she got near it. In very short time, the entire flyer gleamed wetly, a darker red than Ki's, almost burgundy. Zuleikah stepped back and looked at Margot. "So . . . I thought we'd rescue this guy I know."

Margot, who had been expecting information about the paint job—maybe on how the bright liquid would cure to handle atmospheric burn—had to take a moment to focus. "Excuse me?"

Zuleikah shrugged. "If you'd rather not leave right away. We could rescue this guy."

Oh, there was her stress again. "We haven't rescued ourselves yet."

"Police have no idea where we are."

"For now. What about when we try to leave? We have to fly across the sky and someone will see us. Do you have local air traffic controllers? You must, right? One for this neighborhood, one for the community, the geographic range? How do we even begin?"

Zuleikah sprayed a small spot near the canopy latch. "So, don't go, then."

Margot's insides temporarily became goo. She had to push that feeling away. "We have to go! We can't stay here!"

Zuleikah raised an eyebrow at her. Margot felt paragraphs of dressing-down in that motion. Margot said, "Not that I'm agreeing, but who is this 'guy'? What does he need rescuing from?"

Zuleikah dropped her eyes to her work, inspecting the flyer for imperfections. "A prince. He's desperate to get out, and I know where we can get him easily, today."

"I'm all for helping others, believe me, but . . ."

"Smugglers are killed, here."

Margot blinked. "Wait, what?"

Zuleikah met her gaze. "Smugglers are killed. Ki wants to smuggle. If she finds a gem and keeps it, that's smuggling. I think she'd be willing to rescue Thane, instead."

"Oh. I see what you mean. Yes, let's . . . let's not smuggle."

"You need a purpose," Zuleikah said.

Wait, this was supposed to be about Ki. Margot wanted to explain that she knew what she needed, and it wasn't a princely rescue operation, but Zuleikah was on the other side of the room, taking new supplies out of the paint cabinet.

Margot's solo-flyer looked exactly as smooth as it had in the showroom. Not a hint of a dent or scratch. She felt dumb with admiration. Of course, it was now red, and hadn't Margot said yellow? Well, she hadn't *not* said red; she'd said flames. She chewed her lip and considered her new future as an outlaw.

Zuleikah stood over the flyer, frowning in concentration, like a bullfighter poised for violence or a philosopher about to debate. Margot felt compelled to remain silent. The moment stretched, and then Zuleikah moved. She flicked lines of yellow and orange across the red, against a flexible guard that she touched down and lifted up so quickly Margot couldn't believe she was even planning the design. Stylized flames formed from the nose, fluttering and trailing around and past the canopy, growing one curve and slash at a time. Zuleikah lifted the guard and fed more yellow into the heart of each flame.

That was why she'd started with the dark red. Yellow was the dominant color, now, consuming the red and orange with wisps of black soot.

"You're really talented," Margot said, now quite certainly in love.

Pink-lashed eyes narrowed. More paint splashed here and there, smaller and smaller touches now, bringing out the tips of flickers. Margot twisted her fingers together, unsure how to say anything in the face of such beauty.

Zuleikah stepped back, arms outstretched, silently asking opinion.

Margot wanted to say something deeply personal, to offer some part of her soul in exchange. What came out of her mouth was, "I was supposed to have a job interview today."

Zuleikah took off her mask and grinned. "Think you'll miss it."

Ki hacked into the house's security cameras first thing when she woke up. All viewing history was blanked. Clever girl, that Zuleikah. She wished she knew if she'd been spied on, though, or if anyone had tried to sneak in on them. Well, she supposed Z spied on her and had looked for outside trouble before wiping the history. She'd just have to trust her. That felt scary, but well, you had to trust a new best friend sometime.

Ki paused at the top of the steps that lead down to the garage, watching Zuleikah and Margot and feeling very maternal toward them. They were worried she'd get caught smuggling.

Worrying about her! That was so sweet.

And a quest! A quixotic quest! Rescuing a boy.

Ki's heart squeezed, thinking of Ethan. There were a lot of failed rescues in her past. She'd wanted to rescue a kitten, once. She had, almost. She picked its wounded body up, carried it to her tent, fed it and gave it water. It had died that night, purring in her arms. She wanted to rescue her mother, way back when. Hadn't tried, though. Then there was rescuing Margot, which, well . . . yeah.

She could hug Zuleikah. Margot *did* need purpose. It was written all over her. Maybe, being a part of this quest would shake Margot loose from all those fears she dragged around with her.

Ki tucked her screen back in its pocket and stood up, drying her eyes. Time to put the mask back on. She stopped in the bathroom to splash water on her eyes so they wouldn't look red, then she skipped down the stairs, waving the door open early so she could make a grand, bounding entrance.

"Good morning, kids! What's for breakfast?"

09:

HOW TO RESCUE A PRINCE

Shortly after his sister left, Thane's steward came in and
wrapped his feet tightly in bandages. His shoes didn't fit on the
first try so the bandages were wrapped tighter until the pain was
throbbing with his heartbeat.

Shahrukh grumbled. "This is all your fault," while shoving
the delicate embroidered slippers on. He used a thin metal
tool to uncurl the backs. Thane felt like he had to be bleeding
through to the satin, but of course he wasn't.

How had Jolica found out? He'd been so good. He'd never
said anything to anyone. Sure, he'd complained about kissing
girls when he was younger, but all boys did. And he had every
right to hate the sex tutor on principle alone. It was wrong
and sick how she made him touch dolls and diagrams and
then her.

"That'll have to do. Come on, we're in a hurry." Shahrukh
tugged him to standing. He stumbled. His feet were too thick.
He couldn't feel the floor through the pain.

He toddled to the dressing room, where his makeup artist was already waiting.

Amir would know. There'd been that one furtive kiss, when they were in the bomb shelter during the war and thought they were both going to die. He could kill him. How selfish, to tell her!

The makeup woman stepped back. "I can't do this with him gritting his teeth. Give him something for the pain or we may as well not even start."

Shahrukh stabbed his ankle with a needle and a blessed numbness spread out from it.

He tried to borrow that numbness for his brain.

The makeup and hair were done quickly and he was shoved out to follow Stan, who half-ran ahead of him, griping about the schedule.

There wasn't time to breathe, all right. Greet the ambassadors at breakfast. Greet the press at their breakfast. Greet the dignitaries at brunch. By afternoon, he'd welcomed faceless crowds to five meals and hadn't had a bite to eat. He teetered on the brink of fainting. The pain medication was wearing off.

He'd give anything for a distraction, something to think about other than what percentage of agony he was feeling and how that translated into time before he couldn't stand anymore. Or his sister's threat. Could he convincingly deny it? Would it matter if he did? What if his sister's scheme failed? What if he didn't help? His mother burned his feet for texting during dinner, what would she do if she found out what he was really hiding?

He wanted to check his chat account, but his sister and his mother or their representatives were always right next to him. There wasn't a lot of privacy on a stage.

Finally, he had to tilt himself toward his steward and,

whispering through a perfect smile, say, "Stan, I'm going to faint."

Shahrukh grimaced like he'd said he was going to renounce the monarchy. "There's a Royal Lounge in the next corridor. No one will miss you for a few minutes. Eat something."

Thane almost fainted right then. He mumbled his thanks, performed a perfect ceremonial bow to the throne, and beat his retreat.

First, he'd sit down. No, he'd get food first, because he wasn't going to want to get up again. Grab something from the snack table and find the nearest chair. Maybe someone had answered his last post. Rest. Recuperation. Distraction.

He slipped in the door and the makeup artist was on him. "Hold still. What a mess. Were you touching your face?"

"I would never dream of touching my face," Thane said.

She pushed him into a chair. He looked forlornly at a tray of sliced fruit and cheeses while her brushes ran over him, a million cat-licks of paint.

Shahrukh came in. "Are you done yet? We have to get ready for the official summit opening. You're processing directly behind your sister's steward. I'm behind you."

This would be news if it hadn't been repeated to him eight times that day. "Thank you, Stan. Can you hand me a cracker?"

"Are you crazy?" The makeup artist gasped. "I just got these lips perfect."

"We don't have long," Shahrukh said. "We need to go over the procession so you know exactly what to do."

Damn it. He'd murder someone for a cheese slice and five minutes alone. "Skip to the part where anything is different from usual, please."

"Don't talk back." Shahrukh imperiously flipped through paper notes—a medieval affectation. There was a certain type of person who became a royal steward and that type of person loved affectations, the more obscure and anachronistic, the better. "You look forward. After you take the stage, look left and nod to the woman in the red suit."

"The Earth ambassador and eligible bachelorette, Andrea Hoang. I will give her my best smile, whatever that is."

"Without Earth's help we cannot maintain peace." Which was only the eightieth time someone told Thane that in the last hour. "Your crown is crooked."

The makeup artist was poking his hair-curls with the end of a comb. Shahrukh joined her, a veritable party on Thane's head. "Keep your head still. Keep it steady so it doesn't tilt. Do not try to adjust it with your hands."

"Yes, sir." Like he hadn't been living under these rules his entire life.

"We have a lot riding on this treaty and there are several potential marriage prospects in attendance."

None of whom, Thane would have liked to point out, would pick their husband based on his mastery of crown etiquette. Not that he cared why they picked him. He just needed someone, anyone, to pick him so he could finally escape. It would help if that woman respected that he had a mind and interests beyond pleasing her, but he wasn't holding out for that. She could be awful, even. He'd do his disgusting duty by her and be rewarded with not being part of a dynastic struggle every weekday.

Though maybe, just maybe, he'd be lucky and marry a woman less interested in sex with him than he was with her. He stood from the make-up chair and turned in a circle so that everyone could see the crown was perfectly straight and at last made four deliberate steps to the buffet.

Shahrukh slapped his hand away from the cheese. "Get him something caloric he can drink from a straw," Shahrukh barked at the waiting waiter, who bustled to comply.

Jolica waltzed in, then, plucked a few slices of fruit from the buffet, winked at him, and waltzed away again.

Oh right, there was also the possibility his sister was planning a coup today and everything was about to get worse.

⚡

Margot watched Zuleikah spread images and news headlines across her coffee table. "Here." She pulled a map out from the clump of files. She tapped a location and flagged it.

Margot tentatively reached for a picture, and when it quivered under her fingertip, drew it closer and expanded it. Prince Thane of Ratana, in the wide headdress of royal men, flawless dark skin and glittering silver hawk-wings around eyes that were unnaturally large and blue. Margot had never seen eyes like that, and she'd seen every type of person in the navy. "He doesn't look like he needs rescuing."

Zuleikah swept the image out of the air. "Scars can be on the inside."

Ki started drawing on the map with her finger. "This is perfect."

Zuleikah looked at what Ki drew. "Yeah. He has to walk through there after the signing. The transport back to the palace parks here, and he'll probably wait in this room or the corridor itself."

"Are you really okay with this?" Margot asked Ki.

"Mm? Hell yeah. Rescue the prince. A lot easier than smuggling gems. Plus, we'll have the satisfaction of helping a poor, incredibly handsome soul." Ki pulled another image of the prince out and whistled low. "That is definitely my idea of a good deed."

Margot cleared her throat. "So, we snatch him away. What then?"

Zuleikah shrugged.

Margot said, "See, this isn't a plan. It's . . . it's vague ideas. We need a plan."

Zuleikah shrugged. "This is the closest I've ever had to a plan."

Margot wanted to grab Zuleikah's shoulders and hold them still. "Well, I plan a lot. *Not* having a plan is new to me." She looked at Ki. "You never plan more than one foot in front of the next, do you?"

Ki cackled. "Are you kidding? Planning is my thing." She opened a blank document and started scribbling fiercely.

Zuleikah gave Margot a long, studying stare. "You want out?"

Margot ducked her head and felt stupid for doing so. "I want to do what you want to do, but I want a plan."

"Ki's making one."

That was, apparently, that. Margot tried to read over Ki's shoulder, but her notes were in some strange shorthand.

She watched Zuleikah calmly sending information to Ki with little flicks of her fingers. "Will this get you in trouble? I mean, you aren't missing work for this, are you?"

"I don't have a job."

Margot had to blink. "That's terrible. I'm so sorry. Did you just lose it?"

"No. I never had a job. I don't need one. I'm . . ." Zuleikah gestured around her. "I'm set."

"That . . . how does that even work?"

"My parents own mines." Zuleikah said it like this explained everything and went back to her list.

So Zuleikah was one of the people Margot had been sent to save. The mine owners who had almost lost their lives and property. The oppressive class or the real Ratanese, depending on who was shouting at you. Margot felt glad and worried and uncertain about that. "Your parents own gem mines and you stopped in your schedule to bust me unwillingly out of prison so we can go rescue a prince who isn't in danger?"

Zuleikah shrugged.

It was absurd. "You are the one person who could just pick up a gem, aren't you?"

Ki looked up, eyes bright like a cat that just heard a food dispenser.

"I wouldn't," Zuleikah rolled her eyes. "They'd want to talk."

Ki said, "Well, let's see if we can't work a gem-heist into this prince-rescue, just to be nice."

"They kill smugglers!" Margot said.

Ki waggled her stylus. "Only if they get caught."

Margot met Zuleikah's eyes. "We need to rescue your prince fast, before this little kleptomaniac gets us all killed."

It felt good to read complete agreement in those eyes.

Thane had a brief appearance to welcome some schoolgirls who had won a contest to attend the ceremony, followed by four minutes to drink a protein shake while the royal physician unwrapped his feet. It tasted like sweat and glue. "This is disgusting," he gasped.

"Her majesty is concerned about your musculature," the doctor said. "You're losing weight, lately." She clucked disapprovingly at his now-bare feet and fished more supplies out of her bag. "You shouldn't have been walking on these."

Oh yes, like he had a choice.

She scrubbed his soles with something acidic. It burned.

He pressed his knuckles into the table on either side of him and tensed his shoulders. Maybe that would do good for his musculature.

"If you're going to be . . . entertaining tonight, I think it'll be better to just spray on new skin."

So even the doctor knew his mother planned to throw him at the ambassador.

His hairdresser pushed into the small room. "Regina says the whole hairdo needs to be re-done." The doctor scowled, but gestured that he could go ahead. He brushed Thane's scalp sore. For all the effort put into his appearance, no one seemed to care if he kept his hair past thirty.

The doctor stripped the damaged skin off his feet efficiently. The spray-skin was cool and comforting. She slid back and waved, as though the slight breeze of her hand would speed things. "That should be good without bandages. Do you have socks?"

Shahrukh fetched a pair of silk socks with a look of blank panic. "This was supposed to take four minutes. The queen is waiting!"

The bottoms of his feet were now numb, which felt odd, putting the socks and shoes on, but it was a great improvement. The doctor gathered up the discarded bandages, gestured at Stan, and left.

More brushing, hot irons straightening. His crown was set back in place. Immediately Thane's neck began to protest. His back would be next, and the tension headache. After an hour or so, he'd be too sore to notice. So yes, how nice they took it off so he had to re-acclimate. The hairdresser fluttered around him, poking and pinning curls of the recently straightened hair around the silver base of the crown.

Shahrukh helped Thane stand when the hairdresser was

satisfied. One slow turn around while his dresser and Shahrukh checked for slight imperfections, and then he was free to step into the hallway.

Free, that was, to indulge in waiting as more important people walked back and forth. The occasional requisite nod and smile. He slowly transferred weight from one foot to the other when no one was looking. So far, whatever the doctor had done was holding. Ah yes, there was the backache. He concentrated on the pain, imagined it as a slowly growing red sphere.

Finally, Shahrukh waved him forward. This part wouldn't be bad. He'd do his little trick. Smile at the ambassador. It was what came after that worried him. Either the planned evening or his sister doing something unexpected.

He joined the lineup at the stage. The robes made him sweat despite the artificial breeze that chilled his face and hands. His sister's steward glanced back at him. In front of that man he saw the back of his sister's gold crown. Back perfectly straight, eyes forward: she didn't look like she was planning a coup. Would she give him a signal? In front of her, a hedgerow of uniforms and then, already on the stage, raised above everyone else, their mother.

He did his best to avoid looking in his mother's direction as they took the stage. That wasn't easy when you couldn't look up or down and you were required to face forward. He kept his eyes on the back in front of him. One step up, look left. Red suit. Smile and nod. The Earth ambassador gave him a blank look, no doubt unaware of the careful preparation for this moment.

"May I present Her Highness," his mother said, sweeping up to his sister and lightly touching the small of her back. Jolica beamed as if she were delighted to be there. How did she do that?

Then it was his turn. He called it a success that he didn't jump when his mother got close. He smiled; he nodded; he glanced left again and tried to get the Earth ambassador's attention with a small wave, but she wasn't there anymore.

There were people in all directions who would love thinking a wave or a smile came their way, so he imagined the room sliced up like pie and gave each wedge a wink or a nod.

He was sweating heavily now and his eyes itched. Despite the very real possibility that something was about to blow up, he was bored. He tried to play games in his head—how long until that itch stops on its own? How many song titles can I think of before this speech ends? He let his gaze unfocus, and counted. Every time he reached fifty, he checked to see if anyone was looking at him, and if so, smiled and waved.

He wished they would just build a prince robot to do this job.

Finally, he heard his mother say, "But now my son must be excused."

The high-stepping spider of a camera bot swung away from him. He turned and followed Shahrukh off the stage, smiling and nodding at the crowds that were just a blur. He didn't quite believe he'd made it through unscathed. Maybe Jolica was just messing with him? His gaze focused at last on the far door that represented the exact moment he could take the crown off and *slouch*. Sweet, glorious slouching. After his marriage, if he got out of the court, he would just slouch all the time. Even if he didn't feel like it.

He didn't look at the young Ratanese woman in a security uniform halfway down the corridor. She may as well have been a statue to him.

He recalled her presence, however, when her shoulder slammed into him, throwing him against a door. He cried out in shock, and the bodyguards were all pointing weapons at him. Then the door fell open and he tumbled onto rough pavement. Hands grabbed him. His crown fell off. Relief for his scalp.

Precious metal on rough concrete. The thrashing he'd get for letting it touch the ground! He grabbed it. He held the hateful thing to his chest, heart thumping, stupidly more afraid his mother saw than of the strong hands dragging him and dumping him into the smooth plastic bed of a maintenance truck.

Someone threw sackcloth over him and the truck lurched into motion. Thane recovered his senses somewhat. He was getting abducted. Again. Was this the plan? She could have warned him! He struggled upright onto his knees and punched the woman restraining him.

She grabbed his robe and it tore as he flailed to get away. "We're rescuing you!" she shouted. "It's me. It's Liz88."

"Let me go!"

Gunshots very close overhead. Thane threw himself down. So did the woman. She shouted into her bracelet, "Ki! They're firing on us."

The reply was loud enough to hear—the voice girlish. "Hang on. We're almost clear."

Thane lifted himself on his elbows, despite the zipping bullets overhead. Something soft squished under the thick brocade on his elbow. There was a sharp, distinct smell. Manure. He had gotten manure on his state robe. Even being kidnapped wouldn't excuse him for that. He tried to sound like his mother, chillingly commanding. "Stop this vehicle and release me immediately."

Liz88 ducked her head to her wrist. "Ki, he wants out."

"Too bad! Tell him to hang on!"

It was good he overheard that because there was no time for the woman to tell him anything before the truck bed bucked wildly and tilted. Liz88—whoever she was—grabbed his arm and they clung together to the slight ridges on the bottom of the truck.

Another bump threw them into the air and tossed them back against the truck cab, and then a ceiling—no, a bridge—flew over their heads and there was a sound of squealing tires. They dropped down a ramp. Thane and Liz88 were now side-by-side, hanging on to the back of the truck cab. She looked as scared as he felt.

They went up a ramp, and for a moment the summit building appeared, in the distance now and smoking. An explosion spread from its side, an absurd flowering of stone dust, tendrils slowing as they tapered.

"We didn't . . . wait a minute. We're not the only ones doing something," Liz88 said.

Thane lifted himself. It was true. Troops were running and a ship landed in the plaza beyond the building. It was definitely a coup, though they looked different from the outside. Was that his sister's plan? Were these women acting independently? He almost laughed. There was, he figured, at least a forty percent chance he'd just escaped both his sister and his mother!

"It's a coup," Liz88 said. Her face was young and blank. Pink eye-wings in the frilled shape of the middling gentry. "I'm an unwilling participant in a coup."

"It'll blow over by lunch tomorrow," he said, while a fierce, dark part of him hoped this one would succeed while he wasn't trapped, while he wouldn't suffer for it.

The truck bed bounced and he scrambled to stay in it. They tilted around a corner, down a steep ramp, and rocked to a stop in a dark parking garage that smelled of spilled fuel oil and mold.

Thane staggered to his feet and jumped out of the truck bed. Liz88 followed and tried to take hold of his arm. He deftly side-stepped her. He didn't have to let random strangers touch him. Not if they really were kidnappers. If they were his sister's team or his mother's, he'd find out soon enough.

The truck door slammed. A skinny little foreigner with naked eyes clapped her hands. "This is the best diversion we could have planned! No one is even going to care that we stole a truck. I've never had luck this good!"

Thane saw a doorway, white with sunlight. He marched toward it.

A sleek solo-flyer painted with flames landed in the opening. The solo-flyer canopy raised and another foreigner—this one with a round face and a smooth curtain of brown hair—got out. "No one followed you," she said. "Not after those other guys attacked."

Thane saw some stairs. He jogged to them. Liz88 was suddenly in front of him. "Thane. Your Highness. We . . . we aren't kidnapping you. This is a res—" she looked past him, at the other women, as though expecting one of them to finish her sentence. They didn't. She met his eyes. Her brow crinkled. "I . . . thought you wanted this."

That was when it hit him. "Liz88? That's an alias like they use on . . . you . . . you saw me on chat?"

She nodded.

Thane felt a hysterical laugh about to come out of his mouth. He swallowed it. It felt like an ice cube lodged in his throat. The three young women were a lot less threatening now that he had a moment to look at them. He was taller than the tallest—Liz88—by a full head. "You saw me wish I'd get kidnapped to get out of the summit, and you decided to just . . . do that?"

Her face a mask of anxiety, Liz88 nodded.

Thane clapped a hand on her shoulder. "Thank you."

Zuleikah didn't know what she expected. A fight? A hug? She was still in suspense because reality was so much calmer than her fantasies. Thane was heart-stoppingly gorgeous in the flesh.

Pictures did not do him justice. Or maybe it was just that on media feeds everyone you saw was a sort of base-line beautiful. Then he thanked her and her brain seized like a broken engine. He was here. Touching distance! Wow, his eyes. They were so deep, ocean planets she could dive into and never come out.

A series of pops sounded nearby. Margot suddenly grabbed her arm, Thane's too, and jerked them both down to the gritty, dirty floor. "That's gunfire!"

Margot crouched over her. "It's coming from starboard." She grimaced. "I mean the right. We need to find better cover or a way out of here."

Ki tumbled into the pile of them like it was a group hug and not deadly warfare. "I got the building schematic. There's a pedestrian exit up those stairs. But we can't leave your flyer!"

"If it doesn't bleed, it doesn't matter," Margot said.

"Spoken like a rich girl," Ki said. She crawled to the right side of their huddle, closer to Margot's ship, the entrance, and the gunshots. "I'll take the flyer out and meet you guys on the other side."

Margot grabbed Ki's arm and jerked her back down. "You'll lead them to us."

Ki cocked her head. "Do you really not know me better than that?"

"They're too close." How did she know that? The open sides of the parking garage showed light, scrub bushes, and an empty street.

Ki wriggled out of Margot's grip. "You should worry less. You'll live longer." She darted to the solo-flyer. Puffs of dust perforated the pavement around her, each representing a bullet too fast to see. Zuleikah was amazed. Ki didn't even duck her head, just ran straight and hard.

Margot started to follow her, but stopped. She turned back to

Zuleikah and Thane. She pointed at the stairs. "Go. I'll follow."

Thane looked at Margot, and it was a longer and more grateful look than he'd given Zuleikah. And Margot had grabbed him! Without permission!

Thane's wrist was muscular, strong, hinting at the hidden strength under his loose robe sleeves. Zuleikah stared at it and then took hold of it. She felt him stiffen. She pulled him after her to the stairs. He let her. Maybe he was the kind of guy who wanted women to take charge.

The stairs led to a vestibule that opened on a higher street. Ratana City was like that—built in a series of canyons and cliffs, one building's roof was another's basement. What a difference a block made—instead of a war zone, the section of street before them was calm. The glass wall was unmarred, the door propped open for the business day. A food cart a few doors down gave off steam and savory scents. Only the fact that the vendor wasn't at it belied the situation.

Margot sat down by the wall near the top of the stairs. She was breathing heavy, a line between her brows.

Zuleikah asked, "Should we, uh . . . check the coast is clear?"

Margot gave her a look like she thought she was an idiot. "Stay down, stay inside." She rested her arms on her knees and lowered her head.

Someone should be some sort of lookout. There were two glass walls to the vestibule and a solid wall on the other side, where the stairs continued up. Zuleikah flattened her back to the solid wall and inched along it until she was pressed to the glass. She could see most of the street off to the right, and a glass-distorted sliver to the left. Nothing looked dangerous. Zuleikah had never been in public areas when a violent action happened, but she knew the rules. Find a shelter, stay low. She tried to see as far as she could, to scan for the familiar purple star of a nobility safety shelter. All she could see was the diamond for wealthy commoners. It might have to do?

Margot's solo-flyer screamed down from the sky. The noise and color made Zuleikah flinch, her knees bending before she could stop herself. Ki halted the flyer scant inches above the pavement. It wobbled from the sudden deceleration. Zuleikah saw her hard work on the finish flash before her eyes, but Ki set it down gently—perfectly, really.

Ki popped the canopy. "Guys. This worked out better than you think. We're not far from our original rendezvous point." Ki waved to the right. "Two blocks down and one over. You want to take your flyer, Big M?"

Margot crept forward slowly, looked distrustfully up and down the street, and then shook her head. "Zuleikah and the prince should take it. We can walk to meet them."

Zuleikah felt hot with embarrassment. "I can walk."

"I think M's got the right idea." Ki squeezed Zuleikah's arm briefly. "You're the best one to guard him. You know the streets, and you know him."

Did Ki have to say it like that? She hadn't implied she knew him! Well, not that she *really* knew him. "Your Highness," she said to Thane, and awkwardly curtsied. She gestured at the open flyer. "If it's all right? You'll have to get in first."

The ShadowKat could carry a passenger—technically—sitting behind the driver in the same seat. It was tight. Thane was a tall man. This was going to be awkward. She could barely form two sentences around the prince and now she was going to squash him with her butt.

"Aren't solo-flyers dangerous?" he asked.

That was a shockingly grandfatherly thing for a handsome prince to say. There was an article the club liked to re-post about how solo-flyers were no more dangerous than walking.

Or should she appeal to his sense of adventure?

"You know what's dangerous?" Margot snapped. "Standing around here and getting shot."

Thane got in. His knees stuck up and he bent his head under the canopy.

Zuleikah paused before following him. Thane's crown was missing. Disarrayed curls in his hair showed where it had been. "Your crown?"

"Leave it," Thane said.

Zuleikah saw Ki dash down the stairs and suspected she was fetching it. She had a feeling Ki didn't leave anything valuable behind her.

Zuleikah got in. Thane's muscular thighs pressed against her hips and she felt breathless. Had she been sweating? Did she perfume herself that morning? She tried to sniff her underarm as she pulled the canopy closed. She only smelled fresh paint and cordite.

Thane had no choice but to lie against her back as the canopy closed over them. She could feel the shape of his pecs even through his folded brocade robe and her own flight suit. He exhaled, and his hot breath sent every hair on the back of her neck to straight attention. She was going to have trouble flying. Two blocks back and one over. She called up the program for the rendezvous. She'd put it in herself. She had multiple, redundant routes throughout the city already marked. She could do this.

The ShadowKat wobbled as it rose. In the distance, she saw smoke rising. Don't try to show off, she admonished herself. You'll crash. "We'll stay low," she said. "For safety."

"Thank you," he said, and rested his hand on her shoulder. "I . . . I admit I've always wanted to try one of these things."

"We'll be fine." If they didn't get shot out of the sky or she didn't die of a heart attack before they got there.

10:
THE GET AWAY

KI BURST INTO THE SUNLIGHT TO FIND **M**ARGOT SCOWLING AT HER like she'd just killed her puppy. "What? He'll want it." Ki hooked the crown over her wrist like a purse. The sapphire in the center alone could buy a house—and not a small house, either.

Margot started down the street, half hunched over, a hand on the wall, looking over her shoulder every step.

Ki shook her head. "If they're going to shoot at us, skulking won't stop them. Better to look casual."

Margot turned, bent over, hands clawed in front of her. She whisper-shouted, "With the crown jewels in your hand?"

"Easy, girl." Ki unfastened the front of her spacesuit. The crown didn't fit inside. Who had designed this thing? It was way wider than a prince would need, flowering outward from the base like an inverted lampshade. She sighed. "Do you have something to carry this in?"

"Because I was planning to shop for a crown?"

There was a trashcan nearby. Ki pulled its top off and fished around. Ah, a shopping bag with a torn handle. Perfect. She dropped the crown in and gathered the torn handle together with the solid one and tied them in a knot. She held up the bag so Margot could see the Happy Thrift logo. "Voila!" The crown stretched the fabric, but who would guess royal crown before, say, candy dish?

Margot continued skulking down the street like she was in some war movie.

"It's a palace coup," Ki said. "There's no way anyone will be shooting up some random—"

Puffs of smoke rose from the pavement: a series of dots across the road. Ki was still thinking, "Huh, that looks just like bullets in a movie," when a large shadow engulfed the street. Ki didn't see more than that because she dove under the nearest thing that had an under.

It was a flower box, and loose potting soil ground into the concrete under her palm as she tried to get closer to the building wall.

The shopping bag with the crown in it winced like a living thing on the sidewalk beside her. There was a hole in it now. Ki frantically untied the bag. The crown had a long scrape on one silver leafy bit, but was otherwise undamaged.

The shots faded into the distance. Ki crawled out and looked for Margot. She saw a foot under an overturned food cart. She hurried to right the cart.

Margot scuttled away like a roach seeing sunlight. Ki had to pause for breath—the food cart wasn't light!—before jogging after her.

Ki joined Margot in an alleyway that ended in raw rock, climbing upward. "We're halfway there," Ki said.

"We're going to die," Margot said.

"Eventually, sure. Everyone does. But hey, let's put it off, okay?"

The door Margot cowered against had an analog lock. Ki already had her jacket open, so it was easy enough to get out her picks. She nudged Margot aside and found the right tool. "Would you feel safer indoors?" Ki pushed the door open. Margot nearly fell in.

"You're welcome," Ki called after her as Margot ran ahead.

Margot didn't scurry far—the interior doors were all locked—but Ki followed and made short work of them. Margot led the way through two different offices, one tastefully decorated and one a mess, down a corridor, and into a stairwell. Several times they heard the sounds of shots and explosions from the coup in progress, but Ki figured they were at least three blocks away. Each time, Margot went from leading the way to having to be coaxed out of hiding.

"Why did you volunteer to walk, anyway?" Ki asked her.

Margot slapped her offered hand away and crawled out from under the desk. "I've been shot at before," she said. "I thought I'd be better at it."

Ki tried to remember if she'd ever been shot at. Well, she had, of course, run from guns. She'd heard shots fired in her direction. Maybe it counted. She shrugged. "I don't think getting shot at it is something you can get better at with practice. It pretty much always sucks."

Margot stopped in her crawl past a window and gave Ki such a look.

They climbed the stairs to the roof of the building. Ki pointed. "There—that white roof on the other side of the garden is where our flyers are stashed. We just gotta jump that fence. Are you game?"

It was a six-foot security fence. Margot grabbed hold with one arm and vaulted it like a champ. Well, at least this was something that military experience was good for. Ki took a few steps back and made a running start at the fence. She hit halfway up, scrambled the rest of the way and landed next to Margot, who was half under a bush.

It was a lush rooftop garden. It smelled wet and green, in the middle of all this desert and city. Had to cost a fortune. Ki didn't hurry Margot through it, but enjoyed the beauty as Margot felt each empty space out like it was icy water.

A waist-high wall separated the garden from the garage the flyers were in. Every parking space was full. Either people who parked here weren't worried about the coup, or they'd run to shelter without their vehicles.

The ample cover sped things up. Margot ran between the low wall and the noses of craft to the stairs, and then pelted down them like death was on her heels.

They'd parked on the lowest level, bright and early when the garage was mostly empty, next to the exit so they could make a quick escape. Ki felt better as soon as she saw the familiar shape of Ethan's flyer poking out from behind Zuleikah's bat-like vintage model.

Margot was between the flyers, looking out to the street. Ki set her hand affectionately on the red flyer. "How the hell did we beat them here?"

As if summoned, Margot's flyer glided into the garage. Ki repeated herself as the canopy opened. "How did we beat you?"

Zuleikah and Thane both looked sweaty and nauseous. Thane pressed back against the canopy, letting Zuleikah crawl out first.

Zuleikah said, "There were ships. Soldiers. Didn't want to be followed."

Margot gave Ki a look like she thought Zuleikah was an example Ki could learn from.

Ki opened the canopy on her flyer. Trying to hide her

motions, she tucked the crown of the prince of Ratana behind her seat. "Let's see what we can find out about this coup situation and how best to avoid it. You guys look so glum—don't you realize this is the luckiest thing that could have happened? Border control is going to be a mess!"

Zuleikah gave her prince a hand out of Margot's flyer. "We should be safe here?"

The prince looked around dazedly. "What is this place?"

Margot gestured at the wide garage entrance. "It's only a matter of time before someone who knows we aren't supposed to be here comes, or the fighting moves this way, or this place gets hit by debris or any number of other things. This is not safety. It's a place that has been safe so far, but it is not safety. We have to get out of this city. Now."

"My sentiments exactly," Ki lied. She had to maintain the illusion she knew what she was doing. "Off world we go. Let's see what's in orbit." Her console lit up. There were a lot of ships in orbit, more than before, and most of them had the red "communications blocked" symbol. Ki coughed. "Okay, maybe now is not the time to go into space."

"What about the police?" Margot asked.

"What pluck! That's like getting turned down for a sandwich and asking for twenty Trines instead. You want to hitch a ride with the cops?"

Margot looked liable to punch her. "No. I'm asking if the police are looking for us. What do you see from police communications?"

"Their city's getting blown to bits, M. I think they've forgotten about a trespassing case for the time being. If we don't go looking for them, they won't be looking for us."

Zuleikah had, during this exchange, quietly seated herself on the nose of her flyer and turned on her bracelet display. "I have a tool for accessing police band. We can map their reports and avoid those areas."

Margot looked relieved. "Let's do that."

It wasn't all that different than what Ki had said, but hey, she wasn't one to care who got the credit. She needed a way back into Margot's good graces, since following Margot's own plan had somehow gotten her out of them.

The prince leaned over Zuleikah's shoulder, watching her screen. His long, disarrayed curls brushed her cheek and Zuleikah got a scared-pleased expression that made her look ten years old. That was something. Had she managed to bring two lovebirds together?

Margot walked up to him. "Um . . . Prince, um . . . Your Highness? We're not holding you here, so, if you want, you can just . . . go."

"Isn't there safety in numbers?" he asked.

"You don't know these numbers," Margot said.

Ki wanted to groan. Margot was going to mess the whole thing up—the rescue and the romance. Ki hurried over. "Zuleikah has marked the hot spots. Let's get while the getting is good. Prince? Looks like you're with Zuleikah; the Hawk Angel is our only real two-seater."

Margot looked like she was going to start another tirade, but Zuleikah opened her canopy and the prince settled into her second seat. He looked relieved. Probably to be with Zuleikah, but also the Hawk Angel really was a two-seater, and the ShadowKat was not. That trip had to have been cramped as hell.

"But where are we going?" Margot whined.

"Not here," Zuleikah said. Good old Zuleikah!

Ki strapped in. "How about back to Z's place to start?" Zuleikah made an affirmative sound. Margot said nothing, which was probably as agreeable as she could stand to be at the moment.

Ki moved her flyer to just inside the garage entrance. Occasional shadows of aircraft flickered over the pavement at high speed. Nothing moved on the street, everyone who was not involved in the fighting had gone to ground. Ki tried to get a sense of the rhythm of the overhead craft. Maybe it was like trains, and she could guess when one was coming. (Ethan said she was deluding herself and there was nothing but dumb luck behind her excellent survival rate on illegal track crossings.) The airships seemed to come in clumps . . .

She felt, rather than saw, her companions move their flyers close behind hers. A large shadow passed, then sunlight. Like the gap between trains.

"Here we go," she said, and floored it, banking left into the sunlight.

They made it three blocks before something exploded near them, and then a shadow covered them, bullets raining. Ki cut onto the nearest detour on the map.

"They're after us!" Zuleikah said.

Was she completely wrong? Did the prince have a tracker or something? Oh hell, if she had a prince, she'd have put a tracker on him.

Margot spoke angrily, "It's a lazy-ass gunner who was told to guard and doesn't want to move so he's shooting anything that moves in his line of sight. We have to make ourselves hard to hit."

Ki hoped Margot was right. It felt right. It was what she'd do if she were in some ship guarding some street she didn't even live on. Ki led the team under an overpass and through a breezeway—some hotel loading dock—and back around to the planned map. The gunship and its dark delta of shadow did not follow.

Margot was right. The plan was going to work.

Then Ki heard the boom, and saw the plume of smoke rise as a building in front of them leaned with impossible slowness, teetering a moment before gravity took over and it plummeted to the ground in a rain of bricks.

Her ship could barely take the turn, flipping upside-down as Ki swerved into a narrow alley. She couldn't check behind her to see if the others had joined her or been crushed.

An orderly column of troops marched along the next street. Hundreds of them, bristling with gun barrels. Ki pulled a full stop, lurching forward in her restraints.

Zuleikah's flyer bumped Ki's. They landed together in the tight space. Margot's parked at the other entrance to the alley. All alive. And watching their backs. Good girl.

Ki checked her map. "This wasn't supposed to be here. The police bands aren't talking about this area at all."

Margot spoke. "Troops are coming in from the west, and some group over there is moving to intercept. Zuleikah, is there another way to your place?"

"I . . . I . . ."

"They're heading to the Sanwan Canyon," the prince said. His voice was unexpected and muffled. The Hawk Angel didn't have a mic on the rear seat. There was a rustling and his voice came louder: "The military will occupy the canyon as a choke point on the eastern side of the city. That was the plan, if the city were ever compromised. Which . . . well, it is."

"That's the canyon I live in," Zuleikah said, her voice vibrating with emotion.

Ki looked around at the buildings and cliffs hemming them in. "Damn it. Okay. Okay. Zuleikah, how do we get to the spaceport from here? I know a place near there." Or she would, at least, by the time they got there, Crimopedia willing.

There were always places to hide near ports.

Zuleikah said, "The space port is back the way we came, on the other side of the summit building and the heart of the city."

Yeah, there it was on the map. Ki said, "We'll take a long route around that, huh?"

There was a lengthy pause before Zuleikah said, "Yes, I think that would be wise."

Margot, Ki suspected, had her microphone turned off.

Zuleikah's flyer rose to hover near the top of the alleyway. "We should stay below the skyline, since we can maneuver better than those military gunships. Follow me." There was a pause before she added, "Now."

They were clear of the alleyway no more than a second when the first ship fired on them. Zuleikah banked hard and it was all Ki could do to keep up with her. They swooped through the glass-lined canyon of a street, then into a real canyon, also lined in glass, windows studded into crevices and artificial out-croppings. The canyon narrowed and Zuleikah turned sharply again, into a heavily built-up street shadowed by stone balconies overhead.

Ki had never flown while trying to find a hideout in a strange city, but she'd run location searches on her palm while trying to lose pursuit on foot through a busy train yard. She was a lot less afraid of a bullet than a hypersonic train. Game on.

Margot had scant seconds of thinking that Zuleikah had timed it well and that they were in the clear, when the sky filled with the pop and zing of bullets. Was she ever going to escape the war zone? Had all the universe been at war all along and she hadn't noticed?

Something hit her canopy with a wet thump. An arm. It tumbled off and fell, leaving a smear of blood where its cut-off end hit the glass.

Margot almost ran into a wall. She turned back, craning up to see where the limb had come from. There was nothing above her. Or directly in front of her. She lost Zuleikah. The building on her starboard was collapsing with unreal slowness. She saw the vague shape of a body, like a discarded rag, below her in the street.

It was all too slow and too fast, like a nightmare where monsters crawl but you can't move to escape them. She flew higher and caught sight of a dot of red, a dash of black—Ki and Zuleikah's flyers.

That was good. She had a target to focus on. Zuleikah flew like her life's goal was to shake Margot's pursuit. The black Hawk Angel turned almost too fast to be believed, right into a shopping arcade. Margot whimpered but followed, into the tight vaulted space and an avalanche of stuffed animals, their sales cart so much litter in Zulcikah's wake.d Curlicues of white metal supported the barrel vault overhead, flashing by as if to emphasize how fast she was going.

People in the arcade screamed and ran for cover. Margot felt sick and wanted to shout apologies to each one, but Zuleikah was already turning again, into a café courtyard and then straight up. Margot barely braked in time to follow over a terrazzo terrace which jutted out from the building. Zuleikah tore through a cloth awning and was in open sky again.

Margot pulled horizontal as soon as the awning cleared, flying up against her restraints as she did so, but she still nearly missed Zuleikah slipping over the humped roof and into another street.

Thick smoke rolled through the air to the left. Margot found the back of Ki's flyer at last, swooping between them from port.

Ki and Zuleikah swung back and forth relative to each other at each turn. It was . . .

Weirdly fun. Margot was not as afraid as she had been moments ago. Was it the illusion that she could control her fate? The best pilot couldn't dodge bullets as well as luck could. That was something her sergeant was fond of saying.

Luck could hang itself; it felt better to dodge.

Ratana City, she dimly recalled, was supposed to be a tourist destination. The Paris of space. Margot wouldn't recognize any of it if she came back to visit at something below breakneck pace. Could she someday have a quiet meal on that terrace they'd zoomed over, surrounded by polite conversation and clicking flatware? The idea was surreal.

Zuleikah's Hawk Angel vanished in a narrow alley and was not visible when Margot entered it, but she caught the tail of Ki's ShadowKat again, turning a corner. Another alleyway, another barely-missed turn, and the sky opened above, blue and sunny. Ragged white columns stood around her, a ribcage of stone and glass; she was inside a shattered building. She rose and saw troops in the next street, crouched behind overturned vehicles, aiming across a wasteland of concrete at each other.

It had been a different world, that morning. A quiet street and an intact building and people going about their lives. This was new to her; war didn't change the landscape in space. It only obliterated it.

Zuleikah and Ki were finally both visible. They'd gone high, too, to get around the smoldering wreckage of a building half-collapsed against a canyon wall. Margot put on some speed to catch up. Something exploded very loud and so near at hand it sounded like it was inside her cockpit. In a blind panic, Margot pushed the flyer to its maximum in-atmosphere speed. She overshot Zuleikah and Ki and was suddenly out over open desert, the city swallowed by the canyon behind her.

Ki spoke to her, gently, like an elementary school teacher. "Easy, M. A little slower. That's it. Ease off the throttle. Your batteries need to catch up. Veer south. I'm sending you both coordinates for where we're going. That's it, look at the coordinates. You're doing fine."

Margot's hands were shaking, and sweating, and cold. The flyer wasn't damaged. It had been a close concussion, that's all. No seals breached. She flicked through controls, trying to find the rear-view feed. Even when it was displayed, prominently, she couldn't stop twitching because her back was exposed.

Open country. No cover. Paradoxically, she wanted to go back to the city and its explosions. It wasn't safer, but it felt safer. She wanted to find whoever was following them, because this angry, frightened animal in the back of her skull was certain someone was following them and she wouldn't be safe until she emptied lots and lots of bullets into that person.

But that was crazy. She tried to start the breathing exercises.

They passed over low-lying dwellings and random clusters of rooftop gardens and the glitter of glass where homes sat in the shadow of rock formations. Signs of settlement grew less frequent and the ground less uneven, just desert and rock, similar to what they'd flown through before coming to Zuleikah's place. Margot relaxed, somewhat, with another flyer on either side of her.

Fine. The smug, baby-talking VA counselor was right. She had anxiety problems. He was still a condescending asshole.

"We're almost to the spaceport," Zuleikah said. "Where is this place you know about?"

"I'll know it when I see it."

Margot barely acknowledged the map on her dash. She was content to follow.

The empty desert began to develop pockets of human

habitation again, now glowing as the sun was getting low. It was like the land was cracked from the heat and glowing inside. Life was normal here. Mysteriously, miraculously normal. People sitting down to eat or arguing about chores, maybe. How could they do that? Didn't they know?

The spaceport was brightly lit—all of it above-ground as a necessity—established on a particularly flat and sturdy bit of Ratana, a high plateau like a deck above the rock-strewn plain. Searchlights swept the sky and the tiny shapes of ships in holding patterns could be seen against the orange haze.

"Don't worry," Ki said. One of her favorite phrases. "We're not going any closer to the security fences and searchlights. Hey, Zuleikah, I forgot, what is this geographic feature called, anyway?"

"Space Port Plateau," Zuleikah said with the flat confusion the question merited. That wasn't the sort of name you'd forget.

"Huh. I thought it had a cooler name than that." Ki's ship sank into a cluster of slanted solar collectors. They seemed to be floating in darkness above the plain, but as they got closer Margot could see a finger of plateau under them, a peninsula hidden by the brighter lights of the spaceport.

When Margot landed, Ki was already out of her flyer, walking up to a triangular wall. The solar collector farm was bigger than it looked from the air. Each mirror wall was several stories high, the hypotenuse of a cheese-wedge shaped building. Ki was tiny at the bottom of the short side. She rooted around in the dirt and dust by the base and then, with a groan of complaining metal, she pulled back a section like turning a page in a book. It stayed open, curled, leaving a space wide enough for a solo-flyer to enter.

"We'll be safe here," Ki said. "This warehouse has been empty for years. Local kids use it for parties. Anyway, it's popular enough to have a starred review on Crimopedia."

Crimopedia? There were so many criminals in the world they got their own wiki? Margot waited for the others to guide their flyers in before following.

The wedge-shaped interior was lit with softly glowing balls on the ceiling: the cheap kind of industrial phospheres that take all day to charge and fade to darkness before the night is over.

A few scattered boxes and pieces of debris littered the empty, cavernous space. A sagging old sofa, a collapsed hydrofoil, and an upside-down bucket sat in a group around a char-blackened circle of floor. Directly above it was a hole torn in the join of the ceiling. The hole glowed faintly with sunset, its edges black with soot that trailed sharply down the near wall. Someone burned things . . . indoors? On purpose? Now she saw the evidence, she could smell the faint charcoal over the miasma of rot and human waste.

To Margot's abject horror, Ki dropped herself carelessly down on the filthy couch. "It's not Zuleikah's pad, but no one's going to be bombing here."

Zuleikah stepped out of her flyer looking like she didn't want even her shoes to touch anything. Thane stayed seated inside.

Margot walked up to Ki. "Can't we get a hotel?"

"Taking reservations in the middle of a war? With what money? You want to see if we can pawn the prince's crown while the dust is still flying? I mean, geez, M. They're probably still looking for the guy."

"My name's Thane," the prince said. He raised a hand. They all looked at him. He looked embarrassed, and angry. "Stop calling me 'the prince'. I'm a person and I get a vote and my name is Thane."

Zuleikah crossed her arms on her stomach and moved a step away from the craft. "I'm sorry," Margot said, more to Zuleikah than him. She really didn't want this strange man to be there.

How had she let herself be talked into this? "I'd feel better if we knew where we're going. If we knew—"

The quiet but distinct sound of an aircraft flying low overhead cut her off. She crouched without thinking. The sound faded.

Thane's whisper carried, "You kidnapped me and you didn't have a plan?"

Zuleikah turned her helmet over in her hands. "I'll see what I can get from the network."

Ki hopped lightly to her feet. "See? Next steps. Zuleikah will get the lay of the land. Margot, see if you can get a fire started. Just break up anything burnable that's still in here. I'll go find us something to eat."

Margot followed her to the exit. "Are you crazy? Why do we need a fire?"

"For heat," Ki said, like this was obvious. "Get to it."

"I've never made a fire in my life!"

"It's like riding a bicycle," Ki said, which made no sense whatsoever. "You'll have it figured out by the time I'm back."

"How are you going to find food?" In an abandoned solar farm next to a spaceport next to a war zone, she didn't add.

"If I come back with something, I found a way."

With that she ducked under the curled metal and was gone.

Margot turned and sighed. Zuleikah leaned against her flyer, pulling screens out of her bracelet. Thane was still sitting ramrod straight in the cockpit, looking pointedly at his fingernails. Margot asked, "Seriously, why would we need a fire?" They both pretended not to hear her. Margot wished she could get Zuleikah to look at her. Just a glance, so she could show her she wanted to talk where the prince couldn't overhear. But she didn't look away from her data feeds. Margot went to search through the debris in the warehouse. For what, she wasn't sure.

11:
DINNER DATE

ZULEIKAH SAT CROSS-LEGGED ON THE FRONT OF HER FLYER, TO give Thane the interior compartment to himself. He had cringed away from her when she'd gotten out of the cockpit. Maybe she was revolting to him. Something in how she smelled or flew or looked.

He leaned against the cockpit edge. "If you're working for my mother or my sister, you know, you can tell me. It's not like it'd make a difference, if I knew."

He sounded too casual, and his face was blank, like a poker player or business negotiator, like he was sure she was plotting something evil against him. "I'm not. We're not. Like I said . . . we just wanted to help you." She couldn't say it emphatically enough.

He stepped over the seat divider and settled himself in the driver's seat. Anyone else would have looked awkward doing that. He flicked a sleeve end out of his lap and it might as well have been a throne. Abruptly his expression changed, became softer, almost flirtatious. "Can I see what you're reading?"

He was really beautiful with his sapphire eyes and his hair falling in a curtain around his face. He looked shy, but maybe interested. "Got a screen?"

He held his palm up. "Implant."

Zuleikah gestured apologetically toward the dash. He leaned back. She opened the glove compartment. She had to get the receiver sticker from the little pouch of spare parts that came with her bracelet. Implant readers weren't common. Most people would rather have a thing they could put on and take off than make reading a part of their body.

She felt sweaty and messy rummaging through her stuff while he sat back, clean and cool. She peeled the sticker off its backing and hesitated. It wouldn't do to touch Royalty, but Thane stretched his arm out to her and waited until she smoothed it onto his wrist. She shivered at the contact. The connection lit up on her monitor and she sent him the most interesting of the feeds she was scanning.

His eyes widened and she felt a surge of warmth. "This . . . this is the royal private network. How did you get this? *I* can't get this!"

Why wouldn't the prince get the royal network? Still, it made her accomplishment look even bigger. She'd found an exploit in the police band years ago and used it to find a back door through the military to the royal network. "Public news says gangs, no one hurt. I knew that was wrong, so I went private." It was stupid the way the public networks lied. Were they honestly fooling anyone?

"But how did you get into it? Are you . . . ?" His voice got softer. "You're a pirate."

Zuleikah wasn't sure if she should deny that, if he thought pirates were bad, or not deny it, because it made her sound important and mysterious. Was that fear or respect in the prince's eyes as they left the projection above his hand?

"HA!" Margot's voice echoed from where she was, bent over, inspecting the rubble.

Was that aimed at them? At her? Or at whatever it was Margot was pulling out of a collection of boxes? "Wait . . ." Zuleikah had to stop and reread the paragraph she'd been on. No, it couldn't be. But it was. This was a memo detailing how the attack would take place, dated late last night. Betrayal from the closest ranks. An icy pulse ran through her veins. She couldn't say it out loud; she had to show it to him. She highlighted the passage and flicked it to Thane's reader. Then she felt stupid. She should have said something first, prepared him. She watched his face as he read, anxious for his response. His brow knit, and then relaxed. "Figures," he said, and rolled his eyes. He flicked a finger through the projection, moving to another story.

Just like that. "She's your mother's general."

"And? Auntie Ba always hated Mother. I suspected she was involved in the last coup, though no one ever proved it. I'm just surprised it wasn't Jolica."

"There's . . . did you see there's a part about you?"

"Oh, yeah. That looks like Jolica's work. She did a better job covering her tracks than Auntie."

He sounded completely calm, but he had to be hiding some sorrow, some betrayal. She laid her hand on his. He flinched away. "Please, don't."

Of course. You don't touch royalty. She retracted her hand. His skin felt so smooth, like satin. She curled her hand to preserve the sensation. "You can talk to me. About . . . feelings. If you need to."

He scowled. It was so fast it was almost a flicker. Then the flirtatious smile was back, the lowered lashes. "You can talk to me, too. Tell me anything."

Suddenly she wasn't quite sure she should.

A loud clatter made them both jump. Margot straightened from dumping an armload of wood pieces on the soot stain in front of the couch. She frowned at them, her hands on her lower back. "You found something?"

Zuleikah imagined she looked as miserable as she felt. "A message, coordinating the attack. From the royal guards."

"It's not like it's surprising." Thane peeled the reader patch off and held it out to her on one fingertip. "It happens like this two times out of three. The military tries to overthrow the royalty, and they use the guards. I'm just amazed they cared to target me."

"There's a buyer." Zuleikah grimaced at her own choice of words. "A ransom."

"Someone was going to kidnap the guy we just kidnapped?"

Thane laughed. "Joke's on them if they think I'm worth anything."

Zuleikah had been making him wait with the sticky patch outstretched. Was she trying to make him hate her? She snagged it, careful not to touch his skin, and put it back on its backing. "There . . . they can't all be disloyal. The military, I mean."

Margot snapped, "Who cares? Stop studying politics and find us a way out of this mess we're in."

Didn't she see how important this was? "We've been carried into greater events by fate."

"No, we've been dragged into terrible events by Ki. As soon as you find a way, the three of us fly off this planet and leave rich boy for his family to find. He is not our problem and you've already spent too much time on him."

Before her mind caught up to what she was doing, Zuleikah stormed up to Margot and slapped her.

Zuleikah stood, fists clenched, ready for retaliation, but Margot just stared at her. Then Margot's nose twitched, and tears started to well in her eyes. "Fine, then," she said. "Who cares?" Margot stomped away.

Zuleikah felt her arms shake.

"Hey," Thane said.

He'd gotten out of the ship at last. Was he proud she'd defended him?

"You should apologize to her," he said.

Apologize to *her*? His family was betrayed. He'd been sold like cattle. Margot was acting like it was not important.

Thane walked after Margot.

Thane was now 80% sure these women were not working for his sister. Maybe 60% sure they weren't working for his mother. He wished he were sure. It was exhausting acting normal when his back ached and his feet were swollen in his slippers and, well, there was that delicious 20% hope he'd really escaped.

But he still had to hide any weakness and, ugh, appeal to these women. Story of his life. He had one weapon: flirting. Cautiously, he approached the woman he suspected was the leader and mastermind. Margot. She snapped the orders, but her command was shaky. The little, ratty one never obeyed and now her stable subordinate had mutinied. If the group split, he could be left on his own or returned to the palace. This Margot was the least interested in keeping him, so she was the one he had to make like him.

Margot faced the triangular wall at the back of the warehouse, arms crossed. She kept her face averted from him to hide the tear-streaks he knew where there.

He stayed out of striking distance. He knew a thing or two about dealing with people who were in power and upset. "It's personal, to her," he said. "That's why she did that. I'm sorry."

Margot glared her anger at the wall. "It's personal to all of us. We could be captured or shot and killed. People could already be coming for us, for *you*."

She wasn't wrong. Thane was his mother's "special little project," after all. Jolica had called him that. She was weirdly jealous of the attention. That was probably why she'd arranged the ransom. And whatever "unspeakable thing" she wanted him to do after. He didn't want to think about it. He cast about for something positive to say. "Zuleikah is very good at infiltrating networks."

"She's also good at smacking people."

"She's one of the gentry. When someone acts against royalty, they take it personally, even when they don't really know any of us. We're important to their identity." His tutors would be proud. He was parroting their drivel perfectly.

Margot half-turned, rubbing her cheek with the heel of her hand. Her eyes were small and vulnerable looking with no makeup. "She has a crush on you."

Oh no. And he'd let her touch him! She'd expect something from that. He kept his expression neutral. "Who doesn't? It's my job to look good."

Margot looked at him like she was putting together the pieces of a puzzle and that made him feel distinctly uncomfortable.

He concentrated on the pain in his feet, the maddening itch of healing. He ducked his head. "I'm not saying she was right to slap you, but this is a tense situation. Sometimes you have to put up with people until it's over. Right? Then you can fire her, or . . . whatever your arrangement is with your helpers. Crew? Gang? What's the right term? I'm not used to dealing with pirates, or whatever you call yourselves."

She snorted and looked past him, back at the fire ring. "I think the decided title was 'The Galactic Hellcats.'" She sighed.

"I barely know these girls. I don't want to be here. I'm supposed to be at home, looking for a job."

Thane had to shake the confusion out of his head. It was an instinctual, inelegant act. "Wait, what?"

Margot raised her eyebrow at him.

"You . . . you're working-class?"

"Aspiring thereto." She smirked. "Seriously? That's what bothers you? Three amateurs with solo-flyers kidnap you and you're concerned we're beneath you socially?"

"I . . . I didn't mean . . ."

She poked his sleeve with her elbow. "Relax. You're royal. I get it. We probably sound like we're from Cloud CooCoo World."

There was something comforting about her. Calm and steady. He also got this unmistakable feeling that she wasn't remotely interested in his body, which was hugely refreshing. She hadn't looked him up and down, or stared at his eyes or his shoulders.

Actually, she was frowning, holding herself away from him. "Um, Thane? Are we done here?"

"Yes. I. Just . . ." Wondered if you'd marry me and save me from having to marry someone else? "I came over here to make sure you were all right, to ask if there was anything I could do?"

"Not really. Unless you have some royal trick you can pull out of your sleeve to get us out of here?" She glanced at his sleeve with exaggerated curiosity.

Thane couldn't even get himself out of a press conference. "I . . . I can't believe you decided to kidnap me. For fun. It's so daft. But brilliant, I mean. I can't say I'm thrilled to be in a filthy abandoned building, but in a way this is the best night out I've had in my life."

Margot lifted one shoulder, hugging herself. She seemed older with her hair hanging in her face. "I wanted to leave you behind. So . . . sorry for that."

"Uh . . . sure."

With her arms still wrapped tight, Margot walked slowly back toward Zuleikah and the pile of firewood.

Thane had missed a cue. She had wanted him to say something. Maybe touch her in a reassuring way? He'd spent too much time learning to be still. Thane forced himself to follow. Gods, he hoped he could stop walking soon.

She walked around the pile of wood until she apparently decided that one filthy spot was the least filthy and sat down cross-legged, facing the pile like it was a campfire. "Was there some place you wanted to escape to?" she asked him, a hopeful look on her face.

"I'm afraid not. Just places to escape from."

"Would it be bad to go back? We could say we temporarily moved you for your protection. We could get medals or something."

His mother would skin him alive. "That wouldn't work. I mean . . . you'll more likely be executed without trial." Literally skin him alive. She'd threatened it more than once: some cosmetic procedure that would replace his epidermis with one more pleasing to the touch and wrinkle-resistant. Another step in her special project.

Margot still looked like she was considering it. "Please," he said. No, that was bad. Don't beg. Make it about them. "I don't want to be responsible for your deaths."

Even if the coup succeeded, whoever took power would interrogate him. He'd endured days of torture the last time he'd been recovered from kidnapping, and he hadn't even been remotely complicit that time. "Wherever you are going, I think it's best I go with you." He hoped his smile looked easy-going. "I'm not like other guys, you know. I like roughing it." To prove it, he sat down gingerly on the edge of the heap of trash nearest Margot.

Oh damn. Lifting his feet from the ground awakened a chorus of itch and pain just like stepping out of the flyer had.

Zuleikah looked anywhere but at him. This was awkward. Outside, his mother's troops could be closing in, her plastic surgeons waiting for some improvement to his face and his character to be ordered.

$$\displaystyle \notin$$

After breaking into a planet and stealing legitimate crown jewels it was a little beneath Ki to try locks on unguarded buildings, so she walked past the nearest warehouses.

Ki's breath puffed in front of her as her feet crunched gravel. She could feel heat radiating off the ground, but her nose was running and she had to put her gloves back on. The temperature had dropped hard when the sun went down. Well, Zuleikah had said it would last night, hadn't she?

The warehouses were big, the space between them wide and empty. It was a desolate environment. Her tracker indicated a warm body a mile ahead. Ki headed toward it. That was what she wanted: a living guard to outwit.

It was a woman with a machine gun, pacing around and around a particular warehouse. Ki watched through three repeats of the guard's circuit. She made no random stops or side-trips. Just round and round like a toy train. Boring! The machine gun was exciting, though. Ki found a door and waited until the guard passed. She recorded the time it took the guard to re-appear around the corner. Two minutes, thirty-seven seconds. Ki set her timer and waited for the next go round. She ran to the door and fished out her sticker circuits. Crap, she had her screen in her hand so she could watch the time. Four seconds, at least, were spent wondering if she should put it down. Another four deciding not to. Ki didn't have the right circuit. She had to use a pick. Fifteen seconds left. She put the screen in her mouth. The last tumbler clicked. As she shut the door behind her, the timer flashed its "time's up" warning. She held it to her stomach and breathed as quietly as possible as she counted to fifty to give the guard time to get back around the corner. She let the lock snick back into place.

Then she did a little dance.

The warehouse was full of cargo boxes big enough to live in, each one locked. They all had the same logo. Ki picked the one farthest from all four doorways. Its lock was easy—she used the same sticker she'd used back on Earth for the sporting goods store. Inside were stacked storage tubs. Ki dragged a tub off the top of a stack. It was heavy and fell like a sack of sand, splitting one side of the box when it hit. Slippery bags of candy-sized stones spilled out. Each bag was maybe the size of her fist and contained stones of roughly the same size and dusty translucence as wild grapes. Ki had no idea what these were or what they were worth, but she pocketed two bags in each of the zipper pouches on her legs. Hrm. She could fit more. She paused with another bag in hand. She put it down. Best not to be greedy.

She had dinner to find.

It was clear this was a gem warehouse. Not a place to find food. The guard would still be outside circling. Opening any door on the ground level was a risk, so Ki climbed to a catwalk by the roof, where there was a maintenance hatch for the solar panels.

Ki ran along the roof ridge and found a fire escape. It didn't go all the way to the ground. If she lowered the bottom ladder, the guard would suspect the place had been broken into. Ki could make the drop. She waited, crouched on the roof, for the guard to pass by.

The guard passed. She started down the fire escape. Her first three steps rattled louder than gunfire. Damnit! She froze against the wall, willing herself invisible. The guard didn't come straight back. Forty seconds to go until she re-appeared. Ki crept slow and carefully the rest of the way to the bottom of the escape to avoid making noise. She grabbed the side of the ladder opening and lowered herself. She was about to drop when she heard the guard's footsteps. She should have checked the time again. The guard walked underfoot, slowly, boots crunching sand against pavement. The stupid guard stopped. Walked back the way she'd come. What a time to start caring about her job!

Ki's arms trembled with the effort, then burned, then felt ready to snap in half before the guard stopped investigating whatever it was that was so fascinating under Ki's feet and continued on her way. Slowly. Ki bit her lip and concentrated on the sound of footsteps until the building muffled them again. She dropped to the ground.

She held her breath until she could hear that steady crunch, crunch of the guard's footsteps again. She ran for cover, giddy. That delicious old thrill. The thump of her heart was food to her. What an adrenaline junkie. She had just escaped a war zone and already craved more danger.

Admonishing herself, she stopped at a warehouse that only required snapping a standard lock, and scanned boxes for food labels. Sporting goods. Seriously? Of all the luck.

The third warehouse was the charm, filled with a familiar vending machine logo. They even had a handcart parked near the door. She pushed it around the warehouse, casually dropping items onto it like a housewife in some old movie grocery store. She trundled out into the freezing night, humming a jaunty tune as the cart jolted along the gravel.

Zuleikah was getting cold. Icy blasts snuck in every opening. They'd bent down the curled metal of the damaged wall panel as best as they could, but it wasn't as if the un-insulated metal warehouse was going to provide more than a windbreak.

Zuleikah knelt on the gritty floor next to Margot. She cleared her throat. "I found an article on how to create a fire using electrical parts. I think I have everything on the list, but I was wondering—"

"I'm sorry," Margot said.

"For what?" Zuleikah wanted to take the words back instantly.

"We captured Thane, he's our responsibility. We'll get him out of here safely."

Zuleikah furtively glanced toward Thane, who was keeping warm by walking a circuit of the room, his hands buried in his sleeves like a monk. He didn't look like he'd heard them; he was watching his feet and stepping so carefully it must have been a special, royal meditation walk.

The offer to start a fire was supposed to be her apology for hitting Margot. If the woman would let her get through it. "Do you want me to start? I have to take apart the seat warmer."

"Maybe. Academically, I know fire can work, but . . ." To her surprise, Margot grabbed her hand in both of hers. "I'm not normally such a bitch. It's been a hard couple of days."

"Um. It's okay." Zuleikah looked down at her hand. How did you end a handhold? The warmth, at least, was nice.

"I was in the Sol Navy." Margot blurted like it was a secret that had been bothering her, something Zuleikah should care about. "It's not the same as being on the ground. You live here. I . . . I was defending you. Well, my ship was defending your world's government. Kind of. Uh . . . you were on the royal side, right?"

Zuleikah extracted her hand and wiped it on her pant leg. What was with outsiders and always wanting to talk about the war? It was stupid. War never felt quite what a news story or history class made it seem. It was a series of awful things that were awful until one day you realized it had been a while since something awful had happened. Then it would start again.

"So you're from Earth," Thane said, a little too enthusiastically for Zuleikah's tastes. His circuit had taken him back to them. "My mother is terrified of the Earth government. Is there something you can do? To help them take over?"

Margot looked at Thane like he was so stupid she was amazed his mouth could form words. This relieved Zuleikah because it resulted in Thane scowling at Margot. "It was just a suggestion," he said.

He wasn't like this online. In the chat group, he was snarky and funny and self-deprecating. Charming.

"I'm from Luna." Margot stood. "Let's see about getting that seat warmer taken apart."

Ki walked into their makeshift base to find no fire whatsoever and a space only slightly warmer than outside. Thane was sitting on Ki's flyer while Zuleikah rooted around, waist-deep in hers. Margot arranged sticks in a way that would never make a good fire.

"Food's here!" Ki shouted. Three faces started guiltily. Had they been plotting against her or were they just embarrassed not to have started the fire?

Ki parked the cart of food packages and knelt next to the pile of wood, re-stacked it properly and then poked it with the fire starter sewn into her glove. The wood was dry and old and went up like it had been soaked with gasoline.

Margot scrambled back and said, "Where did you get that?!"

Ki looked from one to another of them. "No one had a fire starter?"

They looked at Ki like she'd asked them why they didn't have a telegraph. "Seriously? No one starts fires in outer space?"

"I'm from a colony with a closed air system. We spend half of every day making sure it's impossible to make a fire." She picked up and dropped packages on the cart in an obvious attempt to look like she wasn't freaked out by the teeny, little campfire. "Snack cakes? Candy bars?"

Ki was proud of her selection. "It's food, isn't it?"

Margot held up a candy bar. "This is what you eat to pretend you have food when there is no food. And these taste like glue." Margot tossed aside a package of rolls.

Ki had specifically grabbed those to have something healthy and a little fancy for her friends. Ki retrieved the package. "Well, I'm eating. If you don't like it, you can go find something on your own, out in the desert night with the sky wolves and the armed guards I evaded for your ungrateful butts." She got comfortable on the couch. The fire was already warming the place enough to take off her gloves.

Margot tore open a package and shrugged. She sat on the floor next to the fire. "At least it's not navy food."

The prince looked at the snack cakes like he'd never seen one before. Maybe he hadn't. "I'm . . . not hungry." He and Zuleikah shared an unfathomable look.

"Z, I trust you did better finding us a place to go than M did with the fire?" Oh no. Z looked guilty, too.

Zuleikah went back to her flyer and fussed with whatever she'd been doing to the seat. "There's one option off planet that looks good—ship folk."

Outside, wheels crunched on gravel. Ki felt ice water in her veins, but that was nothing compared to the tells around the room. Margot hit the dirt. Zuleikah threw herself head-first into her flyer.

The sound passed, and silence reigned.

Everyone looked at Z. Margot cleared her throat. "Do you mean the slow-ship colonists?"

Zuleikah slowly climbed out. "They trade with us—with my family. Black Dragon is in orbit now. They can protect our exit, for a price."

"I don't trust those guys," Margot said. "They switched sides in the war. Twice."

Thane went back to inspecting the snack cakes like they were an artifact from an alien civilization. "They aren't a single group. Some ship folk were on my mother's side, some weren't."

"What's everyone talking about?" Ki asked.

Zuleikah squinted at her. "You said you've been to Ratana before."

"Well, yes." Ki coughed. "Once. I mean . . . ship folk. Yeah. I thought you said 'shrimp fork.'" Ki was missing a whole lot of backstory. Would someone who had been to Ratana once before know about these 'ship folk?' Margot seemed to know about them and she was a Lunar rube.

Margot squinted at her as if reading her mind. "Don't they get *Juniper's Song* on Earth? I thought everyone had seen that sappy old serial."

"Not a big serial watcher," Ki said, her biggest lie ever but it came out sounding honest. Apparently, she'd missed the big Ship Folk serial. It must not have had an actress Ethan found attractive, because that steered most of her serial watching. "But stop looking at me like that because I know about the ship folk. They aren't like in the serials." It was a safe thing to say—nothing was like in serials.

"So we trust them," Margot conceded. "What's the catch?"

Ki wanted to shake Margot. There didn't always have to be a catch.

Zuleikah ducked her head. "I can't reach them to ask. They aren't on the planetary network."

Ok, so there was a catch. "Maybe you can reach someone else, who can reach them?" Ki suggested.

Zuleikah sat on her flyer, projecting screens in the air in front of her. It had to be an expensive projector in her bracelet. Ki couldn't see through the screens, even where the light was brightest.

"We're never getting out of here," Thane whined, like he'd hired them to do this.

"Queen's in hiding," Zuleikah read, flicking screens around. "Public news admits it was a coup attempt."

"Attempt." Thane said it like it was a curse word.

"Fighting is still going on," Zuleikah added, as if to reassure him. Then she gasped, "Oh."

That couldn't be good. Zuleikah moved off the flyer. She sat down on the filthy floor like the rest of them. "There's a picture of me. It's not good but . . ." She flicked the picture out and flipped it so they could see. It was a sweet action shot, Z in her borrowed uniform, barreling linebacker-style into Thane, who looked comically surprised.

Margot moved closer to Z like she wanted to hug her. Z turned away. "I have . . . a lot of messages from my family."

Thane groaned and, weirdly enough, lay face-down on the cart of snack foods.

The awkwardest of silences fell. "It feels good to have some warmth," Margot said, with false cheer. She inched closer to the fire. "Ow." She inched back. "It's like there's no place that isn't half freezing or half burning. It's weird." She moved her hand closer and farther from the fire like she was testing its boundaries.

Ki clapped her hands. "We have communications equipment. We have time. We have a very badass coms officer," Ki gestured toward Zuleikah, who rolled her eyes at the praise. "You'll find a way to talk to the ship folk. You'll get us off this rock."

Zuleikah chewed her lip. "Thane's implant reader is pretty powerful. I could network it with my flyer's computer to get more juice." She looked shyly at him. "If that's okay?"

"My hand is at your disposal." He waved it without lifting his face from the pile of food.

Oh yeah, they were in love. Ki tapped Margot on the shoulder. "You and I need to . . . talk strategy. Over there."

"No, we don't. We're talking it right here."

Ki sighed. She stepped in front of Margot and cut her eyes significantly toward Zuleikah and Thane and mouthed the word "Privacy." Margot squinted at her in non-comprehension.

Ki grabbed her elbow. "Just come over here."

Thane was now 100% sure these disorganized girls were not allied with his mother or sister. That was the good news. The bad news was, they had no idea what they were doing. The ship folk wouldn't take him. They'd turn him right back over to his mother.

And he'd moved past starving hours ago to ill. He was pretty sure if he tried to eat one of the chemical-laden packets of poverty food, he'd die.

He watched Zuleikah put a connection patch on his thumb. It was cold and the glue hesitant. She worked delicately, little bird-peck presses, afraid to touch his skin. She had the power to protect him, but he'd ruined it by showing all his emotions left and right. Saying he "wasn't like other guys." That was what all guys said! He needed to get her back on his side. He could complement her?

Zuleikah had artificially fine cheekbones and a sculpted nose. The default nobility look of Ratana. As if they all shared a common ancestor, or a common plastic surgeon. He couldn't force himself to compliment that.

"Some ship folk fought against my mother," he said. Oh, that was a stupid opening.

Zuleikah really was a royalist. She could hardly look at him. "Not Black Dragon. They stayed neutral."

"I don't mind if they did. Would you?"

Zuleikah frowned, scratched her cheek, and otherwise acted like she was entirely absorbed in the instrument panel. Thane waited for her to say something. When she didn't, he said, "I'm sorry if it bothers you when I talk like that. It's not that I'm not loyal to our planet and government. I see things . . . a little more personally, I guess. She's just my mother."

Her lips flattened grimly. "You'll be free of her, if that's what you want, when we get to space."

"I'm not going to meet some beautiful space whale herder and have a romantic adventure. If the ship folk even let me onboard, they'll want to ransom me."

"We don't know that."

"But it's likely. Ship folk are always looking for any advantage they can get, and a royal prisoner is worth a lot."

Zuleikah's eye-wings were flaking. It lent her a less-severe look. She scratched at the edge of one. She spoke without looking away from the flyer's control panel. "What do you want me to do? Radio the government and ask them to come pick you up?"

"No. I don't want to go back." Thane wished he could scratch his own eye-wings, but he knew from experience that once dislodged, he'd never be rid of flecks of painful glitter in his eyes. "We'll go to the ship folk. Just don't tell them who I am, all right? Say I'm your cousin."

Zuleikah stared at his robe-sleeve. She looked like she wanted to say something. She didn't. She had a crush on him, Margot had said. He should suck it up and use that. It wouldn't be the first time. "Or your boyfriend?" He offered with a shy smile. No, it was too much. She looked terrified. Thane shifted as far away as the uplink would let him. "Promise me you won't tell the ship folk who I am," he said.

She nodded, bit her lip, and nodded again.

It would have to do.

12:
MAKING A BREAK FOR IT

MARGOT LAY AS FLAT AS SHE COULD ON THE STILL-WARM SOLAR array. There was a glow on the horizon from the spaceport, and they could see tiny lights and dark towers against the lighter sky. Farther above, the stars were deceptively peaceful, twinkling in that pretty, atmosphere-filtered way.

"You're so high school," she said to Ki, who lay next to her, likewise trying to absorb as much warmth from the surface as she could.

"Never went," Ki said. "But you have to make time for love."

"He could have a royal lover already. And I can't believe we're even talking about this when we're trapped on a war-torn planet, wanted by the law."

"Aw, but it calmed you down, didn't it?"

Margot did feel calmer, but she wasn't going to give Ki the satisfaction of admitting it. "You've never met the slow ship colonists."

Ki smiled up at the sky like it was full of old friends. "No, I have. Twice. One time I was on one of their ships for almost a year.

They made me part of the tribe and everything."

Ki was so wild and weird, Margot believed it. She'd believe it if Ki said she was a holographic musician turned extra-dimensional gangster. "What happens if the ship in orbit is at war with the ship you were part of?"

"In that case, I won't mention it." Ki turned, rising onto her elbow to look at Margot. She was so delicate, like the wind could break her. "You work hard at worrying."

"Believe me, I'm not working at it. This comes naturally." A part of Margot was secretly excited about the possibility of seeing ship folk up close. She didn't believe everything in the serials . . . but they *were* mysterious, with all the glamor and danger that entailed. Even if she didn't meet a beautiful whale singer dancing among the stars, just to have been inside their ship would make her an explorer of uncharted territory.

Or they could shove her out an airlock. That would end the romance pretty quick

Margot groaned and sat up. "I think we've given Thane and Zuleikah enough privacy. It's freezing out here."

"You don't survive on the run without patience." Ki's childish face was serene, but her serious tone made her sound older.

"The prince thinks I'm our leader," Margot said, not above feeling smug about it. "Where do you think he got that?"

Ki nudged her with her elbow. "You don't remember barking orders at everyone when we left the city?"

"If I'm a leader, I'm a pretty terrible one because none of you listen to a word I say."

"We listen; we just don't agree."

Margot brushed her hands over her flight suit. "That's it. I'm going in." Her breath formed little clouds. Like in an airlock.

"No!" Ki tugged her sleeve. "Five more minutes. They need time to get to know one another."

A shadow ran over the moon. Margot and Ki froze together. "What was that?"

The shadow repeated, larger, more distinct. There was the sound of heavy leather wings, and a low, plaintive howl. Ki bolted upright. "Sky wolves!"

They ran and slapped each other to get indoors first.

Margot stopped just inside to compose herself so the others wouldn't know she'd been fleeing. That was ruined when Ki ran into her and clung, huddled, at her back. Thane and Zuleikah stared at them. His hand was out, palm-up like he was serving an invisible tray of drinks. Zuleikah was in the flyer.

Ki stayed plastered to Margot's side as she approached them. "Were you able to contact the Ship Folk?"

Zuleikah looked sad so she expected a negative, but she said, "They say if we can get to them before they get their people off planet, they'll escort us out of the system."

Ki crawled over the side of the flyer like a cat getting into someone's lap, peering at Zuleikah's screens. "Looks like they haven't even contacted their people. We're sure to get there first if we leave now."

Thane frowned. "What business do you suppose they were on the planet for?"

"I don't think we are in any position to care," Ki said. "Let's get moving. One good thing about a war zone—the cops aren't going to be patrolling the border."

"No," Margot said, "two armies will be, and they'll shoot rather than arrest."

Ki nudged her. "You're way too young to be this pessimistic. Zuleikah, you and Thane take point. I'll cover the rear. We'll do the polar shot again, like we did coming in, fly into space under the cover of the borealis."

"I'll plot a course," Zuleikah said, sounding as bored as ever.

Margot sighed as everyone went to work. "I guess we're making a break for it." She went to get another snack cake. As long as she was waiting and worrying and useless, she may as well eat.

$$\lightning$$

Zuleikah once again had to get into the tight confines of a cockpit with Prince Thane. Pressed intimately close. She tried not to think about it, about the icky mess of emotions he was bringing up in her. Just fly. Save the man so you could spend the rest of your life bragging that you had.

Her brother would flip, if she ever got a chance to talk to him again. (If she ever got up the nerve to read her messages. Soon she'd be off-world and out of range. That would be better. Maybe.)

Zuleikah felt Thane's thighs against hers, his long legs extended past the seat back between them. She felt his breaths, smelled his resinous perfume, felt the tension in him. She hated touching him because she wanted to touch him.

As soon as they were safe and sound, she'd start this all over from the beginning.

As she lowered the canopy, he asked, "How did you meet those other women?"

"Ki and Margot?" Zuleikah doubted he'd appreciate the truth. "We just . . . met." She checked her readings. Ki had plotted a clever course between buildings to avoid local security. Zuleikah plotted the rest of their route to the pole and then up to Black Dragon's orbit. There were unknowns, but there would never be fewer. She hoped Ki knew more about the ship folk than she did. They would be relying on Ki to find the docking bay and deal with any customs.

"You don't strike me as a particularly hardened gang," Thane said. "Do you have allies? Colleagues? Someone to fall back on if this doesn't work?"

Ki flew out of the warehouse. Thank goodness, an excuse not to talk. "Hang on," she said.

They wove through buildings and then flew off the edge of the plateau.

Almost immediately, her radio blared, "This is Space Port control. Unidentified aircraft, where are you heading?"

Ki said, "Automated response beam. Ignore it," and Zuleikah urged her flyer faster.

"You know," Ki added, sounding so calm, "if every time I heard that recorded guy's voice had been an actual conversation, you could say we dated."

Was this course taking too long? Or not avoiding populated areas enough? Zuleikah kept fearing both ways as she adjusted.

So her eyes weren't on the radar when something blocked her vision, hitting the flyer. She nearly careened into Margot. Thane's thighs tightened against her as they made a stomach-lurching dive. A sky wolf, screaming and flapping and coming around for another dive. This was why you didn't fly at night. It mistook her flyer for a territorial rival.

"What was that? OH MY GOD," Margot said, having no doubt discovered the answer to her own question.

"Sorry," Zuleikah muttered. The sky wolf's claws skittered over her canopy as she made another desperate lunge to avoid it.

"Why do these things not have guns?" Margot cried.

"Hang on." Zuleikah tried to steer around the beast and do a quick data search at the same time. It … wasn't something she'd ever tried to do before. She got half a word input and lost control.

Someone else broadcast a blast of the challenge call of a

pregnant sky wolf before she could find it. Oh, thank the founders. The wolf screamed and flew away.

"Crimopedia!" Ki shouted delightedly.

"Well," Thane said, letting go the tight grip he'd taken on her upper arms. "That was fun."

No more fun. Zuleikah widened their course around the capitol and sent the updates to her companions.

"You're going to make us late," Margot said. "The folk aren't going to wait for us."

"I don't want to risk the prince." Zuleikah tried to keep one eye on where she was flying while she scanned the network for trouble.

"Don't put this on me," Thane said. "I'm fine with going straight. I'm no more fragile than any of you."

Zuleikah was going to protect him even if he didn't like it. "We're almost to the badlands."

She had the map and knew precisely where she was every moment, but it wasn't until she saw the pinched shape of Twist Arch that she could release her breath. The badlands. Her playground. She raced like she was trying to escape the heat at her back, her eyes on the map because she knew the terrain. It felt good after so much uncertainty.

There was the pole, and their exit point. She had marked where her instruments would go blind and where they would return. That segment of the course was going to be like jumping a chasm. Ki pulled into the lead and zipped upward, an arrow into the sky. The instruments started to haze. Zuleikah kept her eyes on her simulation. Three, two . . . Zuleikah heard Thane grunt as she was slammed against her backrest. The inertial dampeners screamed in protest, trying to keep them from flattening. Zuleikah's vision greyed at the edges. She'd never tried to pull this many Gs. Just when she thought she was going to die, the pressure started easing off. She tried to ask Thane if he was okay, but her teeth were clenched and her throat felt sealed tight.

Stars shone through a tearing veil of atmosphere, and her stomach flipped, the gravity letting them go.

A planetary patrol—loyal to whom she had no way of knowing—sent a challenge signal. Zuleikah squeaked, "Ki?"

"They aren't in firing range, ignore them," was Ki's quick response. "Yeah, see? They didn't change course to follow us. They don't care." Did the woman not even feel acceleration?

At the top of the climb, they maneuvered sharply. Her stomach flipped again as she pressed upward against the restraints and then floated loose. Sensors that had been jittering turned clear and sharp. They were officially off the planet.

Zuleikah and Thane sighed in unison and, Zuleikah suspected, blushed in unison. (She didn't look back to check.) Briefly absent, the tension returned to Thane's posture. He was trying to hold himself down in his seat rather than let the restraints support him—Zuleikah could tell by the angle of his hands digging into the seat divider. His thighs were squeezing her seat, too. She wondered if he'd ever been in space before.

The Hawk Angel shook as though it had hit a strong wind. Lightning sparked across the canopy and the polarization darkened briefly in response. "Energy weapons!" Zuleikah ran her fingers through commands, approving minor circuit resets and repairs. If her ship had been anything but the antique it was, the bolt would have shut her computer down and left her drifting. She belatedly turned on the energy shields. She'd never used them before. People not in adventure serials didn't need them except when flying through thunderstorms.

"Follow me!" Ki shouted, and her little craft zipped and zigzagged back down toward the atmosphere.

"If we survive this, she's going to be insufferable," Margot said.

Zuleikah almost laughed, but her craft bucked again. Someone was firing on her shields.

"Ha! We're losing them already. Those slugs aren't interested in dragging atmosphere," Ki said. "And they won't follow where we're going; we're on the short road to glory—right into the line of fire of that navy ship."

"Stop," Margot said. "No. Are you insane?"

Hanging heavy in space above them like a displaced office building was a Sol Navy battleship. Zuleikah's heads-up display bristled with points of light, each the tip of a weapon. "This is your escape plan?"

"Yeah. Margot's former Navy. She'll know how to deal with them."

Margot said, "There's no dealing in a war zone! The navy shoots first and asks questions *never*!"

Despite her complaints, Margot flew to the front of their little formation. Her voice broadcast on all channels, causing feedback until Zuleikah's audio filter caught up. "Don't shoot! Don't shoot. Sol citizens. We are Sol Alliance citizens. Don't shoot."

An energy beam rocked Margot's ship. Little lightning bolts crackled around it in an egg-shape. The ShadowKat had her energy shields up. Zuleikah didn't remember how many hits it could take. Two? Margot repeated her hail. "Permission! Peace! We request permission to fly to the slow ship in orbit around Ratana. This is a civilian evacuation. Ki! This isn't working. We have to turn around!"

Ki's ship dipped lower toward the planet, but kept heading across the navy ship's front. The navy ship fired glancing shots, not wanting to fire down into atmosphere. Every civilized world considered firing into atmosphere an act of war against all sides on that planet. "Oxygen is non-partisan" was the saying.

Zuleikah could just see Black Dragon behind the navy ship's grey bulk. The folk ships were iconic. Smaller and very irregular, made up of mismatched pods and cylinders bristling with gantries and lights in different sizes and colors. A tiny bright light was disappearing under it, like the ship was swallowing another. Zuleikah checked the communication log with Black Dragon. "The ship folk are powering up," Zuleikah said. "I think they're leaving."

"They aren't going to be there when we get to them!" Margot said. "If we get to them."

"I'm thinking," said Ki.

"Think faster! I've sent the navy my ID number, the friendly fire code we used . . . they aren't responding to anything."

"I don't have enough energy to land and take off again," Zuleikah said. The shields were draining her batteries fast.

No one acknowledged Zuleikah had spoken. More blips showed on her radar. "Three ships closing on us from planet-side." Perhaps those were the patrol ships who had thought them not worth chasing before.

"That's it," Ki said. "Fly toward the planetaries."

"Who are *also* trying to kill us," Margot said.

"And the navy wants to kill them," Ki said. Her ship veered sharply. "Follow me."

Ki dipped in front of a planetary cruiser, who immediately started firing on her. She led him on a merry chase—straight toward the Navy ship. Zuleikah lost sight, being too busy dodging fire herself, but when she looked again, there was a bright starburst expanding and Ki's tiny red craft zipped across the massive front of the navy ship, away into its shadow toward the folk ship.

The navy ship had shot the planetary cruiser. Or maybe it had started the other way around.

"Bigger fish always draw the bait!" Ki shouted. "Get one of your own. I'm calling the ship folk."

Easier said than done. Zuleikah turned hard into atmosphere. The planetary patrol had seen their buddy destroyed and were turning tail. "Margot, tell them we're navy."

"I tried that! I sent my credentials twice *and* I cussed at them."

Zuleikah was feeding random numbers into her flight path, hoping to be unpredictable. She checked for the last shot fired. "They haven't shot us in a while." Of course, they could be saving their ammunition for a clear shot.

Margot said, "Stick close to me, Zuleikah. I'm sending the navy our course and profuse promises to stick to it. All we can do is hope they believe us."

The navy ship's main gun fired, a bright beam through the clouds. The last planetary vessel dogging Zuleikah dropped away. She felt Thane turn to gawk behind her as she straightened her path to match Margot's.

"Huh," Margot said, "Getting shot at does a lot to make you seem trustworthy."

Ki floated in front of the docking bay of the Black Dragon. It was closed up tight. Her power gauge was low and she was expending small amounts, keeping herself in place. "Come on, let me in. Call sign: Kleptomaniac. Your radio operator agreed to give me and two other solo-flyers passage not two hours ago."

"Sorry, Kleptomaniac. Black Dragon is in peril and leaving the system. You're attracting the naval attention."

"Those jerks were here already."

Ki watched Zuleikah and Margot's ships glide up to hers. She checked the battery gauge again. Barely enough to dock. She took a deep breath. "I can get you something you'll want."

No response.

"Why aren't they letting us in?" Margot asked. Always a quick one, that Margot.

Ki made sure her channel to the Black Dragon duty officer was secured so no one else could hear. "Specifically, I can get you Ratanese crown jewels."

Please work please work. They had no place they could land to tune up to go interstellar. This was their only shot out of the system.

Could she hack the door lock from here? How many seconds before the ship up and went FTL? Fuck. She scanned desperately for another ship in system that wasn't from someone's navy. "I stole a crown. You want it?"

There was a pause.

The docking bay, slowly and ponderously, started to open. "Come aboard, Kleptomaniac, and talk."

"Hot chocolate! See you soon." Ki switched to an open channel. "Okay, ladies! Follow me. Easy peasy. I told you these guys knew me."

13:
THE SHIP FOLK

MARGOT HELD HER BREATH THROUGH THE ENTIRE DOCKING PRO-
cedure. They'd burned almost all of their energy evading fire
and now they had to carefully maneuver into a tight little bay
barely big enough to hold them.

"The dock is not pressurized," the controller, who had an
odd, clipped accent, said. "You must seal the environment suits
to exit the vehicles."

Margot was already wearing her helmet, as any good ship
pilot should, but she could see Ki and Zuleikah both scrambling
inside their canopies. The prince was a figure for pity, too large
for the space he was in, lifting one arm at a time as Zuleikah
searched under his sleeves. His hair and the fabric of his robe
floated free, making him even bigger, an anemone. They really,
really shouldn't have brought him with.

Something moved in the darkness, and Margot gasped.
It was a person in a black environment suit, almost invisible
in the dim docking bay, feet braced on a section of wall and

pulling cable hand-over-hand. Inside the black helmet, a sliver of skin and eyes swaddled in black fabric. Margot cut power as instructed and watched in fascination as more of the lumps and projections on the walls turned out to be people, throwing cables over the nose of her flyer and tying it down.

The bay door shut slowly behind them, an eclipse of Ratana's sphere taking what ambient light there was away. Amber-colored bulbs glowed here and there on the walls, coming into sharper prominence as stars did when the sun wasn't in the sky. The walls were studded with tie-downs and sported rings of coiled rope and angled cuts of reflective tape but were otherwise black. Was that paint or some sort of oxidation?

Someone knocked on Margot's canopy. "The flame flyer is secure. Come out."

Margot had forgotten to cycle the internal pressure—no sense losing any air inside the ship. She held up a finger to indicate she was on her way. The ship folk waited. The ShadowKat cycled fast. The indicator flashed and Margot opened the canopy.

As she floated out of the flyer, she saw twenty hard-eyed space nomads arranged in a sphere around them. Some had knives in hand that glinted dangerously in the low light like their eyes behind their helmets. The bottom half of each face was obscured by cloth. Masks, just like in the dramas. It was a lot scarier in person.

Ki floated out of her flyer, hands in the air. "That's the tough part over," she said. "They let us in. It would be crazy to toss us right out again. Switching to public channel. Hi, guys! Hey! Thank you so much. You are not going to regret this. You'll hardly notice we're here."

The ship folk ignored her. They were looking at Zuleikah and Thane. "Black flyer, why have you not exited the vehicle?"

Margot could see the panic in Zuleikah's eyes through her

canopy and faceplate. "My passenger doesn't have an environment suit."

The ship folk turned toward each other. There was no way to know if they were talking, with their mouths covered and their channels secured, but everything in their body language said they were. One of the ship folk broke formation to float closer to Zuleikah's flyer. "Why bring someone out of the atmosphere without the environment suit?"

"What do I say?" Zuleikah asked on a private channel. The ship folk surely saw her lips move.

"Tell them the truth," Ki said, on the public channel. "Thane is a refugee, and he hitched a ride with us at the last second. It was bring him as is or let him die down there. I mean, come on, guys, we're not monsters."

Thane had a helmet on now, probably the emergency guest helmet from Zuleikah's ship. He was looking at Ki like she had his life in her hands. She probably did.

The ship folk consulted some more. "Very well," the first one said. "The airlock fits three. Two of Black Dragon will escort Fire Flyer through, and then two will escort Kleptomaniac through, then we will secure the black flyer close so that he who has no environment suit may be escorted through quickly. His companion will wait to come through last. Is that agreeable?"

"Sounds like a plan," Ki said, "Let's get it started."

"First, you will give us the promised payment."

"Um. All in good time. I mean . . . aren't you guys in a hurry to leave orbit? Come on, we don't want to have our backsides hanging out over the navy guns forever, am I right?"

"You promised payment. Black Dragon will have that before you enter the airlock."

Zuleikah sent a private message to Margot, "What are they talking about?"

"Don't ask me," Margot said.

Ki tried to swim back down to her ship and ended up treading air like a complete rookie. Margot kicked off to join her. "What do you need?" Margot asked, not bothering with a private channel because that was going to do nothing for them but make them look even more suspicious than they already did.

"There's a bag behind my seat," Ki pointed. "Under the safety cage."

Margot hooked the edge of Ki's canopy with one toe and jackknifed into the space. Immediately she recognized the pale blue strip of fabric floating free of the safety cage. It was the shopping bag Ki had fished out of a trash on Ratana. Margot grabbed hold of the flyer seat and flipped around so Ki could see her anger as she fished it free. "This isn't yours," Margot said.

"If you want to be altruistic, it's a long walk home," Ki said.

"What's going on?" Thane asked. His hands splayed on the inside of Zuleikah's canopy. He was wearing tight and shiny black gloves, completely wrong for his billowing white sleeves. His wrists looked shockingly long and vulnerable between the dark fabric and the loose tunnel of his inner, gold sleeve.

Margot held the shopping bag to her chest and looked from Thane to Ki to the ship folk. This might be the only way to save their lives, but it was also wrong.

One of the ship folk glided to her and took hold of the bag. It was a woman with beautiful topaz eyes and dark olive skin showing above her bandana. Her lashes were thick and dark, flicking down as she checked the bag.

"Uh . . . hi," Margot said, her brain suddenly malfunctioning.

The woman tugged the bag free of Margot's hands with a narrowing of her eyes. She was surprisingly strong and Margot was surprisingly frozen.

The man who had first addressed them peeked into the bag,

just a brief glance, and nodded. The woman floated to a hand-hold on the wall near the outer dock door—far from the airlock and everyone else. Margot suspected that was to make it hard for them to take the "payment" back.

"Was that my crown?" Thane asked.

"SO!" Ki clapped her hands. It made no noise, of course, and she flailed as the motion made her start to rotate. "How about we get this road on the show?"

Margot grabbed Ki's leg to keep her from over-compensating into a full spin. She squeezed her fingers into the thin suit, wanting to impart some of her anger.

"Fire Flyer, you are to enter first." Two ship folk each held a hand toward Margot.

She reluctantly let go of Ki and pushed off toward them. "Call me Margot," she said.

"We won't," the man said, and she was bundled into a tight cubicle.

Zuleikah practiced the motions in her head, hitting depressurize, opening the hatch, getting out of the way. She planned a series of countdowns. She would hit the button, count to twelve to let the depressurization run, grab the handhold, count to three for the hatch mechanism, push herself out, probably four seconds to float free, grab the rear of the hatch, float in place. She was unstrapped. Thane had her gloves and spare helmet.

She was ready. She could do this. She hit the button.

And then it was all panic and fumbles and she could scream except screaming would take time to explain. Every motion failed. The hatch wouldn't open on the first try. She hit the canopy with her hip while she pulled the emergency release.

When it finally opened, a puff of snow appeared in front of her, blocking her view. She hadn't depressurized all the way and the moist air that was left frosted. Her foot caught on a safety strap. There was no time to check on Thane. She kicked off too hard and flew across the room. She grabbed on to a tangle of wire that felt like fire and ice and blades on her bare palm. She looked back.

Thane ascended. Flickers of flame ran down his thick wings of fabric. He was an angel! Gold embroidery, that's what it was— lines of metal in the cloth, twisting like a secret code, catching every little light in the room and making them run like water droplets as he moved. He curled around himself, arms tight to his waist, legs bent. She saw his trousers under the robe, ringed with embroidered flowers, and a finer gold fabric blooming underneath. His slippers were golden and his ankles curved gracefully above them in fine golden stockings.

The ship folk moved in slow motion, black gloves pushing into pillowing fabric, guiding him into the open airlock. It took an age for the door to close, covering his slender feet at last. The world was dark and ordinary again.

Zuleikah pushed off straight for the airlock. The ship folk caught her efficiently around the arms and legs. "Patience. It must cycle." Zuleikah tried to escape their hold, but the ship folk were as natural in zero G as fish in water and simply compensated for every move. At last the door rose again. It was a maddeningly short advance to the next closed door. Two folk pushed in with her, calm and dark at her sides as the chamber sealed. She clenched her pained hands. She thought the returning air pressure would be soothing, but the damage was done and she didn't really feel it. The folk guided her feet under her as artificial gravity took hold. The door opened and she surged forward, nearly falling into the opposite wall. Thane was between two black-clad figures. He looked exhausted but unharmed. A speck of glitter winked on his jaw. The guards were holding his arms.

"You can't handle him like that," Zuleikah said.

"This is the way." One of the ship folk gestured to the side.

Was Thane hurt? Her hands felt like the time she'd had to fix her ship out in the desert night, and they'd only been exposed for minutes. It was worse where she'd grabbed those cables. What had she been thinking?

Thane looked through her.

"This is the way," the folk repeated, and hands pushed her to turn away from Thane.

The interior of the folk ship was . . . there was no word for it but filthy. Oddly organic, like it was built of twigs and moss—it was really tape and fabric and wire covering the surfaces, grey and brown and all the colors of dirt. A tear in padding revealed a sudden brightness, like a mushroom on a cave wall. The corridor was narrow and crooked. Pipes stabbed across at odd angles. Zuleikah decided not to take off her helmet lest the air smell as bad as it looked.

"Where are you taking us?" Margot demanded.

"A safe place to strap in for the system-jump. Refrain from the wandering. You are strangers in the home ship."

As the ship folk guided them through the tight corridor, Margot struggled to go back the way they had come. Why was she doing that? The folk restrained her.

Though they had removed their helmets, the folk still wore masks over their faces. Differences in eye color, skin color, and eyebrows became prominent, the only distinct features. Under the loose drape of fabric around their shoulders and the occasional billowing sleeve, Zuleikah could see they were wearing black, patched-up environment suits. Ki fit in with them, there.

Now and then one of the folk would stop and tap on the wall of the ship, like they were feeling their way by sound rather than sight.

"What about my hands? Does anyone have lotion?" she asked. No one answered.

A group of stick figures were scratched into a ceiling panel with short straight gouges. They were . . . sword-fighting? She had a sudden feeling she was going to be sacrificed to an alien god.

They were led to a door. It was short, hexagonal on top. There was a sharp drop inside it to a chamber not unlike an elevator car. It had molded seats facing each other along the walls. Perhaps it had been some sort of transport before the ship folk had found it and mashed it into their ship.

The folk threw Margot in first. She scrambled quickly to her feet. "You can't. We'll die."

The folk bowed. "You will not die. Black Dragon will jump the system in two minutes. Be secured."

The elevator car didn't look very clean or well maintained. Ki scrambled down into it and, after some intense whispering with Margot, who kept swatting her hands away, got Margot to sit down and strap in.

"I'm not going in there," Thane said. Zuleikah was glad someone had said it.

The folk turned their palms to the ceiling in a gesture Zuleikah suspected meant "your funeral."

There were a lot of sharp, random corners around them. It would probably be better to strap in. "These ships are old," Zuleikah said. "They might not have inertial dampening like we're used to."

Thane said, "I'm not used to any inertial dampening. I've never been off Ratana. But I'm not going in there. They'll lock us in, don't you see?"

Zuleikah found Thane less attractive than ever before. The folk walked away as silently as they had come, tapping at the walls as they went. There was something ominous in how quickly the folk vanished from sight. In the car, Margot was wailing, "Just let me in my flyer. Let me be in my flyer!"

Zuleikah shook her head. "We have to strap in or . . ."

The floor lurched up and to the left. Zuleikah tumbled into Thane, whose legs flew up as he hit the ground. Oh no. They were a tangle of limbs and Zuleikah didn't know where to put her hands because she didn't want to damage them and she couldn't grab royalty, but she had to hold on to something and they were sliding on deck-plating that was filthier than anything else they could touch.

Ki was there, tiny hands holding onto her as the world tilted sideways and jerked sharply right.

Margot howled, a sound like a frightened animal.

Somehow, with Ki helping, Zuleikah got Thane into the elevator car. He clung to the unfastened harness of a seat. His face was pinched with fear. "Then again," he said, "skinning alive might not be so bad."

Zuleikah didn't get the joke. She wrapped her wrists in straps to hold tight as the world bucked and shuddered.

"Their FTL was retro-fitted." Margot looked and sounded nauseous, staring blankly as though she could see through the wall. "No thought to comfort. Barely safe. We're jerking along like debris on a string."

"It's fine. They've obviously been using it for a long time without exploding." Ki looked unreasonably comfortable, curled under one shoulder strap. She and Thane had taken their helmets off. Or perhaps Thane's had flown off in the tumult. Now gravity was returning to normal like a liquid settling in a shaken container.

Zuleikah felt her stomach undergo a similar, delayed motion. She longed to check Thane's wrists and ankles for burns. She had a first aid kit in her flyer, if she could get to it. If he would let her touch him. Then, she could moisturize her poor hands.

Margot continued to stare a thousand yards beyond their room. "Nothing is between us and the emptiness of space but cloth and tape and wire."

Ki slid closer to Margot and put a hand on her shoulder. "We've always been surrounded by vacuum, M. It's okay. We'll get through this. We're space travelers!"

Margot jerked away from her. When Ki persisted, Margot smacked her hand away. "You have never been in space!"

Zuleikah was stunned, both at the violence of her action and the accusation. Wasn't Ki the one who had brought Margot to Ratana?

"Hey, big M . . ."

"Stop it. You had no idea how to move in zero G. You haven't been to space before now. You know nothing about the ship folk. Stop lying about everything. You're making this up as you go along and we could die!"

Zuleikah had never had to be around people raising their voices. There had been times she'd wished her parents would scream at her, just to get their long tirades over faster, but now she was experiencing it, she hated it. Where all poor people like this?

Margot abruptly unstrapped and started pacing the tiny space, stepping hard between their knees like she would happily have broken every one of them.

Thane said, firmly but not impolitely, addressing his own knees, "You stole my crown."

"You were going to leave it behind!" Ki said.

Margot said, "No one cares about your stupid crown."

Zuleikah stood. Her three arguing companions turned to her. "You will not address my prince in that manner. Also, I might vomit soon."

"I'm not 'your prince,'" Thane said, soft but firm. And then she doubled over, dropping what food was in her stomach, mostly acid, on the dirty floor.

Margot shoved past her and up into the corridor. An unknown, deep voice said, "The guests are not to wander Black Dragon unattended."

"Talk to Ki," Margot said, "She's 'part of the tribe'. I want to leave this ship. Now."

"That is not safe at FTL."

"I don't care. Nothing in space is safe but the inside of my flyer."

The guards grabbed Margot. Zuleikah didn't know what to say or do to stop this. She couldn't straighten up. She was so humiliated. Ki knelt next to her, wiping vomit up with a dirty pink cloth she'd pulled from somewhere.

The guard let go of Margot's arm, slowly, like he was afraid she would bolt. He looked at his companion. This one was definitely female, her breasts large enough to show through the swaddled, loose clothing. She touched two fingertips to her forearm, and then to her black-draped cheek. The male guard said, "BD will take Flame Flyer where she wishes to go."

Ki said, "No! We need to stick together!"

The woman who must have been BD gestured up the corridor, looking pointedly at Margot.

Hugging herself, Margot preceded the Ship Folk up the corridor.

"Why?" Zuleikah asked.

The man looked at her, inscrutable, silent.

Zuleikah said, "It isn't safe, and she's panicking, and you're taking her to the airlock."

He raised his palm to the ceiling. "There will be a meal soon. Someone will escort you to the washing facilities."

He walked away, ducking around the protruding pipes with the efficiency of a fish in a tank.

⚡

Margot knew she was being irrational. She was on a strange, fragile ship in a strange, violent situation. She just wanted to get into her flyer. Her environment suit wasn't protection enough. She'd seen those fail. The corridors looked different than they had leaving the dock. Had they made a turn?

A sharp corner left her facing a wall. Soft, thick-woven fabric from waist-height down, bolted plates of metal above with circles of mustard-yellow and green painted on it inexpertly.

Someone snagged her elbow. She spun naturally with the tug and swung her fist, which was caught firmly in a padded glove.

It was the same face she'd seen in the dock—what she could see of it: eyes so shockingly amber and angled. Margot felt breathless hope that those eyes could understand her.

"This is not the way," BD said. She let go of Margot's fist. She turned on her heel. She clearly meant more than it was the wrong direction to walk.

Margot didn't know when she'd gotten so violent. Lately all she wanted to do was smash and hurt and break. She held her breath and followed. It wasn't far. She'd accidentally passed the airlock.

BD opened the bulkhead and stepped into the narrow lock. She looked expectantly back at Margot. They were really letting her go. She regretted her anger. "Thank you."

The folk twisted one hand in the air, a gesture she was guessing from previous uses was a sort of shrug. Maybe the folk had to develop gestures that could be done while strapped into safety harness. The airlock hissed, the pressure lowering. BD pulled a helmet from a hook on the wall and put it on a split second before the warning light flashed. It was an effortless demonstration of confidence and competence.

As Margot felt her weightlessness return and reached awkwardly for a handhold, the ship folk hardly moved, stepping off the ground as easily as into a wading pool. Then she was swimming into the dock. Her loose fabric drape floated around her, exposing the close fit of her environment suit below.

Margot knew, in her heart, that it was damn stupid to be in this dock. Any slight mistake could strip them out of the warp tunnel and then it'd be weak points near the hull like this one that would blow. It was brave, that the folk let her do this. She wanted to say that. Instead she said, "Do you all wear environment suits all the time?"

The ship folk touched her shoulder. She was very close, her eyes intent, really looking at Margot. "Flame Flyer," she said, "I know what it is to be outside of home ship, to distrust the walls. The fear follows. You cannot outrun it. Black Dragon will not keep you unwillingly, but do you understand what you are asking?"

She'd asked to leave the ship in FTL. That was near suicide. Theoretically, she could speed up her flyer to match, end up in a random part of space, but more likely she'd be scattered to atoms. Margot felt a hard sob at the back of her chest wanting to rise up and come out. She pushed it down. "I just want to sit in my flyer. Can I do that? For a while?"

The hand on her shoulder squeezed gently and let go.

Together, they opened the canopy and got Margot settled in her flyer.

She felt silly, once she was in it. The fear cut off when the canopy sealed, like it was a sound or a gas. Margot felt her whole body unclench. She saw BD hanging casually from the dock rigging, like she was a part of it, dark on dark, but with such intense topaz eyes.

"Thanks," Margot sent on an open channel. BD made a slashing gesture with one hand. Felt a natural cognate for "Don't mention it."

14:
ONE BIG HAPPY FAMILY

Okay, so Thane was an idiot who didn't know spacecraft moved. His skin was dry and itchy. His wrists and ankles burned. And his feet! They'd been doing all right, itching but all right, largely due to spending a lot of time sitting down. Now though they were buzzing madly, like an army of insects were struggling to escape his skin. He knew these people wouldn't care if he scratched, but somehow, he couldn't do it. Princes don't scratch. Princes don't take off their shoes to see if their socks are full of blood or bees.

Ki pulled a round tin from one of her pockets. "I've got burn ointment. Let me see your hands, Z."

"No." She cringed away. "Treat Thane first."

"I'm fine." He tugged his sleeves down over his raw wrists. The last thing he needed was for them to see him as a needy man. "It's no worse than a sunburn."

Zuleikah looked offended, like how dare he refuse?

"Oh, quit your drama," Ki said, and after a brief, comic

struggle, she had Zuleikah holding her hands out. He saw how Zuleikah didn't look at him, how tight her jaw was.

Margot was the only one he'd really connected with. Of course, she was the one who ran away. If his sex trainer could see how perfectly his flirting skills failed in real life!

"Jeeez, Z. You broke the skin here. Don't grab freezing metal, okay?"

"I panicked." Zuleikah tilted her head back like she was trying to avoid getting tears in her makeup. Thane knew that gesture well.

Ki wrapped Zuleikah's hand with a tiny roll of gauze from another pocket. "Z, I'm sorry. I want the best for you, and your prince, and everyone. We'll get out of this, but we have to do it as a team."

"He's not my prince," Zuleikah said, voice rough and low, accusing.

"He's just jumpy." Ki looked over Zuleikah's shoulder to wink at him. The wink startled him. Were they conspiring? Against Zuleikah? "You just met. We all just met. First things first. Let's find out where this ship is heading, okay? Do you have communications? My pickup is dead."

Ki was smarter than he'd given her credit for. She'd just manipulated Zuleikah into thinking about something else, into action. Zuleikah touched her bracelet and squinted. "I . . . they have us shielded. Nothing's getting in or out."

"Not suspicious at all, huh?" Ki said.

Thane said, "I thought you trusted the ship folk."

Ki stepped on the opposite seat to pat his shoulder. "If someone I trust has a gun or a drug habit, I want to know about it. Helps with the trust."

"I wanted my crown left behind. That helps with trust."

"Come on, some other person would have picked it up,

and they wouldn't have needed it as badly as we did."

Thane's mind whirled at the idea that someone would just . . . pick up his crown. Why would they do that? "I don't want the ship folk to know what I am."

"Oh, sweetie, have you seen you?" Ki patted his shoulder again.

"This network isn't like the one at home." Zuleikah flicked screens up from her bracelet. "I don't understand it at all. It seems . . . dead. I can find connections and drops, but no data is flowing."

Ki said, "Well, if we want to get back to our ships, it's twenty paces, left, seven paces, slight right, two paces. I watched them open it and close it. I think I could do it again."

Were they planning an escape? Already? Would that make three in one day? This was a far cry from his usual mode of transport-by-waiting-on-retinue. Thane wasn't sure if he were amused or exhausted. "You've really thought ahead," he said, giving Ki his flirtatious smile.

She looked startled. "I did, didn't I?"

For a filthy, tiny thief, she was easily swayed by praise. That was a good thing. He should focus on good things. Zuleikah was pacified with work. The ship folk didn't know he was a prince. He was leaving Ratana system!

He really wished he could look at his feet. His hair was a mess, too. He could feel how straw-like and snarled it was when it brushed the seat or his collar. If he were only at liberty to touch it!

A figure appeared in the doorway. Zuleikah quickly covered her bracelet, smothering the displays.

The masked figure bowed. "One at a time the guests will be escorted to the washing facility."

Ki clambered monkey-like over Thane and Zuleikah, never touching the floor of the compartment. "Guess I'm going first!

Wow, am I hungry. What's for dinner?"

Her fast, too-bright words were obviously to distract from Zuleikah's suspicious behavior. Thane didn't like it. He didn't think they should be trying to spy on their benefactors. It could only turn them against them.

When Ki left, the room was significantly quieter and stiller. Thane very slowly and carefully moved his right foot against his left, trying to feel through the slipper and sock.

Zuleikah twisted her bracelet, turning the displays off. It looked like a solid amethyst crystal, and glowed lightly, indicating the processor was working. Hands on her thighs, not looking at him, she asked, "Are your wrists okay?"

Thane rubbed one arm, since her question gave him an excuse to check. The environment suit gloves—her gloves—felt odd against his sleeve. Her hands had to feel worse than his wrists. He peeled the gloves off. He held them to her. "Thanks."

Zuleikah looked at the gloves like they were a dead rat. "Keep them."

"I'd rather not."

Zuleikah folded the gloves together in her hands. After a moment, out of the blue, she said, "I like reading your posts."

Thane didn't know what to say to that. His posts? They were meant to be liked. He used an AI to generate casual, witty remarks.

The tiny petals on her eyelashes were mostly gone, leaving her eyes with a naked, ragged look. "I mean . . . I felt like I knew you."

Thane looked back at his hands. "I'm not who I seem in posts."

"No one is. You are, though. I think. To me, I mean."

Was this a compliment? "Thanks."

"Forget it." She balled the gloves together.

He decided to change the subject. That was the best thing to do with people. Keep them entertained, distracted. "You know," he said, "this isn't my first time getting kidnapped this year."

For a moment he thought he'd made another mistake. She didn't react. Then she said, "There was nothing about it online. Not even your private account."

Was she accusing or shocked? "Yeah, I know we men love to complain, but sometimes I restrain myself." She turned fully toward him, her eyes searching his. He relaxed. "I was visiting my uncle and he decided not to let me leave. My mother didn't want anyone to know because it would look like she was weak."

"Were you scared?"

He'd been terrified. However, he couldn't remember a time since he was ten years old that he hadn't been terrified. He shook his head. "It was boring, more than anything."

Zuleikah sighed and slumped. "I miss being bored."

She looked adorable, young and depressed. Thane touched her shoulder to comfort her. She smiled weakly.

This was good. She was back on his side.

A shadow at the door made him look up. Two ship folk, alike in their dark clothes and veils. One raised their hand. "Black Dragon seeks an answer to a question."

Thane recognized the cadence of ritual. He stood and inclined his head slightly. "Ask it, and if I know the answer, I will provide it."

"Angel of the Black Flyer, are you the crown prince of Ratana?"

Thane froze. Why had Ki brought the damn crown on board? He . . . he was taking too long to answer.

The ship folk lowered their hand. "Angel of Black Flyer, you will follow."

"Why? What have I done?"

"The elders would speak with you."

Thane felt a hand slip into his and squeeze. Zuleikah's palm was rough, and for that, oddly, comforting. All the worst things that had happened to him had involved smooth hands. He squeezed back and let go. "Then lead the way."

The bathroom was tiny, a niche with a privacy screen and a toilet shaped like a bicycle seat. Ki didn't find any active data hookups when she pulled apart the comm plate on the wall and the guy in the hallway coughed in a way that implied impatience more than dry throat.

There was a light-sterilizer and a stick with a spongy end the use of which Ki didn't want to imagine. She put the comm unit mostly back together, used a sonic tool to clean her handkerchief and ran her hands under the sterilizer.

"Sorry," she said, pulling the curtain back. "Big lunch."

The ship folk didn't say anything. These guys were hard to read. "Where are we headed, anyway? Big port of call? I bet you guys go to all kinds of interesting places."

Flattery had never worked less well. He simply led the way back to the guest room.

Zuleikah was pacing the little seat-lined room, two guards on the door. When they stepped aside to let Ki pass, Zuleikah ran to her. "They took Thane."

Ki grabbed the nearest arm—it never hurt to have a hold on someone if you were going to start an argument. "What gives? Doesn't Black Dragon honor her deals?"

"No one is harmed nor held," the ship folk said. "Yet." He looked down pointedly at Ki's hand on his arm.

The other folk said, "Come, Black Flyer, it is the time to wash. The meal is being delayed."

Ki caught Zuleikah's wrist to keep her from stepping up out of the room. They were split up enough! "Where is our friend?"

"The elders wished to see the Angel of Black Flyer."

"I wish to see the elders," Ki said.

Zuleikah tugged sharply, downward, breaking Ki's hold. "You stole his crown," she said, and let the ship folk lead her away.

Ki appealed to the guy she still had a grip on. "We're all friends here. Partners in a business deal—one crown for one trip out of the system. If this isn't working for you guys anymore, drop us off wherever we are now."

He pushed her easily off her feet. The door slid shut, and something clicked inside it, heavy and final like a deadbolt.

Ki tried the door handle. It didn't budge.

Margot knew she couldn't sit in her flyer forever, like a child who needed a particular blanket to sleep. "It's been a weird couple days," she told BD. "A weird life. You make a decision, you know? And you don't really know how it'll change you." She'd wanted the navy to change her, but she didn't feel like she'd consented to all the changes. BD was silent. Just listening. That was nice. "You don't have to stay with me. I know it's dangerous."

BD slashed the air again, twice. Don't mention it. De nada.

The folk would drop them at their next port of call, presumably. That was a start. She wished she'd asked what planet they were heading to. Presumably one near Ratana. She tried to remember her geography. Tiglath was where they'd gone to re-form after the battle of Ratana. It wasn't closest, though. The closest was a place they couldn't go for some reason. Old Hope? Xu?

Something was happening. Margot could tell because BD stirred from her calm float, a hand to the side of her helmet in the universal gesture of asking someone to repeat themselves. BD swam to her canopy and knocked on it. "Ratana is coming. We must go in. There may be fighting or need of this dock."

The Ship Folk led Thane up a ladder and through narrower, ever shorter corridors. They stopped at a sliding door and knocked. The man glanced back at Thane and must have seen some of the terror Thane was trying to hide because he did the most extraordinary thing. He unwrapped his veil, letting it fall from his face. The skin was paler where the veil had been. His nose looked like it had been broken once and his smile was crooked. "Relax. The elders don't eat people. Not anymore." He winked.

He was the most beautiful person Thane had ever seen in his life. He felt a surge of bewildered delight. This was not the time to be thinking how kissable lips could be. "I . . . uh . . ." He had to get his expression under control. How would someone who had no interest in kissing this man look?

The ship folk laughed. "You are overwhelmed by my charm. It happens. But me, I *do* eat people."

The sliding door opened and the woman there, in her black veil, narrowed her eyes at the man. "Honor," she gasped.

The man rolled his eyes and tucked his veil back in place. "Can't one make exceptions for pretty men?"

"No, one may not," the woman said, and stepped aside, indicating that they should precede her into the chamber.

A dark chamber, wherein mysterious elders would decide his fate, and one of those masked faces, at least, knew more about him than he would like.

Ki was trapped, alone, in a sealed room with no network communication. She had nothing, even, to write in her "next time" file.

Ki knew doors better than networks. She pried, tugged, and inspected what she could. The lock was old-fashioned, which actually made it harder to hack. No circuit contacts. Ki needed a magnetic lever. Her magnetic lever, apparently, was that thing she'd dropped during the car chase on Ratana. She emptied her pockets. Could she make something like a magnetic lever from two bags of gems, the plastic clip from her expended bandage roll, lock picks, and a tasty cake?

Not terribly likely.

Network it was, then. She crawled over the room, looking for any physical connection ports. Not so much as an old-fashioned power outlet. She laid out lock circuits as an antenna and scanned passively.

She picked up more vibrations than signals. Engine vibrations. Gravity field vibrations. And something else, like a dance song playing on the metal frame of the ship. She recorded everything and her software dutifully separated tracks by likely source, labeling that one "unknown percussion."

Ki was peering close to the door again, trying to get a sense of some other way to open it, when it suddenly flew open. She fell into the hall. "The meal awaits," said one of a pair of impassive figures in black.

Ki gathered up her things, trying to look like she'd just been taking inventory. "About time. Where's Z? You know, you didn't have to lock me in here. It's not like I'd know where I was going if I wanted to steal stuff."

The folk turned and started walking. How did you get these cats to talk back?

It was bumpy and crowded in the corridor, which was great for picking pockets. The ship folk didn't seem to have pockets, though. Ki spent too long exploring the guard to her left and got a very confused glance from her. She played it off with a wink and eyebrow waggle. The guard moved away from her.

They led her to a room that smelled like a cafeteria and looked like the back of a delivery truck fitted with bolted-down benches and tables. Z and M were already there, each flanked by black-clad figures, at the last of the three tables. It was awkward getting onto the bench, which was bolted to the floor, like the table. Very old-school design from before reliable artificial gravity. A guard slid into the bench first and gestured at her to scoot along with him.

She was opposite the guard between Zuleikah and Margot, with a guard on either side of them and one on either side of her, so they were checkered, ship-folk and non. "What's with the prisoner-of-war treatment? I thought we were your guests."

The folk, of course, said nothing. More filtered into the room. These were wearing soft black pajamas instead of black environment suits under their cowls and hoods. One had his hood down, revealing black hair tightly braided, but he pulled the hood up as he sat down. Were they here to eat? With masks over their faces?

"You look calmer," Ki said to Margot, who had finally lost the helmet, but not her gloves.

Margot may have looked calmer, but she was still in a pissy mood. She turned to Zuleikah and talked like Ki wasn't there. "The folk are upset because some ship from Ratana is following them. Or did Ki tell you that already, since she's knows everything?"

"She tells stories." Zuleikah folded her arms. "What she says isn't as bad as what she does."

Ki rolled her eyes. "Are you both mad at me now?"

"You're a nice girl, Zuleikah. You have everything going for you. Don't let Ki drag you down."

And she was the one who was "so high school"? Ki waved her hand in front of them. "Sitting right here. Getting it. But where would we all be if I hadn't gotten us on board this ship? Where would Thane be? Shot to hell or in custody, right? If one of you had a better idea, back then was the time to suggest it."

Margot looked irritated, but at least she looked at Ki. Zuleikah lowered her head. Tiny, curling hairs were escaping the braid on her scalp. She flicked her glance at Margot. "They took Thane."

Margot lost her pissy look. "I thought he was in the bathroom or something." She half-rose, craning her head over the black clad figures.

"Be still," a woman said. "The meal will be served."

The bulkhead opened. Thane was instantly visible in his white brocade. Also, he was a head taller than everyone else. He was wearing his crown and it passed scant centimeters below the ceiling. He looked like a chess bishop surrounded by pawns. Even the ship folk in the room were staring.

Margot scowled at Ki. Yeesh. How was this part her fault?

Ki spun around on the bench, picking up and putting her feet down to face Thane as he was led to a seat next to her. "What's the good word, Thane? Are they granting you diplomatic immunity or something?"

He looked at her, and then at Margot, like he was hoping they would tell him what to say. Not a good sign.

Someone slid a long metal tray onto the table. It smelled of meat and, oddly, oranges.

The ship folk looked at Ki like she should know how rude she was being. She could read that even with half their faces hidden. If they expected her to be cowed by etiquette, they were going to learn better fast. "How do you eat with your mouths covered?" she asked.

"One of the tribe," Margot muttered.

The ship folk made a large space around Thane, like they didn't know how to get him onto the bench seat. He looked down at the bench like he expected someone to draw it out for him.

Ki raised her eyebrows at Thane. "You have to have learned something since I last saw you."

"My mother has resumed control of Ratana." He said this looking over their heads, like he was making a proclamation to a vast, hidden audience. "Her warships have followed us, demanding my return."

And then, like a kid who'd said his required lines for the school play, he dropped onto the bench and slouched. Chin on his arms, crown askew, he added, "The Ship Folk are going to give me back to my mother. When we reach the end of our jump in Jefferson System. We have like an hour. I'm not hungry."

Zuleikah looked like she was going to crack right apart and start bawling.

Margot said, tactlessly, "But the rest of us are free to go, right?"

Ki wished she were directly opposite her so she could kick her. The ship folk to Margot's right, who had these lovely amber eyes and cheeks that were high and interesting under the top of her veil, said, "You will be released in Jefferson System, and no longer be Black Dragon's concern. The crown prince of Ratana, simultaneously, will no longer be the flyer's concern."

"Hey," Ki said, "Thane's our friend, so he is our concern."

"It is regrettable, but Black Dragon has to avoid angering Ratana. We are one ship and they a planet."

"Stop arguing," Margot said. "There's nothing we can do."

More ship folk filtered in, filling the other tables. They brought another tray. It was mostly rice, with something brown and orange and glistening on top. They ate with chopsticks which were set on the edges of the serving trays, a set for each seat. They lifted each small piece of food under their veils, tidy as you please. Everyone ate from the communal tray in the center of their table, wiping their chopsticks on a napkin between bites. It didn't seem entirely hygienic, but then, living on a ship like this they probably had all of each other's germs already.

Ki wondered how tidy things were under those veils.

Margot and Zuleikah picked up chopsticks. Zuleikah turned the sticks around, separately, with no clear idea how to use them. Margot wielded them like a pro, snatching up a sliver of meat.

Thane stared morosely at the table in front of him.

Ki balled her fist and struck the table hard. Narrowed eyes from the ship folk, who kept eating silently. "The hell with Ratana," Ki said. "Eat up, Thane, because you're not going home and we don't know where our next meal is coming from."

"It is regrettable," a guard said, with slightly more emphasis, "but you will be detained until the handoff."

Ki would see about that. "It is regrettable." She picked up her chopsticks. "Someone show me how to use these."

15:
PULLING TOGETHER

MARGOT HATED PEOPLE WHO DID STUPID, DRAMATIC THINGS LIKE punching walls.

Margot punched the wall.

They were locked in the tiny room they'd spent the jump to FTL in and the ship folk had confiscated all their communication devices. Her stupid brain kept imagining the room vaporizing around her, the cold certainty of vacuum slicing through the molded plastic and metal. She hated that her irrational fear was interfering with her ability to express her perfectly rational fears.

"I'd have thought you'd be happy." Ki curled in a sulky ball in one of the room's seats. She'd wilted the second the ship folk took her ancient handheld.

"Happy? At what? Jefferson system is a terrible place to be dropped. There's no public trade station and the planet is under strict quarantine." If we don't die first, Margot added, silently, to herself.

Thane sat with his crown in his lap, rotating it like a

merry-go-round. "You're not the one being traded like a piece of property."

"Suck it up," Margot said. "How bad could it be? You're going home."

To Margot's utter surprise, the whiney prince jumped to his feet. He looked angry, really angry, like he might hit her, the crown cocked back. Margot set her feet and raised her fists, ready to take it and give it back again.

And he saw it. She saw him see her willingness to fight. She saw him sit himself back down and that wasn't all she saw. She lowered her fist. "What did they do to you?"

"You're right," he said, with an apologetic smile that looked slapped together from cheap parts. "It's enough that I got away for a while."

Margot felt sick. It would be so much easier to dump him and not care if he didn't look so defeated. She turned to Ki. "Problem number one: the door. This door. What would make it open?"

A beat. A silence.

"We need a magnet." Ki straightened and started emptying the contents of her pockets.

Zuleikah, who was tucked in a back corner, her face on her knees, spoke for the first time since they'd been locked in the room. "What good is it to open the door?"

Ki nodded to Margot, like she'd read her mind. "If we get out, get to our ships, we can leave—all of us, together."

"That's right. We only need a second to get in our ships and fly away. If Thane's mother really wants him back, she won't shoot at us."

"But I don't have anything I can make a magnet out of," Ki said, spreading her hands over her inventory.

"What is this?" Margot picked up a weird lump of stacked stickers.

"Flexible lock-picking circuits. Conductive material wrapped in non-conductive film with a sticky back. They're super handy, but this lock doesn't have circuit contacts. It's strictly mechanical."

Zuleikah blinked slowly. "Any conductive material can be made into a magnet. You just need an electrical charge."

"A battery. Does anyone have one left?" Margot looked around the room. Ki sagged. Zuleikah rubbed her bare wrist ruefully.

"Would my implant work?" Thane held his hand out. The ship folk hadn't taken it, of course, because they couldn't. They might not even have known it was there. It would have enough power, but . . .

"Don't be ridiculous," Margot sighed. "We'd have to cut you to tap into the power directly."

"So?" He looked honestly confused this would be a problem. "Cut me."

"No," said Zuleikah. "It . . . we were close to an idea, but no."

Thane met Margot's eyes. "Please. If there's the tiniest chance it'll get us out of here, cut me."

Ki fidgeted. "I can't cut someone."

The fear in those eyes was as irrational and deep as her own. "I can," Margot said. She picked up the sharpest of Ki's lock-picks . . . and frowned. "But I don't know where."

"No. Not you. You're . . . he's a prince." Zuleikah paced the tight little space available to her—the width of a seat. "Are you sure this will work?"

"No," Margot said.

"Yes," Ki said. Of course she said that, but there was that look of hers, like the gears were turning, tumblers falling into place in her internal lock. "Yes, it will work, and you must know it, too."

Zuleikah held out her hand. "I'll make the cut."

"I'll wire the charge," Ki said.

"What do I do?" Margot asked.

"Hold his hand," Ki said. "He'll need that."

Margot braced her arm under Thane's to support it. Ki took her hand and moved it to Thane's other hand.

"Oh," Margot said. Not holding the hand steady—emotional hand-holding. She stepped to Thane's other side. She laced her fingers through his. Was that the right way to do this? "I'm here." She sounded like a bad understudy in a student play.

Zuleikah traced the base of Thane's thumb with her pointer finger and tapped her way down the blood vessel. Thane watched with grim determination.

"This is going to hurt," Ki said, touching Thane's face to make him focus on her. "Squeeze Margot's hand when the pain starts."

He squeezed, hard. "Ow."

"That was a test," Thane said.

Ki nodded. She looked from face to face. "We're going to do this, guys. We are really going to do this. Now."

Zuleikah looked to Ki. They exchanged small nods, and she stopped poking around and started a firm cut.

Margot felt the difference in Thane's hand-squeeze, the stutter of it when the real pain started. Blood welled instantly. It ran fast and bright. Ki blocked Margot's view, doing something with wires. She and Zuleikah struggled with each other for light and access. Margot restrained the urge to intervene. She'd just make it worse.

"This . . . doesn't feel how I thought it would," Thane said, teeth clenched and brow furrowed.

Him squeezing the life out of her hand felt exactly how she thought it would. She said, "We're almost through this. This is the worst it's going to be."

"Not really," Zuleikah said.

Ki said, "I have the contacts. I can feel the charge when I touch the plate." She sighed. "This is going to ruin my circuits."

"We'll get you new ones," Margot said, though she had no idea how.

Thane trembled. Ki grunted, levering her arm up, trying to get something deeper into the flesh. Margot whispered the soft words her mother would say when she was hurt, Vietnamese endearments she was probably mispronouncing.

Zuleikah pushed Thane's sleeve out of the way as a trickle of blood ran down his arm. "We need . . . there's nothing sterile."

Margot used her free hand to tear Thane's sleeve. Zuleikah looked horrified, but took the fabric to sop up the blood.

"Hands bleed," Ki said, her lower lip clenched in her teeth. "They bleed bad, but it looks worse than it is. I've for sure got the power supply directly. Zuleikah, can you test this is magnetized?"

Zuleikah wiped the bloody lock pick on her sleeve and touched it to the film. She lifted it off again. "Are these steel?"

"My picks are non-conductive. It was a selling point. What else do we have?"

"The door lock," Margot said.

Thane was sweating, his eyebrows crinkled. He looked like a man trying not to sneeze. Ki waved her hand in front of him to get his focus. "Are you okay with us trying this? If it hasn't been long enough, it'll hurt worse when we try again."

He opened his mouth and closed it again.

"Just do it," Margot said.

Whites shown all around Zuleikah's pupils. "I'm not sure it's been long enough."

"How long does it normally take to magnetize something this size?" Margot asked. No one answered. "Ki?"

"I don't know."

Margot grit her teeth. "You've never done this before, either?"

"I have! I really have. I've magnetized things to lift magnetic locks. It's just . . . you count to fifty? Sixty? I don't have my screen. I can't look it up!"

"A screen isn't materializing, Ki. Do it."

"Okay," she said. "We're doing this now. Zuleikah, I'm going to pull out the contacts. As soon as I do, put pressure on the cut."

Zuleikah nodded.

It was messy. Ki pulled the contacts out and stumbled backward, Zuleikah dropped the blood-soaked rag as she tried to press it in place. Thane bent to reach for it, turned grey and started to fall. Margot ducked in front of him, catching his weight. She grabbed the nearest fold of robe and pressed it over the wound. Zuleikah helped her. Together they pressed the wound and guided Thane into a seat. It was a small cut, it would close. Margot was pretty sure, anyway.

"I'm fine, I'm fine," Thane repeated, eyes closed. His face was as pale as parchment.

Ki stood with her shoulder against the door. "Wherever the ship folk got this room and its bulkhead, it started its life on Earth centuries ago. I know this lock like a dead relative."

She stared at the door like she could see right through the metal. She ran the little magnet down and then gently upward. Something dragged inside the door, a sound of metal on metal. It fell with a clang.

"It's okay . . . it's okay . . . I might have gone too fast." She bit her lip and moved back to starting position. Margot, Thane, and Zuleikah clung to each other on the opposite seats. Margot wasn't the kind to cling, but she was grateful for the contact. She tried not to breathe. The others were silent, too, so every small sound inside the door could be heard. Ki moved with agonizing slowness. The magnet would lose its power over time. It would get weaker with more tries. How many had this been? Click, scrape . . . Ki shouted, "Push the door. Someone. Someone push the door NOW."

Margot and Zuleikah and Thane surged forward as one.

They tumbled together into the hallway.

Ki was on the bottom of the pile. She pushed and prodded limbs and clothing. "Up. Back in. Up and back. Come on."

"We just got out," Thane said.

Ki was right, they couldn't rush forward with no plan. Margot kicked and pushed and got everyone back. As the bulkhead door slid home, Ki jammed the lock with one of her picks.

Everyone was sweaty, hair disarrayed, and Thane's blood was everywhere: on his tunic, Zuleikah's hands, and even Ki's cheek. They looked like they'd just been through a battle. Ki had a bloody hand on her mouth, suppressing a laugh.

"We need to time this," Margot said, "And we'll all move more quickly if we know where we're going and what we're doing when we get there. I'll lead the way back to the dock. Ki, you said you could unlock its door, right? So you come after me."

Ki shook her head. "I'll take up the rear. Keep space between us—as much as whatever clear line of sight there is. So, like wait for Margot to go around the next corner before you go down the straight away, okay?"

Thane looked ready to run through anything.

Zuleikah looked doubtful. "Take up the rear? Why?"

"It doesn't have to be a good plan," Ki said. "It just has to be a plan."

Margot took Zuleikah's hand and squeezed it. "It's a plan," she said. She wondered if Ki had the same gut feeling she did, that Zuleikah and Thane were civilians, and therefore were safer inside the formation.

"I'll hold up my hand," Margot said, and demonstrated. "Like this, if the coast is clear."

They all nodded. And were silent.

Zuleikah asked, "How will we know when to go?"

More silence.

Ki snapped her fingers. "The vibrations." She jumped up on the molded seats and pressed her ear to the wall. She looked crazy. She held up a finger. "There's this constant vibration. I was thinking about it—how the network in the ship seems dead? What if it *is* dead? What if you lived your whole life on a metal ship with no network? How would you send messages?"

Margot remembered the ship folk tapping on the walls. "With sound."

"Code," Zuleikah said. "The taps."

"But we don't know the code," Thane said.

Ki stayed against the wall. "I don't have to understand it. Just . . . feel it. There's a flow. Conversation has a flow. Faster means trouble, slower means bored. Right before they came and got me for dinner, right? It got louder. That was when they noticed the Ratana ship following."

Margot wondered if this was another story, made up in the moment to make everyone calm. Still, all three of them watched her, ear to the wall, finger raised over her head.

"But how will you know—" Margot began.

Thane and Zuleikah shushed her in unison.

Ki wasn't lying about the rhythm thing; she had been listening since she realized the taps were a code, and she'd broken plenty of codes. She had even figured out that three sharp taps together were a sort of punctuation; it happened too often to be anything else. Maybe it was how they separated discrete packets of information.

Taps were coming almost desultory, like the first pops of popcorn. There was a pause and she almost said "Go" but just when she'd pulled in the breath there was a short flurry of taps—long long short long. Repeated, three sharp. She held her breath and counted. Another tap-tap. Three sharp. Seconds passed. And then it was at least as long as the previous pause . . . popcorn slowing. For now.

Ki dropped her raised hand. "Escape time."

Margot felt better with a goal, even a stupid one. She pushed open the airlock and led the way as planned. She made it around the first two turns. The third corner was a junction with another hall. Someone could come at her from three different directions. It was a perfect kill pocket.

She was afraid to look around the corner. She was afraid not to. She was afraid she was holding the escape up, her team exposed behind her to any number of surprises.

This was also when she realized she didn't have the helmet for her environment suit. None of them did. The ship folk had taken them. What better, easier method for keeping them all prisoner?

Margot inched forward. Her knees ached from crouching so low. Nothing to see in the left corridor, which came in at a sharp angle and inclined upward. She looked to the right.

Two coltish teens were seated, cross-legged in the middle of the corridor, holding cards.

Margot fell back around the corner. There was a childish scream, half delighted, and running footsteps.

There was nothing to do but backtrack. She scurried to the previous corner, grabbed Zuleikah's hand and tugged her up a side-corridor. "Is Ki following?" Margot whisper-shouted to Thane, who dallied at the last juncture.

"I don't see her," he whisper-shouted back.

They were trapped. Margot didn't want to spare a second. "Wait there. As soon as you see Ki, make sure she sees you and then catch up to us."

"I'll stay with him," Zuleikah said.

"He's not an invalid." Margot had gotten a glimpse at who Thane really was now. She kept her grip on Zuleikah's hand, dragging her after.

There were no sirens. Margot expected sirens. Or warning lights. Something.

If they turned right at the end of this corridor, and then another right when they had a chance . . .

The corridor dead-ended in a bulkhead.

Margot turned her back to it. Zuleikah's eyes were wide. "I don't know how to open it," Margot said.

"Maybe Ki can?"

"Back," Margot said.

Ki and Thane were running toward them, they met in the middle of the hall. "Locked door," Margot said. "And someone saw me the other way."

Ki looked back the way they came. "I choose lock," she said, and slipped between Margot and Zuleikah like a bird darting between trees.

They followed. What else could they do? Ki felt the edges of the door like a lover. "This is good. This . . . crap."

She turned to them. "We fried my circuit that would open this door opening the last one."

"Back?" Zuleikah asked.

Thane pushed between them. He was holding his wounded left hand against his stomach. "Let me try to force it."

"With what?"

"With my body." He pushed her out of the way with his shoulder and slammed into the bulkhead. It made a loud, hollow sound.

A man's voice shouted, "Stop!"

Three ship folk filed into the corridor behind them. Two held short daggers.

Thane threw himself against the door again.

Ki gathered his sleeve in her hands. "Easy. I think we stop now."

Margot put herself between her friends and the men with knives. She held her hands out, but couldn't think of anything to say that wasn't stupid.

Now there were the sounds she had expected—running feet, from many directions. The ship folk in their soft slippers. Bodies packed in behind the first three, blocking them utterly.

BD appeared, her beautiful eyes unreadable. The others deferred to her, stepping back to let her forward.

"This was the wrong corridor," she said. She tilted her head to the left. "You wanted the next one aft, port to the docking bay."

"There was someone there," Margot said. "I hoped we could go around."

She shook her head. "That is an engine room behind you. Dead end."

Margot felt a hand on the small of her back. Ki. Was it an expression of support? A warning? Margot said, "So . . . what now? We talk about this?"

There was a commotion advancing through the crowd of black-suited figures. A grey head appeared: an old woman. She wore no veil across her face.

The old woman stopped two ranks back and the ship folk parted like automated doors. "There is blood on you," the old woman said.

Margot didn't know how to answer.

"We had to get at Thane's implant," Ki spoke from behind her. "To open the door. Hands bleed a lot, you know?"

The old woman approached Thane, who held the bloody rags to his chest. "You let them do this to you?"

He held his chin high. "I'd rather die than go back."

The old woman frowned. "And you a royal?"

"I'm more royal property," he said, and though he was shaking, he looked ready to fight.

Zuleikah tried to step between them and was restrained by the ship folk. "We won't leave without him! And we won't let you hurt him!"

The old woman gave Zuleikah a look like Margot's grandma gave her when she said something rude. "Well," the old woman said. She set her hand on the wall, briefly. She lifted her hand away and a suppressed gasp went through the crowd. That meant something? "No, I think the path is clear," the old woman said. "Get the things that came with them," she said. "And an environment suit for the angel."

More ship folk arrived. There was something funereal in the way they carried everything in front of them. The formal way they walked forward and handed each of them a helmet with a bow. Then they presented their reading devices. Margot had never had her bracelet presented to her like a sacred object before. She almost couldn't put it on. The last gift-bearer to come forward held an environment suit up as high as he could reach, holding the shoulders so it was like a curtain before him. He bowed low in front of Thane.

"Please suit up," the old woman said.

Zuleikah turned her helmet over in her hands. "I thought you were giving Thane back to Ratana."

"You are very clever," the elder said, smirking.

Thane tried to step into the environment suit, holding it with one hand, drawing it up under his robe, which bunched around his waist, halting progress.

One of the ship folk touched Thane's sleeve. He backed against the bulkhead. The man bowed and gestured at the sleeves. Margot stepped in. "Let me help you take that robe off."

He looked so embarrassed and afraid that Margot half expected to find his skin covered in hideous sores or something, but his arms and chest were just normal, though a bit exposed in the semi-transparent gold shirt he wore under the robe.

Zuleikah looked like someone just uncovered an enormous box of chocolate bars. What was it with straight women and guy's chests?

Thane zipped the environment suit up quickly, almost before they got the robe all the way off. He caught the shirt fabric twice. Margot handed him the ball of robe and crown when he was done. She sure as hell wasn't holding on to it.

They were herded back down the corridor. Toward the airlock. Margot couldn't think of a reason why they would be thrown into space after being given suits, but her irrational fear was ratcheting up with each recognized pipe and weld. What were Ship Folk funeral rites like, exactly?

The woman stopped at the airlock door and turned to face them. "We will not hand over four young people so determined to be free. We think you may just grow to be a powerful ally in the future. Black Dragon releases you to take your own fate."

"Wait," Ki said. "What about our star drives? We'll be stuck in this system without a re-tune. They've gone through FTL in your dock."

"This is no less than what you requested: passage out of Ratana's system."

"For payment," Thane said. He held up his crown.

"I don't know what use we will find of it," the woman said, lips pursed just like Margot's grandmother when she tried to get a shopkeeper to drop a price. She smiled and took the crown. "Go quickly. Ratana will not take long to realize Black Dragon has changed its mind."

The airlock opened. "Three at a time may fit," said BD. "We'll start with Flame Flyer."

"Wait!" Ki cried out.

Everyone froze. Ki bounced a curtsey to the old woman. "Before we go, could you make us part of your tribe?" she asked.

Everyone was stock still. Margot wanted the floor to swallow her whole. The old woman laughed and folded Ki into a hug.

16:
PERSEPHONE

Ki FLEW STRAIGHT OUT FROM BLACK DRAGON, TRUSTING THE others to follow. Zuleikah shrieked over the radio, "Five Ratana Navy vessels in the system! Five! They could have seen us already!"

"Get behind that moon," Margot said, and well, there wasn't much else they could do. They couldn't outrun the Ratanese ships and they had no weapons unless they wanted to open their canopies and throw their helmets at them.

It was a tense, silent, short run to the far side of Jefferson's largest moon.

They regrouped, hanging in the shadow of the moon, afraid even to scan lest their scanning be seen. It was half-dark, the moon an absence of stars below them, and half-light, the bright green and blue marble of Jefferson to their right.

No one was talking. Ki confirmed their private message network was still working. "So," Ki said. "What do we know?"

"The Ship Folk are wonderful," Thane said.

Uh . . . thanks, prince, really useful.

"We could wait here. Jefferson is an unaligned world," Margot said. "They won't let a foreign navy stay in their orbit forever."

"Persephone was named after the goddess of spring," Zuleikah said. It sounded like she was reading. "Because it only appears in the sky of Jefferson six months out of the year, and it's shaped like a pomegranate seed."

Ki wondered how everyone else could know so much more than her and yet not know anything at all. "We have two choices, out-wait the Ratana Royal Navy, who have food and showers and room to stretch their legs—not going to happen—or contact the locals for asylum."

"There's another moon named Hades," Zuleikah said. "It's smaller and rounder. Hades was Persephone's lover."

"How does that help? It's also further out," Ki said, checking her map. "Doesn't look like there are any stations on either moon or orbiting Jefferson. What's up with that?"

"It's Jefferson," Margot said. Like that meant something.

Ki couldn't believe how badly a lifetime of serial watching had prepared her for space. "No other planets inhabited in the system? Not a single moon base?"

"Jefferson is just Jefferson," Zuleikah said. "What do they teach in Earth schools?"

Two hundred light years from home, and still getting shamed for dropping out. Ki looked up at the bottom of Margot's flyer. Zuleikah had done a great job painting it. "You're saying what we need is a way onto Jefferson. I'll try to tap into their communications network, see if we can direct a signal straight at the planet so the Ratanese craft can't hear it."

"Please don't," said Zuleikah.

"Why not?"

There was a long pause. Thane spoke, "Zuleikah is busy with the defense network."

Margot said, "Let Zuleikah do it. She's better than you at this stuff and if we get caught trying to break in, this planet will fire on us. Jefferson is the only human colony on a world with native life. They maintain a strict biological quarantine to protect that life. They will vaporize us rather than risk contamination."

There was a space elevator extending from the planet's equator to a low orbit station. Ki saw tiny craft—one or two—descending from it, and an atmospheric plane dragging a teeny contrail over Jefferson's southern continent. "I don't get it," she said. "How do they trade with the rest of humanity?"

"They don't," Margot said. "Mostly. I wish the ship folk had dropped us in any other system."

We should go back, Ki thought. Black Dragon could still be in the system. Sure, they said they didn't want to cross the Ratanese, but their grandmotherly leader had lifted Ki in her arms and declared her one of them!

Ki fingered the black fabric they'd tied around her arm as a symbol of that. She really, really wanted to go back.

"I have something," Zuleikah said.

"Thank you," Margot said. "Anything. What?"

"I caught a broadcast from Black Dragon to Jefferson air traffic control, telling them about us and asking if they can dock for commerce. Jefferson replied that they could only dock if they had something they wanted, and sent them a list. It's mostly advanced tech and chemicals."

Ki read over the list as Zuleikah sent it. She didn't recognize half the words. It was unlikely any of these things were in the three solo-flyers, as well-provisioned as they were.

Ki's console lit up. "Oh crap. The air traffic controllers are calling us, now."

"Solo-flyers, you are to leave this system immediately."

Ki didn't bother waiting for the others to weigh in. "That's going to be a problem since our star drives aren't prepped."

"Not our problem. Approach the planet and you will be reduced to component atoms."

Ki sent on the private channel, "Let's call Black Dragon and get them to pick us up again."

"Wait," Margot said. "Wait."

"What? You have some Earth navy secrets that can help?"

"Sort of," Margot said. "These people need a stock clerk."

Ki could not think of a statement she expected to hear less. "What?"

"Jefferson planetary forces," Margot said. "This is Margot Santiago-Nguyen, formerly of the Sol Alliance Navy. Are you aware that your list of items you have to trade contain a compound you are asking for?"

Ki opened a private channel directly to Margot. "Is that true?"

"I think so," Margot said.

The voice from Jefferson was dripping with sarcasm. "You think we wouldn't catch such an obvious mistake?"

"It's not a mistake," Margot said. "And if you let us just dock at your elevator station, I'll show you why."

"Margot, you are so full of it right now," Ki said.

Margot switched to the private channel, too. "No, I'm not. This compound, it's used to pack ordinance. Shock-absorbing, moisture-absorbing. But we ran out of it all the time. People would steal it to pad their bunks. We had to mix more, and they have the ingredients. I don't know much, but I do know this. And if I can bluff that I know more . . ."

"M, you haven't told a lie in your life."

"Well, then, you tell it. I'll stand behind you and look mean."

That, Ki believed Margot could do.

Jefferson control said, "One of my guys just checked the list and says there's no way you're right. And if you are, we don't care. The Ratana craft are asking about you and we don't like getting involved in other people's squabbles."

"Margot?" Ki asked. "Maybe give them a hint?"

Margot sighed, loud. "If I tell them where to look, that's the end of our leverage."

"Which part of the trick would be harder to guess?"

"The source material," Margot said. "I think I see what you're saying." There was a click as she switched to the public channel. "Jefferson control? I'll tell you what compound on your wanted list I can get for you if you please don't tell Ratana where we are."

"And it's not the only one," Ki said. "The girl's a chemical genius."

Margot growled, "Don't over-sell me, 'member of the tribe.'"

"I won't. Everyone, turn off your radios. We have to ignore them. Nothing makes someone more interested in talking to you like ignoring them. Trust me." This was a huge gamble. Ki wasn't sure it would work.

"How will we know if the Ratana ships have locked on to us?" Margot asked.

"We'll know," Zuleikah said, grimly.

"Yeah, I'd rather not find out because I'm getting shot at. How long do we wait?" asked Margot.

Ki didn't know what to say. "A minute? Just make sure they contact you first."

"What if they don't? What if Ratana sees us?"

Ki turned off her radio, darkened her canopy, and curled up tight in her seat.

Thane sat in a cramped compartment, wearing a rough suit that smelled of someone else's sweat, in an absolute cornucopia of pain. The sharp, focused pain in his hand where the implant had shocked him against Ki's intrusion; the dull throbs where his shoulder had hit the wall and where his hip had hit the deck plates when he'd foolishly failed to strap in; the pinching ache of his back from just being in cramped places; the elaborate, worming sting of his feet.

The litany of irritation expanded: his robe was constantly threatening to float out of his lap. It could hardly be called a robe anymore. It was torn, stained, mutilated. His mother would definitely want to skin him, knowing he'd touched so much dirt. If he took his helmet off, he wouldn't smell the suit so much, but he would smell Zuleikah, then. The whole compartment smelled of her cold panic-sweat. It was a more intimate stink for being associated with a particular person.

Zuleikah muttered to herself and fussed with different displays on the inside of the canopy. Her right elbow frequently invaded his space.

He'd ignored worse. Many times. He should be patient. He wasn't. "Could you not do that?"

Zuleikah twisted around, her hand on the headrest between them. "Do what?" She dropped everything, focused solely on him. Such the royalist.

"Never mind," Thane said, losing his nerve. He'd interrupted the important work of his own rescue. He tried to sink back farther. There was no gravity to aid him, and pressing himself back squeezed the environment suit, expelling fresh stink on his face.

She turned to her work, elbows moving toward his face again. "The Jeffersonians use some of the same security protocols Ratana uses," Zuleikah said. "I'm being cautious, but I think I . . . no, no this is impossible. Maybe if I . . ."

Thane itched to be out of the tight space. Every second was a second unsure, not quite free yet. His mother's people were *right there* and no one was doing anything to get rid of them. He tried to remember what he knew of Jefferson. Their ambassador had been a man, he remembered that. He'd had exquisite skin.

"Don't look so worried," Zuleikah said. Her braid rose in the air behind her in a half-coil, like a question mark, a record of her past turns. "They might not let us on the planet, but all we need is a few hour's docking for a tune up."

"Will you stop? I'm not weak. I can't stand your simpering." And immediately he regretted the words, but they were out. Bullets fired.

Zuleikah's eyebrows canted toward each other. "I—"

Thane took the helmet off, knowing he was doing it too late. "I'm sorry. I . . . this is all very stressful."

"No." Zuleikah's hair bobbed, following on a delay as she pushed herself lower into her seat and re-fastened her seat belt. "Don't take your words back."

Now he was stuck in a tight space with someone upset with him. "Can I help?" he offered.

She looked down at his hand. The makeshift bandage was stiff under the environment suit glove. Was she thinking about how she had cut him? Was that making her sympathetic enough to forgive him? He flexed the hand.

Zuleikah turned her back to him. "No," she said, "you can't help."

She went back to work with stony silence, and when her elbow poked at him, it felt intentional.

Margot's voice came over the radio. "I think we should hail them again."

"Wait," Zuleikah replied. "I almost have something. I . . . yes!"

Thane loosened his restraints so he could float higher and see Zuleikah's console. She was typing furiously. It was too small to read.

"That's brilliant," Margot said. "It has to work. Should we check? How do we check?"

Thane asked, "What did you do?"

Zuleikah said, "I couldn't get into Jefferson, but I was already intercepting external communications, so I inserted a fake one."

"Wait," Margot said, "You told the Ratana ships we were shot down entering the atmosphere? Zuleikah! What if Jefferson decides it's easier to make that true than explain it was fake?"

Zuleikah didn't respond. She reached overhead, flicking a switch. A system map appeared, showing the location of the Ratana ships. This was the general scanner, the one they hadn't used because it could give away their position. Thane wanted to strangle her. He held tight to the headrest between them.

One of the ships winked out, returning to FTL. Then a second. Then they were all gone.

The Jefferson control officer's voice was amused. "You cheeky scamps. You got rid of the competing bid for your hides. You have permission to dock at our elevator station long enough to prove you have useful knowledge to trade."

"Wake up, Ki." Zuleikah flipped another switch. "I just saved our lives. You're welcome."

Thane stammered. "I . . . look, I don't hate you. I . . ."

"Stop digging," she said, and turned the craft toward Jefferson.

17:
NEAR JEFFERSON

ZULEIKAH DID NOT EXPECT THE OPERATOR WHO MET THEM IN THE loading dock to be quite so exotic. He had pale peach skin, yellow-blonde hair, and a suit of iridescent fabric that clung to his body, emphasizing his fit, muscular form, and his pinkness.

The docking bay was shaped like a slice of pie, a segment of the outer ring of the station at the top of the space elevator. Everything was very, very clean. *He* was very, very clean. He looked at them with open disgust. "First thing first—showers for all of you." He tilted his head back to address the air above his head. "Autumn? Are we cleared to start decontamination yet?"

A melodic woman's voice responded, "Nearly so. Just getting confirmation on the third microbe scan."

He smiled. "We are being bathed in a harmless, cleansing radiation. You may feel some prickling or dryness in your lips and other *sensitive* tissues." He emphasized 'sensitive' in a way that was suggestive of a dirty joke, but Zuleikah didn't get it.

"Thank you for letting us in to talk," Ki said.

"Please," the man said, "Exhale as little as possible until we finish the decontamination."

Zuleikah was not used to seeing such disgust directed at herself. It was true, she desperately needed a bath, but did the Jeffersonian have to look at all of them, even Thane, that way?

"Call me Andrei," the man said, waving Zuleikah forward. He gestured at a door. "Step through there, please? Hold your breath when you see the light blink."

"Huh?"

Zuleikah was still wondering what he meant when the door closed behind her. She was in a small cubicle. Well, it would have been considered small to her before spending the day on Black Dragon. It was almost as big as her shower stall at home, and felt more spacious for being a perfect rectangular shape.

A red light on the wall opposite started to flash. "Oh." Zuleikah sucked in a breath just as a mist started spraying from every direction. She choked and coughed, unable to hold the bitter air in her mouth, much less her lungs, but that meant she took another breath, which was even wetter, and her lungs burned.

The spraying stopped, the light ceased flashing, and then wind was blowing all over her, flipping her braid around over her head.

The wind stopped. "Ten in one thousand chance of microbe contamination," a voice said. "Turn, please."

"What is going . . . ?"

The light started flashing again. Zuleikah slammed her lips shut.

Twice more she was sprayed and dried, and then a light shone hard on her, hot, like the sun at noon. She covered her eyes with her hands and still saw light.

It reminded her of the films in school about sun exposure, to scare kids into not wandering into the desert.

The wind whipped her again. Her ears ached from the force of it.

The red light turned green. "Coleman-Sagan threshold reached," the woman's voice said. "Please proceed forward."

The wall with the light on it slid upward, exposing another cubicle. Zuleikah stepped into it, and the wall closed behind her. There was a hum, a buzz, and a ding. The opposite wall opened.

The woman before her was also exotic, exotically dark, with black, wooly hair, and an iridescent tunic less form-fitting, but no less scanty than Andrei's. She held a large screen in her hands. "Welcome to Near-Jefferson," she said. "I'm Autumn. Thank you for your patience. It will take a little while to get the rest of your party cleared for the station." She smiled a quick, professional smile, and then turned her attention to her screen. "Cleaning cycle complete. Andrei, the decontamination booth is ready for the next visitor."

Zuleikah coughed. It burned all the way down. "Why not just talk to us in the docking bay?"

"It's against regulations to spend long periods of time in the docking bay. Besides, it will be unlivable in there while we decontaminate your ships. Four in one thousand chance of microbe contamination. Turn, please."

Autumn was talking to whomever was in the decontamination booth now. Would Margot have come through next? Not Thane. Thane wouldn't want to be stuck alone with Zuleikah on this side.

"Detecting slight bacterial infection. Remove your shoes, please? Yes, those, too." Autumn nodded in satisfaction and tapped her tablet. "Nine in one thousand chance of microbe contamination. Turn, please."

"I never thought I'd actually visit Jefferson," Zuleikah said.

"You're not going to," Autumn said. "Coleman-Sagan threshold reached. Please step forward." She smiled at Zuleikah. "You've made it to Near-Jefferson, and that's as far as any of you will go. Now, step back, your companion is about to walk through the door."

The door opened and Thane stepped into the corridor. His hair was sticking up from the wind-treatment. He was carrying his helmet and boots. He looked from Zuleikah to Autumn. "I never thought I'd actually get to see Jefferson," he said.

Zuleikah wasn't ready to make small talk with him. He sank onto a low stool. He had his slippers and stockings in one fist like a limp, golden bouquet. Zuleikah looked away when she caught a glimpse of fresh blood. Had he been hurt in her flyer? By the Ship Folk's terrible suit?

Autumn spoke in her calm, professional voice about microbes and thresholds. The corridor was gleaming white with milky light-strips overhead and chrome frames around the bulkheads.

Margot came through next. None of them were surprised that Ki took the longest time to decontaminate. Then Andrei came through himself. Andrei and Autumn hugged as if they'd been separated for months, cooing and running their hands over each other.

"I'll start docking bay decontamination," Autumn said. "Take the visitors to the lounge, Andrei?"

He put his hand on his heart and inclined his head to her. "It will be an eternity until we speak again."

"You," was all Autumn said in response, her eyes on her tablet, though her cheeks dimpled.

Andrei spun on his heel and waved one hand overhead, gesturing for them to follow. He was even more colorful against the white corridor.

Zuleikah wasn't sure if she should offer Thane her arm. The others had hurried ahead. He got to his feet stiffly and limped after them, back ramrod straight. He left little smudges of blood in his footprints on the pristine white tile.

They were led to a crescent-shaped room whose larger, convex wall was transparent. The room had mauve carpet and tan chairs. Through the transparent wall was an identical room, which had the addition of a control console and a potted plant. Thane sank into the chair closest to the door.

Zuleikah went straight to the window, figuring it was important. A door opposite slid open, and an angry-looking woman entered. She wore a severe white uniform with a high collar. She walked up to the control console and touched it.

Her voice was amplified through speakers in the room, though she spoke at a reasonable tone. "I am Commander Wong of the Jeffersonian Protection Force. Which one of you is the chemist?"

Margot raised one hand and said, "I'm a stock clerk, actually, but I know about chemicals. Some chemicals."

"More than our chemical database, or so you claim."

"I know one thing your system doesn't. In exchange for the knowledge, we want our three solo-flyers retuned to get us back to Sol system."

"Or we could go back to Ratana," Zuleikah said.

At the same time, Thane said, "Or anywhere but Ratana."

Ki said, "Not Sol! Let's not go home yet!" How old *was* she?

Margot stepped closer to Zuleikah. "It doesn't matter where. We just want to get out of here, since we can't land on Jefferson and Ratana's forces may come back looking for us. We'll go to Old Hope or Woolworth's World if that works out to be less trouble. It's up to you. Don't you want us out of your hair?"

Commander Wong did not look like she thought any option

was less than too much trouble. "Andrei? Open a communications panel for them. You will transmit your information, and if it turns out to be useful, we will retune your ships. If not, we will hold your ships as payment for the expensive decontamination we've done on you."

They would be trapped! Zuleikah would be trapped! In a . . . a public waiting room? "Where will we go?"

"You will stay in the hospitality station until you can arrange transport. We aren't barbarians. We'll feed and house you at a reasonable rate minus the value of your craft and any work you do on our behalf."

Andrei bowed and walked to the far wall, where he slid open a panel.

Zuleikah stared at the Spartan, uncomfortable furnishings. "We can't live here!"

Ki gave her a very odd look.

"We have no reason to cheat you," Commander Wong said, looking like she thought she would be well within her rights to do so. "You will survive as long as it takes to secure transport. Perhaps you could call those Ratanese ships? They seemed keen to take you aboard."

"Ice wouldn't melt in her mouth," Ki muttered.

"Here you are," Andrei said, cheerfully, a little forced, waving a hand over the exposed console. "Any time, now."

Margot hesitated.

"You can do this," Thane said. "You'll save us all."

Margot didn't acknowledge this. Zuleikah wanted to smack her. After she finished saving them, of course.

Andrei stepped in front of Zuleikah. "You're clenching your fist, and your heart rate has elevated. I'd like to move you to a separate location if you're going to be violent."

Zuleikah was surprised out of a portion of her anger and fear.

"Are you even human?"

Andrei waved a hand. "Of course not. Only androids work on this side of the station. Fully autonomous, of course."

A humanoid robot? Zuleikah took a step back in horror. They were illegal on Ratana, and she was pretty sure on other planets they were only used by perverse people to be . . . perverted.

Andrei frowned. "I've upset you. I apologize. Perhaps you'd rather speak with Autumn? She should be free to take my place now."

Zuleikah tried to grab Thane's arm, to feel his reassuring Ratanese respectability. He flinched back deeper into his chair.

On the other side of the glass, Commander Wong's expression changed completely. "Excellent. This does check out. How amazing. I guess there can always be an oversight in the system, especially when you assume there isn't." Commander Wong looked up. "Are you seeking employment?"

Margot said, "I . . . a job? Yes, I would love a job here. You have a job?"

"It's not often our systems are found wanting. You have an extraordinary eye for detail. Andrei? Run the tests for emigration and I'll have legal check into processing this . . . Ms.?"

"Santiago-Nguyen. Margot Santiago-Nguyen."

"Ms. Nguyen as a valuable asset. Of course, you'll have to live here on the station; non-native-born aren't allowed on the surface, but in a few months you'll be cleared to enter this side."

"Wait!" Ki asked, "What about retuning our ships?"

Commander Wong ignored her and left the room. What did that mean? Were they being released or not?

Margot beamed at the room. "I have a job offer!"

18:
THE J-O-B

THANE FELT THE TENSION IN THE ROOM. IT WAS AS BAD AS A family dinner. Ki marched up to Margot. Andrei stepped in her way. "Could you stay away from others while your heart rate is elevated?"

"Shut up, Gort," Ki said, and punched Andrei in the chest.

Andrei made a disappointed moue. "Was that a kind act?"

Ki knocked Andrei's arm down when he tried to keep her from stepping around him. She shouted at Margot, "We are almost out of this, and you're going to break up the band?"

"It's me," Thane said, very quietly, but then, everyone was listening. He tried to look as dignified as he could in an environment suit that did nothing for his figure, holding his helmet and boots on his lap. "She doesn't want to have to keep dealing with me, and my mother chasing us."

"It's not about you." Margot gave Thane a disgusted look.

The door opened and Autumn arrived. She joined Andrei, standing on the other side of Ki. They bracketed her like extremely eager-to-please riot police.

Ki glanced from one android to another. "Oh relax, robot twins. I'm not going to hit anyone." She crossed to a seat across from Thane and slumped into it, drawing her legs up and hugging them. She glared at him like it was his fault. Well, he'd already said it was.

"Look, none of you really want me hanging around," Thane said. "I'm just . . . I'm cargo to you. Something you could sell."

"Not at all!" Zuleikah said. Because of course she would. It was more true of her than any of them.

Thane considered his prospects, and nothing sounded as good as never getting up again. "So maybe I should stay, too. On Jefferson, I mean. There's no reason we have to stay together."

"There is a reason. Because we're a gang!" Ki said.

"No," Thane said. "We're not. Anyway, I'm not."

The androids fidgeted nervously like children stuck with arguing adults. Andrei laughed brightly. "There's no rush to decide anything until your craft are ready to go. This lounge will be at your disposal for your wait. Autumn or I can also show you to the sanitary facilities. It's not far. Would anyone like a glass of water?"

"Yes," Margot said. "Please. Water for everyone. We shouldn't refuse that when we can get it. Right?"

Ki sniffled. "Yeah." She looked very young, now, with her un-made-up eyes and her small body curled. She looked like she'd been betrayed by a close friend.

Margot let the female android lead her from the room.

Thane felt guilty. Guilty and stupid. What if he couldn't stay here? He'd alienated Zuleikah and Ki and disgusted Margot with his egotism. Some seductive prince he was.

"What happened to your feet?" Ki asked, looking over her arm at him.

"My . . . what? Nothing."

"You've been limping since we left Ratana. Everyone's noticed. The robots noticed."

This was his fault for not putting the boots back on. "They were hurt before you rescued me."

To his horror, Ki slithered out of her chair and onto the ground at his feet. He flinched back, but that just lifted his toes into her grasp. He yelped. Her fingers were icy. "My gosh, it looks like you walked over hot coals and didn't stop to wipe after." She turned his foot over in her hand with surprising gentleness.

Thane felt he was going to die of embarrassment. He hadn't looked closely, himself. He knew they were ugly and puffy. "Please... it's fine."

Worse, now Zuleikah was staring at him, and the robot, Andrei, squatted to frown over his foot. He wished he had his robes on so he could hide it from view. "It seems some idiot put spray-skin over a wound that was leaking. Small gaps in the adhesion let all sorts of bad stuff in. I . . . I can tell you don't want more detail."

Ki set his foot gently down and pulled a dirty, much scratched box from a pocket.

Everyone was staring at his feet. His ugly feet, sticking out like raw meat from the ankles of the ratty black environment suit. He wanted to die. He wanted the chair to swallow him whole from sight.

"Oh no," Andrei waved over the meagre medical supplies Ki was laying out. "We'll take care of everything. The decontamination did wonders for him, believe me, and letting the wound breathe. I'll be just a tic. You poor dear, whatever did they do to you?" He shook his head and sashayed blithely to a wall panel, which opened to reveal many tightly packed boxes of supplies.

"Sanitation is our top priority, and that includes keeping your insides on the inside!"

Why wouldn't any of them look away from him? For a moment! Zuleikah had been poking consoles and seams in the room since they'd gotten to it as though convinced it was one big puzzle. Ki was the self-admitted thief. Shouldn't they be seizing on the new cabinet Andrei had exposed to them? But no. Ki held his feet, one at a time, while Andrei peeled away the ruined bits of spray-skin, which certainly looked worse than it was. Zuleikah knelt next to her, looking at him like she was about to cry.

"It's nothing," Thane said, again. He looked at the ceiling, feeling tears starting, damn them. His makeup would run. "I was caught using my implant during a state dinner. It was important, I assure you. Someone was wrong on a fan site."

Andrei sprayed his feet with something cool and numbing, then slipped a strange, papery bootie over each foot. It felt... comfortable. Dry. He didn't dare look down, though.

He felt Ki's small hand on his arm. "Can he walk?"

"Oh, certainly! This is a durable and flexible covering that—"

"Great. Come on, we're going." Ki urged him up. "Show us to the restroom, Andrei?" Her cheeks were streaked with tears, but they were old ones. She held one hand out to stop Zuleikah from following, and that, at least, was a mercy.

Margot filled four real glass drinking vessels in the elegant dispensary, and Autumn gave her a tray to carry them back to the waiting room, where, to her surprise, she found Zuleikah alone. "Where's the other one?" Margot asked, and then realized how vague that question was. "Andrei?"

Zuleikah raised and lowered one shoulder, not looking away from the control panel she was poking at.

Autumn said, "Andrei is in the hallway outside the sanitary facility. He is giving your colleagues privacy to complete their ablutions."

Margot turned her back on Zuleikah, to block whatever it was she was doing from robot sight. "Aren't you worried that we might be plotting?"

"Oh, no. Nothing you've said since coming on station has remotely worried our security intelligence. It listens to all conversation on Near Jefferson and alerts all staff if something suspicious comes up. For example, right now your colleague is trying to gain access to internal communications, but it's aware and stopping her."

Zuleikah abruptly stopped typing and muttered, "I knew it."

Margot felt uneasy. She set the tray of glasses on a little oval table before she dropped them.

"Is there anything else I can do for you before my brother gets back?" Autumn asked.

"You aren't . . . your superiors aren't angry that Zuleikah tried to hack into your security system, are they? Will this affect their decisions?"

"I can't say." Autumn rolled her eyes. "You know humans!"

Margot sat down and pressed against her temples, which were aching. "I feel like I'm going mad."

"You didn't have to be so mean to Thane," Zuleikah said.

Speaking of mad. Was Zuleikah living in some alternate universe? "He's a grown man."

"I'm his loyal subject," Zuleikah said.

Margot snorted.

Autumn snorted, too. "Men," she said. "Am I right?"

The android sat down next to Margot and crossed her legs.

She had the eerie poise of a news anchor. "Not to alarm you, but it looks like Queenie is secure enough in her seat to send an ansible straight to Jefferson Governance. She wants footage of the destruction of the flyers, residue evidence, and recompense. Yikes. She wants lots of recompense." Autumn rolled her eyes. "Heads of state, am I right?"

It was like a small explosion went off. Zuleikah strode forward, fists clenched. She seemed to think better of attacking and stopped, growling, "How long until the star drives are finished?"

"We'll get to it," Autumn said. "Have patience."

With the same stern determination, she said, "Thane needs to be out of here before Ratana comes back."

"Our priority at the moment is to process Ms. Nguyen's employment."

Zuleikah turned to Margot. "Tell them you don't want the job."

"I will not!"

Autumn said, "Women. Am I right?"

"If the queen has asked about Thane, she's going to come here. The station isn't going to lie for us forever. You can't want to spend the rest of your life on this tiny, miserable elevator station."

Tiny? Miserable? What a snob. "I want a job. Stability. This is both of those."

Zuleikah looked disgusted. "What about a purpose in life?"

Spoken like a rich girl who'd joined a gang because she was bored. "A job *is* a purpose in life."

Zuleikah groaned in frustration and went back to her console.

Autumn set her hand on Margot's. "I know just what you mean," she said.

Margot wasn't sure how to take that.

Thane stopped abruptly, confronted with his reflection, larger than life, under unforgiving lighting. His hair was an unkempt lion's mane. His eye-wings were nearly gone, revealing the tattooed line his stylist used every morning as a guide. Helplessly, he sank his hands into the tangles on top of his head.

Ki hopped up on a counter behind him, meeting his reflection's gaze. "I get it."

Ki's hair was the color and consistency of dye-festival grass. She must have seen the incredulity in his gaze. "I mean, I get you didn't want us pitying you. Especially Z. She's probably a little too close to the people you're supposed to impress back home, huh?"

Feeling a little too clearly seen, he found the sink taps and a basket of grooming supplies, including a cellophane-wrapped hairbrush. He tore it open and wet it under the taps. "It's my job to impress people. To look good."

"She really likes you, you know."

The brush stuck immediately in the tangles. He grimaced and worked it out. "That's her job."

"Not really. I thought maybe you two could have a thing ... but now I'm seeing that's not going to happen. Look, Margot can't take this job. We have to keep the gang together. Say you'll take my side in this."

He didn't like the way she was looking at him; like he could do something. Like he was capable of doing anything. "It wouldn't matter if I did. There's no real way out of this for me." He kept his eyes on his work, separating locks of hair from the tangle so he could brush them smooth. "I keep thinking maybe I can escape, but I can't. My mother will keep coming after me wherever we go." He knew Ki was disappointed in him. He rinsed the brush and smoothed it over the small bit of neatened hair he had hanging in his face. "It's safe here, and I'm sure Zuleikah would rather have her flyer to herself."

Ki chewed her lower lip. "Can you fly a solo-flyer?"

"What? On my own? No."

Ki drummed her heels. "That narrows our options. Would you rather stay on Jefferson and wait for rescue from some unknown future source, or come with us? What if we can catch up with Black Dragon?"

"When my mother hears that Jefferson supposedly blew me up, she'll come running and they will not back up our story for the price of some . . . chemistry knowledge. But if I stay here and find someone local who wants to marry me, then I'll be one of their own." Maybe Margot. He admired her. She was smart, capable. If he could make himself halfway decent-looking ...

Ki was staring so steadily at him it was unnerving. He brushed more hair into his face. He heard her drop to her feet. "How's your hand?"

His hand? Oh. He'd hardly thought of it. The cut was puckered, purplish. "Fine."

She rinsed a washcloth and touched his wrist. "Let me check."

Slowly, he let her take his hand and inspect the cut. She gently pressed the cloth over the wound twice. "Please stay with the group. You shouldn't marry someone just to feel safe."

"I don't think I'll have a choice."

She released his hand and reached up, fingers deftly picking apart a knot in his hair. "We'll all get out of here, and we'll do it together."

"There's nowhere we can go my mother can't follow."

Ki smiled ruefully. "Leave that to me. It's my job."

He wanted very much to trust that, to let this sudden burden of decision fall into her tiny hands. "But . . ." He shook his head. "I thought Margot was the leader?"

Ki threw down her washcloth. "It's not fair. I came up with the name!"

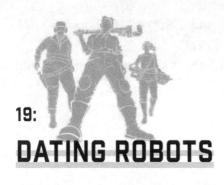

19:
DATING ROBOTS

Ki **knew** **he** **was** **incapable** **of** **sleeping, but** **Andrei** **perked** up like he'd been dozing off when she stepped into the hallway.

Andrei frowned. "You aren't much fresher," he said. "I would have thought you would have at least used the hairbrush. You . . . did look in the mirror, right?"

Ki patted him on the chest. "Thane needs some privacy, he said. You are an astonishingly shallow artificial intelligence." His chest felt real, all warm and muscled.

Andrei plucked her hand from his pectoral and kissed the inside of her wrist. "I am *deeply* shallow." He gave a saucy wink.

"How does that even work?" Ki marveled, feeling him take a breath.

"Wouldn't you like to know?"

Ki searched his eyes. Gorgeous sky-blue. The pupils dilated while she watched. The iris had to be some elastic polymer. "Someone programmed you to flirt."

"Darling, it's almost the first thing AI were trained to do. Right after sell insurance."

She heard the hiss of the air-shower. Ki bit her lip. "Oh darn, we have time to kill."

Andrei tilted his head and licked his bottom lip, a quick swipe of tongue. What was the liquid inside his mouth? The texture looked genuine. His teeth were too perfect, ruining the realism.

His fingers, though, dragging gently up her neck, felt just perfect enough. He purred, "It gets dull visiting Near Jefferson Station. Our government cares about your entertainment." He kissed the underside of her jaw. "What did you think I was built *for*?"

"I love technology," she murmured, closing the distance.

Andrei's tongue felt as real as it looked, though it tasted a bit . . . antiseptic. Whatever he washed with left a tingling burn on Ki's lips, but hey, so did stubble. Her fingers slid into his soft locks. They were silkier than normal hair. Andrei moaned with pleasure. Someone put a lot of thought into him.

A loud throat clearing brought her back to the present.

Thane stood behind her, looking off to the side, jaw tight with clenched teeth. His hair looked a lot better, and he must have washed the environment suit itself. It shone wetly.

Ki hung off Andrei by one arm. "Is this a terrible place to be stuck in or what?"

"He's not real," Thane said. "And we're in a public place."

"Barely public," Ki muttered, but she let go of Andrei with a last, fond squeeze. "Fine, let's go meet up with the rest of the gang and decide what we're going to do—if we have any choices left, that is."

Thane caught up, shoulder to shoulder with Ki as she hit the control for the lounge room door. "I bet Margot has been making real progress," he said, "not making out with robots."

The door slid open and Margot jumped back from Autumn's lap, lips puffy and dark from kissing. Autumn waved to Andrei with an unmistakably smug expression.

Zuleikah looked over her shoulder from the command console and raised an eyebrow. "She likes the benefits package."

Margot straightened her clothes. "Hey, guys. So, we're learning a lot about Jefferson."

"The queen is asking for proof," Zuleikah said. "I'm trying to make it look like communications are failing."

Thane looked like a man whose mind was breaking.

Ki felt him sway on his feet and took hold of his elbow. "We've all been under a lot of stress."

"That's not even an artificial *man*," Thane said.

"Yeah, I noticed." Margot stood. "I guess I'll go wash up."

Autumn rose gracefully and met Andrei. They clasped hands. "Did you hear that?"

"I did. Good news, I think."

What were they talking about? Despite their very different appearances, Andrei and Autumn moved and talked like the same person.

"Darling, the male is anxious," Autumn said, pressing her cheek to Andrei's. "I think he'd prefer you talk to him."

"I don't," Thane said. "I don't prefer either of you. Please stop acting like . . . like you're people."

"Don't be mean," Ki said, instinctively hurting for the artificial intelligence. She knew how it felt to be treated like you weren't people.

Andrei, however, just dropped the arm he had around his "sister" and said, "All right. Mr. Thane, will you come with me? I have some things to say to you in private."

"Uh . . . I'm not . . . I mean . . ." Thane looked like he was going to blush to death.

"It's a message from the human staff. I won't even wink." Andrei walked to the door in the most automatic, unsexy way, one step in front of the other, without a wasted motion, no sway to his hands, even. It was funny the things you noticed only when people didn't do them.

"They are incredibly detailed," Margot said. She'd come to stand behind Ki, watching Andrei lead Thane outside.

"I know! I bet neither of us could afford a minute with one of these back home in Sol system."

"I don't think I could afford to even look at one," Margot said. "Did you notice the eyebrows? Each hair had to have been individually injected into the skin."

Ki hadn't. She marveled at her memory of running her hands through Andrei's curls. "I wonder how they do it."

"It's not that complicated," Autumn said, with an air of modesty. She sat down, hands folded on one knee, like a guest at a cocktail party enjoying the ambiance. Her eyebrows were exquisite.

"If you're done drooling after the furniture," Zuleikah said, "The ships aren't being worked on because the station is processing Margot's employment first, and they're waiting on replies from Luna and the Earth Navy about her references."

"I wish they'd let me talk to them first," Margot said.

Ki took hold of Margot's shoulders. "Kid, if you don't turn down this job, Ratana will get back before we can get out of here and you'll be sending that boy back to an abusive situation."

Margot knocked her hands off. "That's not fair. It's the station's choice how they prioritize things."

Ki tried to keep her voice calm and steady. "Is a job worth his life?"

"We don't know he'd be hurt," Margot said, obviously not believing herself.

"Hurt more, you mean. And what about our lives? Do you think they're going to let his kidnappers go? Because that's us. I've made a life out of running, M. You can't trust the cops to be slow."

⚡

Andrei led Thane to a smaller, duller room. It had a single rectangular table with four swing-out disk seats. The walls were uninterrupted, slightly glowing white. Andrei walked to the far side of the table and set his fingertips on it. "In this room, I represent to you the voice of Commander Wong and the human staff of this station. They are communicating with me directly via radio. They want to know that you understand this. Indicate so by saying 'yes, I understand.'"

"Are you being intentionally more robotic?"

"A little." Andrei's eyes curled a little in smile.

"Yes, I understand."

Andrei pulled a chair out, sat down, and folded his hands together on the tabletop. "We are aware that you are a special person, Prince Thane of Ratana. And we are aware that diplomatic ties must be maintained, especially with a planet as important and, frankly, as war-like as yours. We would like to be able to call Ratana and tell her we have her prince safe and ready for pickup."

Thane felt something sink inside him, but just a little. It was what he assumed he'd hear. "I understand."

"However, we're not idiots. We have monitored your conversations and it is clear you don't want to return home. We are offering you asylum, if you are willing to make formal charges. This asylum does not come with a guarantee. Under threat of force, we will hand you over."

"I don't understand. What are you asking me?"

"To make a decision. Do you want to go home, do you want to stay with your companions, or do you want to stay here? Things you said in casual conversation aren't binding, but we need an official response from you to proceed. What do you want us to do?"

Thane felt paralyzed. He'd never been required to make a decision on anything in his entire life. Decisions were made for him.

Andrei leaned across the table and touched the back of his hand. "Try to keep breathing, sugar."

"What do you think I should do?"

"Giving advice right now might be construed as coercion," Andrei said. "It's really up to you."

"I shouldn't be talking to a robot about this," Thane sighed, then realized how that sounded. "No offense."

"I am incapable of being offended, but I can fake it if you want."

"Please, don't." Thane blinked. Andrei blinked. Thane had no idea what to say. He wanted to scratch his scalp, but Andrei was almost certainly a camera. "I've been trained a great deal in . . . pleasing women. And I look . . . well, I've been told I look okay. I think things will go best if you can find a woman on your planet willing to marry me."

"Sweetie. You like men."

Thane jumped to his feet. "I didn't tell you that. No one told you that!"

Andrei rolled his eyes extravagantly. "Trust me. Reading clues to human sexual interest is my top priority. My report on your sexual orientation was part of the evidence used to approve your asylum. We don't do this for just any head of state. Ratana is an awful place to be gay, or so I'm told." Andrei shrugged.

Thane felt distinctly uncomfortable. "What did I do wrong?"

"Nothing. But if what you're asking is how I picked up your orientation, it was simple. I measured the time you spent looking at me against the time you spent looking at Autumn, and your biometric states while looking. You hardly noticed Autumn was there. She'd be offended, if she could."

It was getting hard to breathe. "Anyway, that doesn't matter," Thane said. "I've never been particularly interested in romance. It's all just . . . treaties and economics."

Andrei, the little bastard, didn't appear to be paying attention. His gaze was unfocused, his face still.

Then the robot shook his head, ruffling the unfairly attractive artificial curls. "Sorry about that. It was a lot of data all at once. Ms. Nguyen has turned down our job offer."

Thane felt relief. "But why? I thought a job was all she cared about?"

"She's concerned about your safety, and so she's turning down the job offer so that we will prioritize re-tuning the star drives on your flyers."

Thane stood up. "Then I've made my decision," he said.

20:
BREAKING RULES

MARGOT PACED, WATCHING THE ANDROID AUTUMN—DARN BUT she was cute—calling up readouts and controls and doing a dozen small tasks that were *not* opening the landing bay airlock. "You didn't even *start* the re-tuning?"

"The commander sets our priorities and if a task has top priority, all other non-life-essential tasks are halted. I know, so inefficient! Human programmers, am I right?" Autumn shrugged. She poked and frowned at the control panel. "There. I've halted the disinfection. Now we may enter the bay safely. As soon as it cools."

Zuleikah leaned against the far wall, arms crossed, looking tired but relieved. "There's time. If things are still unstable back home, the Queen won't send someone right away."

Autumn made an adorable worried whine. "I wish you hadn't said that, sugar." She flicked a display up on the wall so they could see it. "A ship is on its way. The governors are going to throw you guys under the bus so hard you won't feel the impact."

Margot turned to Zuleikah. "How soon could Ratana get a ship back here?"

Zuleikah said, "I'm not sure . . . an hour?"

Autumn said, "It's going to take another fifteen minutes to cool the docking bay and vent the toxic chemicals for human habitation."

"So we go in in environment suits," Margot said.

Autumn looked horrified. "That goes against regulations. We have to use the quarantine protocol."

Margot pointed at the airlock. "We don't need quarantine protocols; we're not coming back in."

"Oh no, no no! We always use the protocols. I have to go out with you to perform the maintenance and *I* have to come back in. I don't even know how to log a request to sidestep these procedures. It isn't done."

"So you stay here," Margot said. "If that speeds things up."

"But who will re-tune the star drives?"

"Zuleikah will," Margot looked back and got a tiny, less-than-enthusiastic nod. "And she'll show me and Ki how so we can get it done quickly."

"Organic labor! That's . . . that's archaic! You'll never be as efficient as I would be."

At least the android acted concerned. A human in her place would probably tell them off. "I'll go wake Ki up now. This won't be as long a nap as she wanted, but we can all sleep when we're in FTL."

Margot had just turned when she saw Thane marching purposefully toward them, Andrei following like a bright balloon on a tether.

She didn't want to deal with him now. She'd done the right thing; she didn't want to have to act happy about it.

"I'm coming with you," Thane said. "Wherever you're going."

That wasn't what she expected. Was he coming along because she'd given up the job? He'd better not be putting this on her. "Tell me why and make it a good reason."

He looked slightly angry. "I can either give up, run away, or do something different. So let's do something different, because those other two options suck."

Margot blinked. That was a good reason. "Okay. Go wake Ki. She's back in the waiting room. Zuleikah and I want to be ready as soon as this door opens."

He didn't move. "Why did you? Not take the job, I mean."

Did he really want to do this now? She sighed. "I already have a job: keeping you guys alive. The pay is terrible. Now go; I have a feeling Ki takes a while to wake up."

That taken care of, she looked at Zuleikah, who had her head back against the wall, eyes closed. "Are you going to be okay to do this?"

Zuleikah slit one eye open and gave a thumbs up.

Andrei and Autumn were canoodling during this time, and Andrei took over Autumn's place at the room controls. Autumn turned shyly to Margot. "Are you sure you won't stay?"

"I don't care how pretty you are, if it turns out that you're delaying things to try to get me to change my mind, I will never forgive you."

Autumn played with the hem of her tunic. "I think it's awfully noble, what you're doing, but where could you run that the queen couldn't follow?"

"Earth."

They all turned to see a bright-eyed Ki marching forward with her environment suit helmet under her arm. "Earth has the strongest military in the universe, doesn't give a flip about Ratana, and I know the local security systems like the back of my lockpicks."

Oh boy. Margot could only be sure the first two statements had any truth to them. "Can you re-tune a star drive?"

"I've seen it done, and I read the manual," Ki said.

It would have to be good enough.

⚡

Zuleikah was so tired her eyes hurt. When had she last slept? It felt like weeks ago. Manually re-tuning a star drive wasn't easy. Hopefully the docking bay would have an auto-tuner she could hook up.

Why was she even doing this? To save her prince? It was like every time she opened her mouth, her mother popped out. What did she care about Ratana? She'd only liked Thane because he was hot and sarcastic. She liked that he rebelled *against* Ratana. In person he was more like her brother than the men she fantasized about.

She should have been a better sister. If she'd set down her data feed once in a while and actually talked to him, maybe her brother could have prepared her for the crazy ways boys behaved.

Margot gripped her shoulder. "Come on," she said, "The door's opening. I promise you can rest when it's done. We'll all get a real good rest when we reach Earth."

"You think so? You think we're ever going to stop running?"

"No, but it felt good to say it."

Ki wriggled between them as they entered the air lock, whooping with delight as the room made a briefer cycle than it had letting them onto the station. Then Ki ran off to her flyer, touching it like it was an animal that had been left alone and might be anxious.

Zuleikah got that. She loved her flyer, too. And Margot's. The flames were the best she'd ever done. She'd never had the guts to go all out on her own flyer the way she had on Margot's.

Ki had the cover off the star drive by the time Zuleikah found the bay's auto-tuner. The interface was different than Zuleikah's, but the leads were the same and she could work out the rest from context. "Bring it over," she said, motioning.

Ki and Margot obediently got Ki's flyer in place under the tuner. Margot then went to her flyer and popped the panel over the star drive.

Well, great, Zuleikah's was going to be done last, of course. She was annoyed, but that made her feel less sleepy, at least.

The airlock flashed and Thane entered the room. He really looked different in an environment suit. More normal? More human. "My mother knows I'm alive now," he said. "The robots just told me."

"It'll still take her a while to get here," Margot said. "Help Ki move her ship out of the way when Zuleikah says it's done."

Thane obediently got into position at the nose of the craft.

Ki's flyer had only one buckle in the harmonics. It must not have been flown much. The first crosscheck came back clean and although she should really do a second or third for safety, Zuleikah undid the leads. "Next," she said.

Thane and Ki pushed her red flyer out of the way and Margot nudged her flyer into position.

Brand new, more or less, and only flown twice in FTL. But it had wrinkles in the waveform from rough handling. Zuleikah set the tuner to flatten everything and re-sculpt.

"Is there anything I can do to help?" Thane hovered at her elbow.

"No," she said, and, remembering how she'd snapped at him before, quickly added, "Thanks. Help Margot move her ship so I can get mine next." He picked up the nose. The wave harmonics modulator screamed. "No! Not yet! Not—I'll tell you when."

Thane looked chagrined, but there was no helping that. She had to start the flattening over from the beginning. A reflection on her helmet visor obscured a reading. In anger, she took the helmet off. The poison gas was gone by now, right?

Andrei's voice came over a speaker. "Ratana has ships en route, darlings. It's hard to judge while in FTL but I put them at an ETA of, what would you say, Autumn? Twenty minutes? About twenty-two minutes. Ugh, I hate being imprecise. Commander Wong wants you secured and arrested if you aren't out of here in ten. No hard feelings, but we'll only help up to the exact second it becomes us or you."

There was not enough time to finish Margot's and get her own ship hooked up. "Margot? Get over here." When Margot was close, Zuleikah grabbed her hand and pulled it toward the waveform level readout. "When that indicator is zero, press this button. It'll say 'good' after a minute or so. If it doesn't, press this thing that says 'fine-tune'. Then press this button, and after it says Good, disconnect the leads. I'm going to do my ship manually."

Margot looked confused, but there was no time. A manual tune would take at least ten minutes and that was all they had.

Zuleikah popped the side-panel on her baby and felt the soft plasma-sack. She grabbed the tuning wand and bent close, tapping it to the surface to get micro-readings. This too high, this too low. One hand to test, one hand to adjust. She could do this.

"I got the manual," she heard Ki say.

"Look up code 71," Margot said.

Well, great. The auto-tune had an error.

Zuleikah forced it from her mind. She had time to do one thing, and that was fix her own flyer.

The Hawk Angel warped in familiar ways. There was always

a bulge near the front. Zuleikah attacked that first, then worked her way back, more quickly than was safe, but she knew the top-middle tended to stay smooth.

"Darlings?" Autumn's voice announced. "Sweet, beautiful, dear people . . ."

This was bad news, obviously.

"You have only three minutes left, so I'm just going to start cycling the air lock in the assumption that you'll all be in your ships and not sitting next to them in three minutes? Okay?"

Thane was at her side. She didn't look at him. She was mad at him for jostling Margot's flyer. "Hold still," he said, "I'll get your helmet on."

It felt intimate and dangerous, but she kept it out of her mind as much as she could as Thane gently lifted her braid from her neck. He eased the helmet over her hair and bobbled it on her forehead. She dropped her tools. She shoved the helmet down and picked the tools back up. Thane did the catch while she resumed smoothing the waveform.

"I think mine is done," Margot said. "Thane, get in with Ki for now. We can't disturb Zuleikah. Zuleikah, how much time do you need?"

As much time as you'll give me, Zuliekah thought; she didn't waste it speaking. She made it to the back on the top and turned her tool to inspect the bottom. Damn, there was a triple-bend ripple.

The sirens alerting everyone that the airlock was cycling became silent as the air left the room. Gravity let go gently below her. Almost done.

"This is it," Andrei said over her helmet speaker. "It's leave now or we have to hold you. The Ratana ship could appear any second."

A large shadow passed over her. Ki's ship. Then Margot's.

Zuleikah slammed the hatch shut and dove into her cockpit with the tools still in hand.

She turned the engine on and followed the others out. She hadn't run a diagnostic check. Either Zuleikah had done her tuning right the first time or she would scatter herself across space in a half-formed warp bubble. Ki sent her coordinates.

A Ratana Royal Naval Cruiser—the Queen's own flagship—blinked into the system, far closer than normal safety protocols would allow.

Ki vanished. Margot vanished. The Royal Navy Cruiser slowly filled the sky. Zuleikah closed her eyes and hit the star drive.

21:
THE CITY

KI FELT THE ADRENALINE DROP OUT OF HER SYSTEM LIKE A VALVE had opened when she saw the other two flyers had entered FTL. They were safe. They'd made it. She closed her eyes for what was meant to be a second, but woke to the warning bells that they were coming into Earth System. It had been a hard, dreamless sleep. Her body must have needed it.

After all that near-death excitement, slipping into Earth Traffic Control felt like putting on an old nightshirt. She knew every hole and loop, and she even knew the waiting patterns. Because they were the way they were supposed to be. She checked for the others. There was Margot. "Margot? Did you see Z in the tunnel?"

Margot's voice came with a yawn. "You're joking, right?"

A second later, Zuleikah's ship appeared. Ki breathed a sigh of relief and threw coordinates and instructions behind her on double-encrypted private channels.

She was bringing her friends home.

They followed, silently. Through the orbital authority and then into the backwater that was North American airspace and finally the Cleveland municipal air authority, which sent demands for final destination and all sorts of warning flags. Earth didn't just let you zoom around like Ratana did once you were in the atmosphere. Too many people. Too many aircraft. They would have to land fast, and pay for parking.

Ki had one advantage: a storage locker.

She registered a flight path, confirming twice that she had ample parking reserved and did not need to pay the "no reserved parking space" fine. She checked on the ships behind her. Did they see they were in a poor country? A poor neighborhood of a poor city in a poor country? Not even the more picturesque part of that neighborhood? She waited for an objection that never came.

It was dingy and small, but it was home. She flew over the river, each bridge an old friend. The commuter trains along the shore were clacking away and the sun was shining bright on metal and water. There was that old graffiti mural of a super-hero eating a hot dog. She wondered how it looked to new eyes. Did they love it instantly like she did when she first saw it? It had faded, and flaked off in places since then.

They landed on the roof of the storage facility. Ki jumped out as her ship was still settling and sprinted to the parking pay machine. It was scratched and covered in a thick layer of graffiti. "I think this is a Warner-Swaysey? Let me see if I can get into it." She missed her scrambler. The others were probably looking around themselves, realizing what a shithole this was, and making plans to bolt. If it had been a Lockway . . . Ki spun through interfaces on her screen. Yes! The poor thing had been busted already. Someone had left an account called "TAGGEDITBIOTCH" with infinite credit.

Ki straightened, relieved.

Margot and Thane were gaping at the street below like it was the Macy's Thanksgiving Parade. Zuleikah stepped out of her flyer and took off her helmet. She looked exhausted, her skin ashy, her green hair sweat-plastered. "I can't ... I didn't see if they followed."

Oh no. No, if they started worrying about that they'd never stop. Anyway, she hadn't had anything to eat since Black Dragon. Ki waved to get everyone's attention. "There's a food market downstairs. How about some lunch? Anyone have credit on them? I've got two trines."

Margot groaned.

"What?"

Margot shook her head like Ki had made a joke and walked away. Oh, that was probably because Margot knew Ki had three trines. Right. You stick around the same people, you have to remember your lies. Ki ran ahead of Margot before she went down the wrong stairs—the ones she was headed toward ended at a locked door at the bottom.

Hot-dog carts and propane stoves on wheelbarrows competed for space on the gravelly grass strip between the parking garage and the road. Ki scanned the wares, trying to decide what people would like, but Margot walked up to the very first cart. "Whatever you have, four of it," she said, and held out her bracelet to transfer credit.

The surly teen behind the cart looked up and got a nasty grin. "Hey it's a Loony."

Ki held her breath. Sure, Margot looked like a Loony. Something about growing up in low gravity made people round-cheeked well past the age they should be. It was a look. But you didn't just say it! What if she hadn't been from Luna? Or was it worse that she was?

Margot didn't respond, anyway. She just shoved rolled flat-breads in paper at each of them.

"What is it?" Thane asked, looking up from the bouquet of paper and food.

"Delicious," Ki said. The odds were good. "Eat it." Please, please, like my town.

Margot dropped onto a milk crate with a sour expression and bit into her roll.

"She'd have to get through border control to get to us," Ki said, obviously not calming anyone. The roll was hot and savory-smelling, but Ki was too nervous to eat.

"It didn't seem that hard to get through," Margot said.

"I bet by the time we finish eating, we'll have a plan." Ki should probably fence her Ratanese gems as soon as she could—unless they triggered an alarm with law enforcement, in which case she should hold off and fence them when they were leaving. Where would they go? Was Zuleikah about to flip out? Or Margot? Ki still remembered the impact of Margot's fist when they busted her out of jail. She needed a plan! And fast, because she didn't know if the Earth would do anything to stop Thane's mom from collecting their asses.

"We should get Thane a solo-flyer," Zuleikah said, matter-of-factly speaking into the uncomfortable silence.

Thane looked at her like she used to look at him, like he'd never seen such a wonderful person.

The two Ratanese stood in the middle of the pedestrian pathway, ignoring several free milk crates to sit on, holding their food like leaky bags of biowaste. They stood out with their desert-dark, smooth skin and their bright, dyed hair. Like a pair of wealthy colonists on vacation, slumming it. People stared as they passed by, shaken out of the ubiquitous "not my problem" field that most city dwellers carried around them.

Ki paced the invisible boundary between their food-vendor's seating area and the next—milk crates giving way to pre-molded stackable seat-boxes in teal and orange. She turned around. "I can think of two options. The first is a pawnbroker not far from here. Which could be handy if we want to divest ourselves of some rocks while we're at it."

"You have rocks?" Margot covered her face with one hand. "Of course you have rocks."

"Relax, Big M. Just a bag of little beads from one of the warehouses I searched for food." Ki patted the pocket on her leg where the two bags sat.

"The gems you stole," Zuleikah pronounced that word far too loudly and clearly for Ki's tastes, "should be more than enough to purchase a flyer for Thane."

"Yeah, that's not how pawnbrokers operate. We'll get a fraction of the value, and the flyer they're selling will be marked up past retail."

Zuleikah frowned. "How does that work?"

"Just trust me, it works. Since time out of mind. No, I think our better bet is the vehicle showroom on Cedar. They always have a solo-flyer in the main window."

Zuleikah frowned. "But if the pawnbroker won't give us enough to purchase a used flyer from their own store, surely it won't be enough to buy a new flyer, either."

"I wasn't thinking about buying anything," Ki said.

Margot wiped sauce from her chin with the back of her hand. "Can you not talk casually about breaking the law on a public street?"

"Come on, M. What else do we got to talk about?"

Margot bit her lip. Just when Ki decided she wasn't going to talk, she said, "I was thinking I should check on my parents." She fiddled with her bracelet. "Not directly. I don't think I can talk to them, yet, but I could check their calendars and my messages."

Zuleikah stared guiltily at her untouched food like it was a dead baby now.

"Will you sit and eat?" Ki was sounding as testy as Margot. She took a deep breath. "Don't go contacting anyone. I'm trying to plan our next move. We're in the city now. Non-paying customers don't get to sit around. Once the food is eaten, we'll have to start walking and stay walking."

Zuleikah frowned. This, of all things, got her to sit down at last. "That sounds needlessly cruel."

"Try living it. We want to have a destination in mind when we leave here."

"Mm!" Thane looked up as they all turned to stare at him. He wiped his mouth. "It really is delicious," he said.

There was something heartbreakingly naive about his expression. Ki peeled back the paper wrapper on her wrap: spiced chickpea mash. It was hot and mustard-sour.

Thane sat down on a crate, legs wide, nothing elegant about him, his hair hanging in a messy tousle as he chowed down and talked with his mouth full. "I think getting me my own flyer is the most important thing. Not just for me, for the whole group. So if I'm chased, I can break away. And then we'll be safer and more mobile." He paused to chew. "What's a pawnbroker?" he asked. "And how is it different from a traditional vehicle merchant?"

He looked excited. The heck. Also, he had a dribble of sauce on his chin. Ki surveyed the gaudy group of them. "Yeah, I have an idea where we can go."

Flying into the crumbling factory reminded Zuleikah a little too much of flying through the destruction of Ratana city, except it was clear this building had not fallen down recently. It had been falling down for a very, very long time. Vines thickened the incomplete traceries that had once held windows. A mature oak tree bowed its head against the remains of skylights. Nothing on Ratana was this old. Earthquakes and wars took care of that.

Ki landed on a clean patch of pavement with yellow stripes, still labeled—in paint! "Landing Zone."

Ki hopped out of her flyer and ran up to a rusted metal door. She squatted in front of it and fiddled with her thin metal tools. Then she pushed it open. The hinges squealed in protest. She paused to wave at an ancient CCTV camera. Could such a thing still be in use? It looked like it came from the era of magnetic film.

Inside they went, into a musty, decayed interior. Zuleikah hadn't realized how afraid she was of an aerial attack until there was a roof over her. Up two flights of metal stairs and down a corridor lined with gaping doorframes, there was a bright blue ceramic door, so sharp a contrast to the weather-chewed walls it seemed to jitter. Ki waved at a camera spot on it and said, "Ki for Sally."

"What does that mean?" Margot crowded close behind Ki. Thane crowded behind Margot. He seemed comfortable, and Zuleikah was oddly annoyed by that.

Ki said, "Sally's always here at this time of day. Um . . . it is a weekday, right? Did anyone check the local calendar?"

The light over the door blinked twice and the door opened with a hermetic pop. It hung slack until Ki pushed her way through.

The room on the other side was full of light and greenery: stacked hydroponic beds in rows under industrial skylights.

A tall woman with a square jaw approached them. "I let you in even though you aren't alone, because I know you wouldn't be stupid enough to bring me trouble." She glared at Ki and then directed her gaze at the rest of them.

"Sally! Pal! I have had such a weird and wild week. I was going to come see you, too. I got a real nice duffle bag. Nylon. Swordbreaker brand, double-knit decoration."

Sally's stern glare softened. "Rip-stop Nylon? Where is it?"

"Um . . . the moon, I think. But I have something even nicer." Ki held out a silken pouch.

Zuleikah recognized the type of bag used to hold raw gemstones for wholesale markets. She wondered if the pebbles inside came from one of her family's mines. A part of her hoped they did.

Ki's friend led them through a forest of vines and leaves hanging from white plastic trays to an old-fashioned wooden counter. "How is Ethan, anyway? Haven't seen him in ages."

Ki muttered something indistinct that might have been "fine." Margot looked at her strangely. Zuleikah wondered what that was about.

Sally took a velvet-lined tray out from under the counter and spilled the gemstones onto it.

They were dull green nodules. Beryls, if they were lucky. Aventurine if they weren't. Zuleikah's family mined a lot of both.

Sally passed a wand over the tray. Instantly the air above it filled with information, including crystal structure and composition. "Tanzanite. Unusual color for it." Sally poked at numbers. "Nice quality. Useful in the crystalline computing industry. This sort of stone isn't found raw in the wild on Earth anymore."

"Huh," Ki sounded fake-casual, "I hadn't realized. So, can you sell them?"

Sally's eyes went straight to Zuleikah. "Any reputable

wholesaler will suspect these came illegally from Ratana and refuse to take them."

"If they were hard to sell," Zuleikah said, "We wouldn't worry about smugglers."

"Relax, I said 'reputable' wholesaler." Sally flicked her hand, clearing the projection. "It's not my usual wheelhouse. How much were you looking to make?"

"Eighteen trines," Zuleikah said, quickly, before Ki could make some ham-fisted guess. She'd heard her mother and her cousins complain endlessly about base unit prices and eighteen trines was a figure frequently quoted as unreasonably low.

Sally took a step back as though the gems had scorched her. "No way."

Did prices change that much on Earth? Zuleikah wished for the first time that she'd paid more attention to the family business. "That's half what we'd get for it through our regular wholesaler. And these gems were taken before processing. There's no holo-mark."

Ki put her arm on the table. "You should really listen to Ratana here. She knows what she's talking about. Born into the business."

"Then have her sell your stones."

"Come on, Sal! Don't be like that. I'll let you give half of it in credit."

Zuleikah was aghast. Credit? With thieves? "Why would we need credit?"

Ki waved her hand at Zuleikah and mouthed "shush."

Sally smirked, slow and easy like she was savoring a sinful treat. "You're planning a heist."

"A big one," Ki said, grinning wide. "Something so grand it's symbolic. Are you in?"

Sally moved to another point on the counter and opened a

drawer. It was full of long rows of Trine coins, like speed bumps. She counted some out. "I'm going to regret this," she said. "But you always give me the very best regrets."

22:
TO PLAN A HEIST

MARGOT WONDERED HOW SHE ALWAYS ENDED UP FEELING LIKE the designated adult. Sally seemed mature, with her crows' feet and floor-sweeping, shapeless gown, but she cackled like a schoolgirl when Ki asked, "So, where would you go to steal a solo-flyer in this town?"

"There's an assembly plant just outside the city. Why stop at one?"

"I dunno . . . sounds like a big target that's probably got nothing around it but security. Oh! What about a shipment? Do they send the flyers out to retailers in batches? We could hijack a train!"

Sally cupped her face with her hands. "Oh! A train heist! I've always wanted to watch one of those."

Could they trust this woman? Margot quietly tapped into the public information network. First, she checked her messages back on Luna. Twenty messages from her parents with increasingly panicked titles. "Ratana?!?" "Police said you are on your way?" "Where are you!" "Answer please if you are alive."

Well, not exactly a surprise. Quickly she sent a short message that she was okay and following up a job lead.

It wasn't entirely wrong.

She didn't look at the rest of her messages. She didn't know how to check if there was a warrant out for her arrest or if the queen of Ratana was on her way to Earth. So she scanned for solo-flyer retailers. Motorcars Spaceflight was nearby. It proudly advertised itself as one of the largest and oldest vehicle warehouses in the city. The inventory was publicly available for potential shoppers, along with showroom hours and (legal) points of entry. She passed the info to Zuleikah, who nodded and projected it in front of one of the grey chicken-wire-laced windows.

"How about this place?" Zuleikah asked.

Ki and Sally immediately descended on the display, not mourning their more ambitious dreams. Good.

"They have two ShadowKats and a brand-new Legacy 150 in stock!" Sally pointed. "I like what I've read about the Legacy."

The Legacy was steel blue and had sweeping fins reminiscent of the Hawk Angel's wings, but more shark-like. Margot was not surprised when Ki jumped up and down and said, "Oh, that one. Thane, look at this. It is *you*."

Thane frowned and flipped back and forth between the varied images. "What's the difference?"

Ki bounced. "It has *fins*!"

"It's the more expensive model," Zuleikah said. "It's supposed to need less re-tuning."

"Are we really doing this?" Margot asked. "We could get a hotel room, rest, take showers. We just got some money."

"Not enough," Ki said. "We need to think about our future."

It was too much like something Margot's father would have said. She felt a tight squeeze in her chest. "So, your plan, to be responsible adults about this, is for us to steal enough to finance our next caper?"

"Sustainable thievery," Sally said. She brushed Ki's wild hair back from her forehead with a maternal smile. When she looked at anyone else, her expression was cold, all business. Margot wondered if her own mother softened when looking at her, but it must be something you could only see from the side.

"I'll underwrite this project," Sally said. "In exchange for the other two flyers in the showroom. That seems fair, doesn't it?"

Ki said, "Steal three ships and only keep one? That sounds kind of dumb to me."

"You haven't seen what I have to invest." Sally led Ki down the long, windowed wall to a steel-banded and riveted door. Sally made a gesture which opened a cover on a retinal reader. What would require that level of security when she had a plain wooden drawer full of Trines?

Sally tugged the heavy door open. It was a dark space. Weirdly, a white string hung in the middle of it. Sally tugged this. There was a strange, spring-like sound and a buttery light flooded the space.

Ki squealed and ran in. Margot approached more cautiously. The room smelled pleasant, organic, like oil and wood. Various shelves and bins lined the walls of a long, narrow closet. It was a stock room!

Ki bounced on her toes and dove to peek under the bottom shelves and then jumped up again. "Look at all of this!'

Sally handed Margot a wire basket like you'd have at a market. Ki plucked it from her before Margot could think what to do with it.

The basket tinged and twanged as Ki threw things into it. She squealed and swept an entire shelf's contents into the basket.

"Hey," Sally said. "I said I'd underwrite the heist, not your entire life of crime."

Ki whined, "But if we're going to be intergalactic outlaws, we're going to need all the jammers we can carry."

Margot patiently pulled the odd flower-shaped disks out of the basket and put them back on the shelf.

"A whole roll of contact circuits." Ki's eyes were comically large as she took a cylinder of silver tape down from a high shelf. "Can I have this?"

"You may have two feet of it," Sally said. "And be grateful."

Margot left them to it and went back to the main room.

Thane was projecting images of flyers over his hand, oblivious to the drawer full of money his rear end was resting on.

Margot stopped and turned around to address Sally, "You trust us in here?"

"I don't have to," she said. "My security is microbial."

Margot wasn't sure what that meant, and wanted to remain ignorant.

Zuleikah was sitting cross-legged on the floor, eating a carrot. She glanced up. "Give me your bracelet."

"Um . . . why?"

"You're not using it."

Margot made the unlock gesture on the back of her data bracelet. "I still want to know why you want it."

"Increasing our private network security. For the heist." Zuleikah said.

Zuleikah was absorbed in what she was doing. Margot couldn't help asking, though, "Can you tell if they're after us? I mean, if anyone is after us?"

Zuleikah shrugged.

Not very comforting. "Have you contacted your parents? It was pretty dangerous back in your hometown. Are your family all okay?"

Zuleikah frowned. "Best to hit the shop during shopping hours. More points of entry."

"You really aren't worried about your family?" *Tell me I shouldn't be worried about mine,* Margot thought.

Zuleikah rubbed her eye and finally looked right at Margot. "My family . . . we're sort of a group of strangers who have invested stock in each other." Her eyes dropped. A tear was trembling, trapped in her lashes. "Anyway, it'd take an ansible transmission. The royal fleet could be waiting for us to give Thane's position away."

It was impossible to track ships once they went FTL, but if the Ratana fleet had telemetry on their flyers as they were entering star drive, or if they just guessed Sol system, it was an obvious choice . . .

Zuleikah turned back to her displays. "There'll be alarms and anti-theft devices. On the heist, I mean. I'll be the lead on that. I'll hack from afar while you three walk in and get the physical ships."

Margot got it. Worrying about a heist wasn't worrying at all in comparison to their other problems. She decided to play along. "If the store is open, though, there'll be people. Not just bots. Sales staff and other customers. We can't hack people."

Thane leaned over to see them more clearly, where they were sitting on the floor below him. "I can do that." He looked surprised at his own words.

"No one can hack people," Margot said.

Thane turned off the projections. "It's what I was trained to do. Politics is the art of influencing people. I can attract attention by being something I've been before: a wealthy shopper." He tilted his head back, like he was posing for an inspirational poster.

Margot rolled her eyes. "Shoppers don't attract attention in a shop. They're like part of the decor."

"You think so? Whenever I went out to buy something, shop clerks fell over themselves."

Did he even see himself? His second-hand ship folk environment suit and a smudge of dirt on his nose? "We aren't on Ratana. No one here will recognize you as a prince on sight."

"A prince!"

Sally popped out of the closet door, her hands clasped in front of her with delight. "Now it makes sense. That's how you got Ratanese gems before processing."

"Uh . . ." Margot felt her brain seize up like an overheated gun. How did one ask politely if someone could unhear what they just heard?

Sally didn't look like she needed to be dissuaded from calling the police, however. She hurriedly dragged Ki from the storeroom, took a few things out of her basket, shut the door, and walked around Thane. "We'll have to clean you up. Polish you back into wealthy shopper form."

"I would like fresh clothes," Thane said, touching his fingertips lightly to his chest.

Sally grabbed his wrist. "I've always wanted my very own life-size Ken doll. Come with me."

Ki sulked with the shopping basket hugged in front of her. "Sally's a cheapskate," she said. "Did you see all that stuff?"

"Don't be greedy," Margot said.

"Like I *can* now that she's locked up the treasure room!"

Margot followed Thane and Sally back to the dilapidated part of the factory.

The room had rounded corners. A row of high waxy windows stood over a narrow ledge. Half of the floor was raised a step. It was tiled in tiny white squares with a row of beige squares marking the raised edge. It was an odd room that clearly had some specialized use in the past, left cast in all that ceramic and brown-glazed brick.

On the raised platform there was a desk and a folding screen of carved sandalwood. A pink sparkly scarf hung from the top.

Sally went behind the screen and brought out a fat tackle box streaked with various pink and purple smudges. "I don't have Ratanese gem-dust colors for your eyes, but I held my own in makeup back in my clubbing days." She set the box on the desk and opened a drawer, laying dishes of colored powder out for Thane to look at. Then she opened the top drawer of the desk and drew out a seemingly endless array of scarves, filmy little squares that expanded like smoke as they were freed. "That's how I met Ethan, actually, and Ki through him. Clubbing. You should have seen him! He was a human disco ball some nights. You could hardly look at him. Have you met him? I assume you must have, since you know Ki."

Margot remembered Ki holding that bundle of "Deceased's Belongings" and held her tongue.

Sally sighed in reminiscence, hugging a silver shawl. She put it down. "He's been sick lately, poor dear. Let's see if we can't make him proud." She looked Thane up and down and vanished behind the screen again. There was the screech of hangers on a rack. "Back in the day I had to do a lot of quick-changes. For business. Here we go." She came back with several garments draped over her arm. "These are my most Ratanese styles, I think. You'll want to be the judge of that, of course." She dropped the heavy stack of fabric on his arm. "Try them on, we'll wait."

Thane looked at Margot like he was hoping she would save him. She shrugged. "I don't . . ." he began. "I mean . . . I was just getting used to looking . . . messy."

"It's for the team," Margot said. She gestured forward.

He looked terrified. "Will you . . . um . . . can you see me back there?"

"We won't even try to look," Sally said, and then turned to wink at Margot.

Thane ducked behind the screen.

Margot grabbed Sally's arm and pulled her away from the screen as the older woman craned her neck to peek. "Will this outfit be deducted from your underwriting?"

"Only if you don't return it." Sally's eyes narrowed. "You'd better return it. I charge for emotional value."

"He'll have the money to buy something for himself after the heist," Margot said.

Thane popped out from behind the panel, wearing a red silk belted robe. "You mean I'll get to pick my own clothes?" Sally looked very excitedly at his bare chest.

Yeesh. He really had needed to be rescued. Margot held up her hands and backed out of the room, "I'll leave you to it."

Zuleikah was where she'd left her, dragging images in the air. The green-topped stub of the carrot lay beside her. Ki sat on the old counter, dangling her feet and watching. She had the twitchy look of someone unused to waiting on someone else.

Margot realized that she didn't feel twitchy at all. She hadn't for a while. She was so used to being anxious she forgot to notice when it stopped.

She sat down next to Zuleikah and gestured at the two bracelets in her lap. "About done with that?"

Zuleikah nodded. "The public data network here is a lot less secure than on Ratana."

"Not having a brutal dictatorship does that," Margot said.

Zuleikah shrugged. "There's a rival dealership across the street from Motorcars, and a public parking lot adjacent to that. I can park close to the property line and break into the rival dealership's network, relay my attack on Motorcars through there."

"Sneaky," Ki said. "And kinda evil. I like it."

Zuleikah held Margot's bracelet up for her to take. "If the information I've gotten on the make and model of their security system is correct, I should have no trouble unlocking the flyers so you can fly them out of the showroom."

"We'll need energy," Margot said. "They won't keep them charged up, but they'll have a system to charge them quickly. Someone will have to find that."

Ki hopped down. "I'll break all the physical locks and Margot can get the energy to the flyers."

Margot wasn't sure how she'd do that, but how hard could it be? It was the sort of thing stock clerks did. "Then Ki and I get two flyers and Thane will be in the third, test-driving," Margot said. "This is going to work. We each have a role and we'll all be playing to our strengths. I almost don't believe it."

Ki cupped her face in her hands. "I love that you guys look like you're having fun, too. For once."

Zuleikah snorted. She stood, putting her bracelet back on. "This is not fun," she said, "this is the joy a suicide feels after jumping."

23:
THE VERY BEST REGRETS

ZULEIKAH GOT UP FIRST THE NEXT DAY AND LEFT WHILE THE others were still sleeping. Ki had felt it would look most natural, and ensure a good spot, for Zuleikah to park in the public lot at the start of morning rush hour. Zuleikah paid cash for her spot to avoid the transaction being traced. She had enough time before the others would get there to walk to a nearby coffee shop.

Earth had tremendous food. So far, at least, it had all been amazing. The coffee shop did not disappoint, with a display of row upon row of delicate pastries and fruits and sandwiches. She didn't even know what half the things on display were. Most didn't look edible.

A pale-skinned man leaned on the counter and smiled at her bemusedly. "What are you in the mood for?"

Zuleikah scowled and pointed at random. He wrapped the pastry in paper. She didn't even see what it was until she was back in her flyer.

It was a seashell of flaky pastry, buttery and sweet. She pulled it slowly apart, reveling in the different textures, brittle to chewy. She needed to find out what it was called and order ten more as soon as possible.

This was living. This was why she didn't get along with her mother. It wasn't that the life her mother wanted for her was boring—it was *small*. It was all tied up in how this inner circle felt about that inner circle and gathering numbers in an account like life had a high score. Everything was designed to make it easy for her, so that anyone with half a brain could succeed in her place, but she didn't have half a brain! She had intelligence and she wanted to really use it. Really experience life. She thought that had meant something like a romance with Thane, but that had been small thinking. It meant affecting things, going places and being affected by them, accepting the gross smelly unhygienic parts.

Zuleikah felt like writing a poem or something.

But first she had to start infiltrating the vehicle showroom's network. She checked the time. A half-hour spent indulging in sweets wasn't so bad. This network would be easy to crack for a hard-boiled Ratanese hacker. Earth didn't even have DNA-encoded data drops!

So Zuleikah licked her fingers, thought about the exotic boy in the coffee shop, and fired up her sniffing bots.

She expected to find an exploit before she took the lid off her coffee.

She didn't. The coffee tasted pretty much the same as coffee did on Ratana, which was disappointing. She checked the bots and activated more.

An alert showed that Ki was on her way.

The bots still hadn't found a way into the private secure network. What the hell was wrong with Earth? Did businesses have tighter security than the government here?

A long, clear bubble stopped in the road, disgorging passengers, including Ki, who wore a blonde wig with a glittery pink scarf over it and huge round sunglasses.

If that was intended to be inconspicuous, Ki had a lot to learn. Zuleikah watched her walk to the end of the block and cross the street. The network was supposed to be cracked by now.

The fantastic pastry became a cold lump in Zuleikah's belly as she began, seriously, to worry.

Ki stepped off the bus and touched Sally's scarf to make sure it was still secure. Also, she touched it because that's what a celebrity would do, right? They were always lightly brushing their coiffure or their collar, to draw attention to it. Ki felt decadent, riding the commuter bus, which smelled as clean as a strip of tape fresh off a dispenser and whose doors sealed with a sound like lips closing.

Zuleikah's flyer was in place, conspicuous to Ki's eyes despite the coat of white chalk-paint and the fake, printed spoiler designed to make it look like a later, less valuable model.

This was going to be easy. Ki walked briskly, enjoying the autumnal air, savoring the job like a dinner still in the oven. The best part was going to be flying out the front of the dealership. She tried not to ogle the building proscenium with its Romanesque columns and giant's doors. Mums and boxwood trimmed into balls lined the walk.

Down the street and behind the showroom was the service department entrance. Human-sized and dull, but still lined with perfectly round bushes and that savory boxwood smell.

A steady traffic of vehicles zipped in and out of the building. Ki walked straight forward, like she had no interest in the building at all, until she saw her opening and jumped into the shadow of a cargo bot. She scrambled along the line of bushes and into the garage entrance, checked herself and darted to the left, where there was, as the online blueprints had promised, a supply closet. The closet was locked, but like supply closets everywhere, it had a stack of neglected supplies outside of it to hide behind.

Ki's job was to unlock the energy control room, which was on the other side of a glass-walled office, and then make her way to a staff entrance at the back of the garage bay to let Margot in.

Piece of cake. She had sixteen door circuits in her pocket, plus her picks. She stuffed her wig, sunglasses, and scarf in her shirt and made her way to a coat rack to steal a pair of coveralls.

She sank into the row of coats while a mechanic walked by, whistling. A hovering bot followed him, probably a nanny-cam for the customers to watch. Ki kept her head down until she could no longer hear whistling.

She tucked her hair into a ball cap she found on the ground, slipped on a greasy overcoat, and walked past the office window like she had every right to be there. She only looked back to see if anyone was in the office when she was safely behind a parked passenger car. The office held one guy, his back to the window, reclined in his chair. A display in front of him showed camera angles of the entire shop. He was letting a supervisor bot watch them while he watched a drama, something with puffy clothes.

Bot security was a good sign. Easy to fool so long as the bots didn't catch her face. The security companies made you pay extra for body-language recognition, and most places figured rightly that the presence was enough to deter the casual trespasser. Mostly places only paid for the tagging and nagging of their employees. The bastards.

Ki was almost to the power room. Another mechanic walked

by. She bent over the exposed engine of a passenger car and pretended to fiddle with things. He continued on his way. She went to the door, one hand already on her stack of stickers.

She stopped dead, staring at the metal handle and lever, deadbolt and sliding card reader. What a hunk of outdated junk! With a giant Greek temple of a front entrance, this place had a door from the 1970s.

And she had no idea how to crack it.

Margot dropped behind a dumpster. Why was she the only one who had to take a commuter train and walk two miles? Her back, knees and feet were killing her from the gravity and her bowels were cramping from the effort. She could see the back of the vehicle dealership and the door Ki would soon open. At any moment, now, Sally would drop Thane off at the front door in a rented luxury car.

Margot sent a text message to Ki to let her know she was in position. They had agreed on text-only communication. That way, there would be no sound to be overheard.

So, it was a shock when Ki's voice responded, hot and angry. "I can't get the door open."

Margot moved away from the dumpster—it smelled awful. She leaned against a fence and looked through foliage at the door she was supposed to go through. "What do you mean you can't get it open?"

"I mean I can't get it open. I don't have the right tools. I need a card key. I can't even tell if it's magnetic or holographic. This is . . . this is like trying to hijack a carrier pigeon with a radio."

"What can I do?"

"I don't know."

Margot didn't like the helpless, young sound of that. She'd put all her trust in Ki being a brilliant thief. "Where are you?"

"In front of the stupid door!"

"Out in the open? Talking to me?"

Ki groaned. "Just . . . just give me a minute. I'm so mad I could spit."

Margot bit her lip and called Zuleikah. "Hey, Ki's in trouble and . . ."

Zuleikah tersely cut her off, "Can't talk."

"What? Why? We need to get this door open."

There was a long pause. Zuleikah's voice cracked when she spoke, "I still haven't gotten into the network."

"WHAT?"

"They keep blocking me. These keys worked on Ratana government sites. They work on Earth government sites! I don't know how this is possible!"

Margot breathed hard through her nose. "Keep trying," she said, and set her communications to silent.

She could see the door. She had no idea how the lock worked. She hadn't paid attention to that portion of the planning. That had been mostly Ki and Sally talking over each other during dinner in the cavernous former manufacturing floor of Sally's quasi-legal factory home. Margot could picture the long, slanting light that came in from broken skylights. She could smell the savory hot soup. Sally's bowls were thick, handmade ceramic. Margot recalled the feel in her hands and that the one Thane used was the nicest. She could not recall a single thing about the door locks.

There was no time to worry about the door Ki had to get through. She had her own door to get through. It had a sensor eye over it. It had a plain handle. It probably measured people and if they matched the roster, unlocked.

It also had a wooden frame. Wood. Expensive, fancy . . . brittle stuff. Margot felt herself get a bad idea.

She snuck from the fence to behind a bush to behind a sign next to the door. She could see the frame clearly, and a metal plate covering the part with the lock. Could she force it?

Margot had assisted in the kidnapping of a prince. She had assisted in escaping a spaceship with living families on board and flagrantly blasted her way out of a space station. Somehow, though, breaking a door felt like a hard line to cross. She would be choosing to commit a crime, on her own, independently.

She zipped up her jacket and wiped the sweat from her hands on her knees. It was high time she stopped being the gang chaperone.

She put her foot on the wall next to the lock plate. She gripped the handle with both hands. She breathed out, slowly, flexing her grip and making sure it was solid. She adjusted her stance.

She yanked as hard on that door as she could, grunting with the effort and kicking the wall.

The door . . . banged against its frame. Loudly. It otherwise did not move.

Well, crap.

Thane wore a broad-shouldered blue robe that was fastened with two twisted scarves in complimentary colors. His eyes were once again heavily painted, though the makeup felt more comfortable than he was used to. Lighter. He'd picked colors for a member of the upper gentry, but not too important. The darker tones favored by independent men who held jobs. He wondered if the others noticed and appreciated the subtlety.

"Break a leg," Sally said, lowering the car to the ground. She looked back at him expectantly.

Thane realized no one was going to open the door for him. He bowed to her and got out. His hair immediately blew in his face. He batted it back, but strands stuck to still-wet makeup.

The entire front wall of the establishment was glass, behind this artificial temple entrance in stone. It was a self-contradiction of a building, fragile and stolid. But then that seemed appropriate for Earth, with all her jumbled history.

Sally's car lifted up and away, leaving him alone.

His knees were shaking. It was hard to walk forward. Was Earth's gravity higher? He recalled hearing it was.

Ask to see the Legacy. Ask for a test drive. Act snobby. Those were his instructions.

How did one act snobby?

The glass doors slid obsequiously back. Two sales reps and a receptionist all turned to look at Thane. The receptionist, a very dark man with muscular shoulders shown off by his wide, pale collar, jumped up and ran forward, a hand extended. "Welcome, Your Excellency. It is an honor! Regan! Molly! Come help this man. This is the prince of Ratana!"

24:
HOW THANE GOT HIS RIDE

ZULEIKAH KNEW EVERYONE ELSE WAS IN PLACE. THEY WERE ALL waiting on her. And then she got the call from Margot that Ki was in trouble.

She'd given up on the competitor dealership and tried hacking Motorcars directly. How was this so hard? The government . . .

The government! She'd already found a backdoor in local law enforcement. Perhaps there was a law enforcement back door into the showroom. She felt stupid for not thinking of it before!

"So," Ki's voice came from her radio. "I'm hiding under a car now. If anyone has any idea how to defeat a Kryptolock 2000 please send those ideas my way. Any time. No rush. Oh, also there are camera bots flitting all around this place and at any time a real human may spot me. But still—no pressure. Take your time."

Margot's voice then. "Uh . . . brute force isn't working on the external door. I'm hiding now, too."

Ki again, "Zuleikah? Zuleikah, you're online, right? Run a search on this door."

"Busy," Zuleikah said.

"Come on, Zuleikah! You're not cowering from sight. Makes searching a little easier for you."

Yes! There was a backdoor for law enforcement. It was limited, but it was there. Zuleikah set about giving herself a police account. An idea popped into her head. "Camera bots?"

"Three that I've seen, plus a stationary supervisor."

"The bots have to be able to go through doors on their own if they get separated from the people they are watching."

There was a weird sound that Zuleikah feared was Ki kissing her radio receiver. "You're a genius."

"Not yet I'm not." She had to find a way to get the police account to disable the security lock-down on showroom vehicles. So far it looked like it only had access to log files and security cameras.

Oh, cameras. "Let me know when you want those cameras to go dark," Zuleikah said.

Ki rolled onto her back. Catching a camera bot without attracting attention was going to be tricky.

Three hovering cameras followed the repair shop staff around, a foot or two above and three feet behind, more or less. Sometimes bot and employee would get separated, if a repair guy ducked through a door quickly or went inside a vehicle. Sure enough, the doors opened to let the bots follow.

One guy kept going back and forth to a break room. He was keeping tabs on something in there, maybe.

Every third time or so, his camera bot would be separated from him for a second before it activated the door to let itself through.

Ki went back to the coat rack and got a jacket big enough to fit over the camera bot.

"Annnd . . . now!" she said, jumping and throwing the jacket. It hit but did not envelop the camera, which wobbled drunkenly but held its position in front of the door. Ki picked up the jacket. The door opened. The repair guy gaped at her, two steaming mugs in his hands.

Ki threw the jacket at him, then, and pushed him further into the break room.

He fought the jacket off and onto the floor, spraying rich-smelling coffee everywhere. "The hell?!"

"I just need your camera bot," Ki said. She kissed him on the nose. That distracted him long enough to nab the bot. She held it to her chest. The man was staring at her. He was tall, rangy, with a weather-beaten face. His coveralls were splattered and his fingers dripping.

He had no reason not to call for help.

"I am really, really sorry about this," Ki said, and smacked him in the face with the camera bot.

Thane shook all over. His hands were sweaty, he was sure. People were watching him. People who could snap a photo or send a video to their friends tagged "Prince Thane of Ratana." His mother wouldn't even have to come. She'd call the local authorities to collect him. He was pretty sure he saw someone peeking in from a back room.

"What can we help you with? Please, let us know. Would you like to look around?"

Stiffly, he nodded.

No! He was supposed to ask about the Legacy. Still he found

himself led to a table, offered a seat and a cup of tea.

The three solo flyers were in the front window, sharing a platform covered in blue felt.

"Are you interested in recreational craft, or is this for a business use?"

"Re . . . uh . . . rec . . ." His mouth was not working. This was terrible. The one thing that they had asked him to do—that he had assured them he could do!

He felt the twinge in his wrist that meant he had a text message. "Excuse me," he said. That came easily, at least. He shielded his palm with his other hand.

The sales people were going to wonder why he was being so standoffish and why he was checking a message. How long before he was on the local news?

The message was from Zuleikah. "Can't unlock ships. The sales reps should have a key on their person. Look for a grey or silver ball about the size of a kumquat."

What was a kumquat?

Was she asking him to steal something from the sales reps? Something in their pockets, maybe? The woman sitting next to him had small pockets over her hips, flaring out slightly to accentuate her shape.

"Is everything all right, Your Highness? You look distressed."

Thane licked dry lips. Lie. Didn't he remember how to lie? He cleared his throat. "Yes, my . . . my entourage was supposed to meet me here. I don't know if I can proceed without them."

Good, good—the sales rep relaxed her shoulders. She was buying it. "Well," she said, "It won't hurt to review your options. We can get a jump on business before they get here. What are you looking for?"

"Legacy," he said. He cleared his throat again and straightened his spine. "I was interested in the Legacy 150 you have in your window."

$$\lightning$$

Margot spent five minutes terrified under a shrub, her every nerve screaming, her joints like ice. How had no one come running when she'd yanked on that door? Was there an alarm on it? A silent alarm? The police could already be on their way.

Her bracelet buzzed. A text from Zuleikah. "Alarm intercepted. Don't do that again."

Margot rested her head against the fence. Like she was going to do that again. But what could she *do*?

Ki yanked open the door, leaned out, scanning, and found Margot. "Get in here," she said.

You didn't have to tell Margot twice! She ran for it.

Instead of diving for cover like Margot expected, Ki led the way straight across the open shop floor. She had a bundled coat in her hands. Margot quickened her pace to stay on her heels. "What . . . where is everyone?"

"One guy I knocked out. The others are ogling the foreign prince. Which is good for us."

"Wait—someone recognized Thane? We're toast."

"Let's worry about that after the toaster pops. Here's the power control room. Watch my trick!" Ki banged the bundled coat against the door. Something inside the fabric made a metallic thud. She banged again and the door opened. Ki stepped aside and extended her arm. "You got five seconds and you might—"

Ki finished her sentence after the loud clang of Margot throwing a metal can into the doorway. "—want to prop it."

You didn't have to tell a former stock clerk to prop a door. This part Margot knew how to do. She found the inventory interface, located the proper control and ordered energy dispersal to all showroom models. The system quickly charged vehicles on display without inconveniencing test-drivers. Ki hovered behind Margot while she entered commands. "There," Margot said. "That's done." She turned. "So, how is the rest of the plan? When do we break into the show room?"

Ki bit her lip. "Yeah, so . . . Thane still hasn't gotten this fob that we need to disable the lock."

"A fob? It's a physical thing?"

"The salespeople have them."

Margot felt a headache starting. "And you're waiting on Thane to slight-of-hand these fobs out of the pockets of professional sales representatives?"

"You say that like it won't work."

Margot quickly entered a command to stop the charging in ten minutes, even if it wasn't complete, so the launch locks could disengage. "Come with me," she said. "And put on your wig."

Thane walked around the Legacy. He patted it and tried to pay attention and look interested as the sales rep talked about power and speed and options. He glanced down at his hand to check the time. She asked, "Am I boring you?"

"Hm? Oh, no. I . . . It's a fine machine." Curse his mother insisting that the heads-up option on his implant be disabled. He couldn't so much as check the time without showing the world. "Can I sit in it?"

"Oh absolutely!" Her grin was ravenous. She popped the canopy open. "Just sit right down. Feel the upholstery."

The interior of the Legacy smelled lovely—like lilac and leather. The seat was long; like the ShadowKat's it was designed to be straddled and leaned over, not sat upright in like the Hawk Angel. Thane gathered up his robe against his legs and stepped over the seat. It felt clean and smooth and comfortable, but vulnerable. He didn't like having his back exposed.

He felt over the controls. Here was the recessed disk Zuleikah had described for manual steering. Here was the manual attitude control. Here was where the display would appear when it was turned on. Here was the spot to touch to turn it on.

The display did not come up. He looked at the rep. "Where's the control display?"

"It's not powered. We keep our showroom ships uncharged so that there is no wear on the systems."

"I want to see the display."

The sales rep tilted her head, her eyes narrowing while her smile stayed the same. Thane recognized the expression from people trying to tell his mother things she didn't want to hear. "It's a standard display. If you are really interested in purchasing, I could charge the ship up for a test drive."

"Yes. I am interested. I am committed. I want this ship."

Had he spoken too quickly? Too enthusiastically? Her smile dimmed a bit. She stepped back and held out her hand. "Perfect. Let's sit down and sign some initial papers. Just a statement of your intent to buy, in case, oh, your entourage arrives and disagrees?"

She waved toward the table. Documents popped into existence on it. What would happen, if he signed his name? He imagined his mother receiving an alert, her military swooping in, the Earth government politely complying.

Thane held still. When the sales rep put her hand on his arm, he stared at it until she let go. "Don't I get a test drive, first?"

"It takes a few minutes to charge the ship. Let's use the time. You don't want to take too long on all these silly details."

"I can wait."

"Of course." Broader smile. "You do have your operator's license?"

Thane bit his lip. He had no license to operate any kind of vehicle. "Um. Yes. Yes, I do. Do you need to see it?"

"Does your entourage have it?" There was something knowing in her eyes, for certain now. He had gone from a bigwig to the son of a bigwig in her estimation. Someone who might not have authority to buy. He was losing control.

"They'll be here any minute." Thane tried to return to the Legacy, but the sales rep stood in his way.

"Shouldn't we wait for your entourage, Your Majesty?"

"It's 'Highness', and no, I really want to do the test drive now." He resisted the urge to check the time again. He knew it was past the time he was supposed to already be in the air. He also had no idea how to get hold of the kumquat-thing. Or even get them to show him the kumquat-thing. "Do you . . . have to do something so I can fly it?"

"Why don't you sit down, sign the paper, and then I promise we'll get you in the air right away."

Thane could see no way out of it. He let her guide him back to his chair. He started reading the contract as slowly as he could without looking like an idiot. No doubt the sales rep had an implant that tracked customer's eye movements. He'd read about those.

A door banged open and a voice shouted, "Darling! That's where you are!"

Margot strode across the show room wearing Sally's pink scarf, Ki in tow.

You could have knocked Thane over with a puff of air. Margot dropped into his lap, draping her arm around his shoulders. "I thought you meant the service part of the dealership! Don't you already own a solo-flyer? I mean, that's what you drove to mama's soiree last week!"

"Excuse me, who are you?" The sales rep spun in place, glaring at Ki, who backed up away from her. "Who is *this*?" she added, like she considered Ki something less than human.

"That's my driver, darling," Margot said. "Don't mind her."

Margot was speaking in a ridiculous accent, like her teeth were clenched in back. Thane flushed with many levels of embarrassment. "Get off my lap," he whispered.

"Of course, darling." Margot kicked her crossed legs over, getting up in the showiest way possible. "He's shy, the silly dear." She waved her arms around dramatically. "Arranged marriages, you know. Dating is all hush-hush."

"Please stop," Thane said.

"Hey!" the other sales rep called out, reaching toward Ki, who was crawling in to one of the ShadowKats on display.

Ki tossed something at Thane. He caught it against his chest.

A little silver ball attached to a ring by a bit of chain. Margot was already crawling into the second ShadowKat when he realized what he was holding.

The fob.

"Don't you dare!" The sales rep physically blocked him, her hands on his chest. "You aren't a real prince, are you?"

"Actually, I am," he said, and pushed her out of his way.

There was a sound of breaking glass. Ki had decided to fly through the window. Right. He tripped on his robe, nearly dropped the fob, and then got tangled in his skirt getting back into the Legacy.

This time, though, when he touched the spot on the dash, a control screen sprang into being over the burl wood. He touched the controls Zuleikah had told him to, in the order he'd rehearsed.

His stomach rocked as the ship lifted off. He could hardly hear the alarm sirens and shouts of the showroom staff over his own beating heart.

He barely knew how to fly this thing. They had better not be chased.

25:
THE CHASE

ZULEIKAH GOT ALL THE POLICE ALERTS AS HER FAKE ACCOUNT WAS "the closest officer to the scene" and she quickly replied that she was in pursuit and had the situation in hand, but there were still private security companies and video logs to deal with and she had just broadcast her location. It wasn't going to take long for an AI to flag that location as the source of lots of suspicious network activity.

She looked up from a report of a broken store window to see, well, the store window opposite her was completely gone. Ki, Margot, and Thane were in the air.

She pulled the plug on her many strings of communication. Alarms rang out, instantly, and metal bars descended over the gaping hole in the building—and over the intact windows as well.

Zuleikah ran nonsense data over the flyer's scratch memory, erased it twice, and then exited her flyer. This was the most absurd part of the plan. Calmly, she started walking around the block. She had to stay until the others were clear. If she flew off after them, she'd effectively be a tail. This seemed like a great plan the night before but now it felt like dancing on a trap door.

She didn't think she could eat with her stomach clenched, but she stopped at the coffee shop again, anyway. The same man was behind the counter and he gave her a knowing smile. "No one can resist our croissants," he said. "Another?"

She nodded.

The plan was to rendezvous outside of the city at another abandoned factory. She had the coordinates memorized to keep the Hawk Angel memory completely blank. Nothing that could be used against anyone. Also, none of them were to use public traffic control. She would have to be on the lookout, constantly, for vehicles that would not be looking out for her. And she had to get back to her flyer without arousing suspicion.

Living a more authentic life was stressful!

She looked down at the beautiful pastry, fat and indolent on a ceramic plate. "Um . . . could I get a dozen, actually? In a box?"

"No problem," he said.

There was something, Zuleikah was sure, innately trustworthy about someone carrying a pastry box.

Despite the cool temperature of the day, Zuleikah sweated profusely all the way back to her flyer. There were police flyers in the area now. They were black and white, like the police cars in old movies. She hadn't thought Earth actually did that. The uniformed personnel were more drab than on Ratana, too—a watered down version of the blue and grey of police in old-fashioned movies. She allowed herself a few glances at them. Would an innocent person stare? They would. Innocents gawked. She opened her flyer, but didn't enter. She stared at the broken window, pastry box in hand, until a police officer saw her and said, "Move along."

Zuleikah ducked her head to hide her relief and closed her canopy as quickly as possible.

She joined air traffic control heading south, toward a suburb in a different direction than their rendezvous. It was the most popular direction for traffic at this time of day. After a few miles, she dialed out to drop into a fly-through auto-wash. Two passes through removed the white chalk-paint, leaving her flyer its original, badass black. She tore off the gooey remains of the printed starch spoiler and checked a passive police band listener. So much chatter, and most of it about her and her friends. Police had an astonishing habit of not saying what direction they were traveling.

Zuleikah descended into the abandoned car factory. A scrap of fence here and there and security towers poking up through thick vines marked the insane extent of its lands. Earth used to use up its green space like it had an unlimited supply.

The main building still stood—a part of it, anyway. There was a large hanger entrance, half hidden by a stand of scraggly pine trees.

A tiny figure ran out and jumped around, waving her hands overhead. It was Ki, fluttering a tiny pink piece of fabric. Perhaps she thought the visual cue would be useful. Zuleikah's flyer had already mapped the terrain and kept a steady count of how far away every object was as she guided the ship down and into the building.

Four ShadowKats in a row, and one Legacy. If it weren't for the indifferently grassy floor and rust-stained walls, it would look like another vehicle showroom. Zuleikah parked at the end of the row, on the other side of the Legacy.

She still expected sirens as she stepped out into the forest-smelling cool.

Margot sat on the nose of her flyer. She glanced up from her display only briefly as Zuleikah approached, but she smiled when she did.

Sally was frowning, inspecting her pink sparkly scarf against a phosphere.

Ki ran up and hugged Zuleikah hard around the waist. "We did it! Our first real heist as a gang!" Ki let go. "Well, our first that didn't involve trying to save our own lives."

"What a difference that makes." Margot stretched.

"The cops will almost certainly ID you all." Sally folded her scarf and tucked it into a duffle bag. "Now could you all skedaddle? I don't want you here when my chop crew arrives."

Margot touched Zuleikah's arm. "Don't look so freaked out. The company will get insurance money for the stolen flyers. No one was hurt. No one will have any reason to chase after us."

No one to care. She must have looked sad. Margot hugged her and she found, to her surprise, that she was hugging back.

Ki coughed and moved away, awkwardly feigning interest in an ancient chain hoist.

Thane jogged up, his face was pink and wet and he smelled of rainwater. A dark line around each eye and a thinner wing-outline remained, tattooed in his flesh. His smile was unrestrained, almost dorky. "We are so screwed. There's definitely going to be news coverage that I was at a daring daylight robbery. My mom is on her way. Let's not hang around?"

Margot left Zuleikah to tug Ki back to their group. "Where too, gang leader?"

The child-like wonder instantly returned to Ki's face. "There's dozens of inhabited worlds we haven't visited."

"If you steal anything big and need it fenced," Sally said,

packing up her phosphere, "*And* you get away clean, you know where to find me."

Margot took a step backward, toward her flyer, and hit her fists together in front of her. "Let's start with Old Hope. I always wanted to see it."

Zuleikah felt something unclench in her chest. "Old Hope," she said, nodding.

Thane opened the canopy on the Legacy. "Just don't get too far ahead of me, okay? I'm still learning this thing."

Ki saw stars and blackness before her, seemingly empty, like a field of untouched snow waiting to be run across.

She remembered one winter, romping through a vacant lot, destroying graceful curves of glittery white with Ethan. The sky was so clear overhead, even with the city light pollution you felt like you could touch the stars.

Ethan hadn't worn nearly enough clothing, as usual. He was so vain. A skimpy fitted jacket and a wooly scarf. A thin sliver of perfectly-formed abdomen showed whenever he raised his arms over his head, which he did a lot. He fell into the snow back first and waved his hands, laughing while clumps of snow melted on his eyebrows and bellybutton.

"You're going to freeze to death." Ki threw a snowball at him. It hit his gut and he curled up with a satisfying "oof" but then he grabbed her and pulled her down into the snow with him.

"Gah! I got snow in my pants. You're going to make us both wet."

"Hush. Look at the stars, will you, little kleptomaniac?" He spread his fingers overhead. "We're going up there, someday, me and you."

She wriggled, trying to get warm against his side. "Where could we possibly go? Where do they let dust like us seep in the door?"

He squeezed her shoulders and nuzzled her cheek with a freezing cold, damp nose. "You'd be surprised what you can get away with when you're not alone."

Ki called up the rearview camera of her flyer. Against the sinking blue and white of Earth, she could just make out the dark shapes of three other flyers. Black, flames, and now the blue Legacy. Ki remembered the cold and wet and felt warm and dry. She sighed in contentment. "Almost to the out-system gate," she said. "Everyone ready? Thane, you understand how to switch to FTL?"

"I watched the tutorial," Thane said. "You can all stop asking."

Ki grinned. A hail came in from law enforcement. She muted it. "Right. Okay, gang, here we go: together."

⚡

THE END

ACKNOWLEDGEMENTS:

I WANT TO START BY THANKING THE WELFARE SYSTEM, WITHOUT which social safety net I might not have survived to write this, and also thanks to free public education so I could put my thoughts in words. Thank you to all the hard-working English teachers that put up with me and my inability to spell.

Way back in junior high, my twin sister drew a sketch on a spiral notebook of three punk girls lounging around a motorcycle. They were Margot, Ki, and Zuleikah in their earliest form, so this is all thanks to Grace's art.

I owe a huge debt to Mary Grimm and Mary Turzillo for their teaching and guidance. The Cajun Sushi Hamsters from Hell workshop read and critiqued and provided invaluable insight, including Mike Substelny telling me to change the name of the gang to "Galactic Hellcats." (I had "The Stardust Gang" which sounds exactly like the sort of thing one makes up in junior high, because it is.) Geoff Landis helped me feel confident breaking the laws of physics. Charles Oberndorf urged me to slow down and focus on character. Darrin Bright gave me all my best jokes. Nyla Bright enabled my love of hurting the pretty. Editor Eric Bosarge fought nobly against my non-standard punctuations. J. M. McDermott plucked my dream from obscurity when he replied to a tweet about space girl gangs asking if I could send the manuscript to him.

Finally, the biggest thanks to my partner in life, Brian Crick, and his brother John, for doing all the housework while I typed on the sofa like a matriarchal queen, and to my dad, Ken Vibbert, for raising me to believe in a better future.